MILKED

A Modern Mommy Tale with a Retro Twist

Cover Art by Amanda Mullins www.designbyamanda.com

MILKED
ISBN-13: 978-0-9853520-8-0
Simon & Fig
4343 Ocean View Blvd. #282
Montrose, CA 91020

For bulk order prices or any other inquiries, please visit
www.simonandfig.com

Dedication

For Colin

In Loving Memory
Dennis McCann
1950-2014

MILKED

A Modern Mommy Tale with a Retro Twist

By
Lisa Doyle

PART ONE

Let me just start off by saying that, for the record, I didn't think this was how things were going to go.

I am a college-educated, thirty-two-year-old woman originally from Naperville, Illinois. My parents are still married; I have one older brother; I grew up in a ranch house with three bedrooms, two bathrooms and a cat. I've never been late on my taxes. I've always paid my credit cards on time (before the last year, anyway). I've never highlighted my brown hair, not even when the first streaks of gray have popped up. I send out Christmas cards the day after Thanksgiving. I've never gotten a speeding ticket.

I certainly didn't think that in the span of two years, I'd be an unemployed, single mother with my tits for rent.

1

My phone buzzed:

JOY: "We're here!"

I downed the last of the single glass of Riesling I'd poured in my own honor, grabbed my purse, turned off the light and locked the door behind me. I walked up the handful of steps from my garden apartment and out the door, dodging raindrops and smiling as I saw my best friend and her husband in the taxi awaiting me.

"Happy dirty thirty, lady!" said Joy, as she gave me a squeeze.

"Happy birthday, Amanda," echoed her more polite husband, Jonathan.

"Thanks, guys," I said. "So, who is this—"

"Where to?" interjected the cab driver.

"Diversey and Halsted," said Joy. We were heading out to at least one, and maybe a few, Irish pubs in Lakeview. We had a pretty open agenda—I'm a little over the whole pub crawl idea—but the plan was to meet up with some friends at Daly's to start, and see where the night would go from there.

The driver pulled away from the curb and took off with a screech.

"Okay," I said. "So, tell me again who this guy is that I'm supposed to meet?"

"His name is Anthony, and he's an internist," Joy

said. "He's very, very nice."

"Nice" is what you say when someone has no personality. Still, I hadn't been on a date, much less in a relationship, for an embarrassingly long and dry year now, so I had agreed to let Joy invite him along. There would be about seven or eight of us altogether, so if we didn't hit it off, the whole night wouldn't be a washout.

"What does he look like again?" I asked.

"He's tall—"

"He's not that tall," Jonathan said, without looking up from his phone.

"Yes, he is!" Joy protested. Jonathan gave her the side-eye. "He's tall, like 5'11" at least. He has dark hair, and has a little bit of face scruff. And he's really good with his patients from what I hear, and the nurses all seem to think he's nice."

"All good things," I said.

"Yes. And he's single, never married, no kids. I think you'll like him."

And if I don't, I'm not going to worry about it, I thought. A few minutes later, we pulled up to the pub and darted inside as the summer rain had quickly turned into a downpour. We grabbed a table near the bar. We were the first of our friends to get there, which wasn't too surprising. It was only eight o' clock. Our friends Meg and Henry were probably still wrangling their two-year-old into bed or waiting for their sitter to get there, and Meg's twin sister, Leigh, was always running late.

My friends are the same ones I've had since high school. Actually, that's a lie. They're the same ones I've had since middle school, plus their husbands (when applicable) that we've accepted into our little world. That probably makes me sound like some kind of loser, but I don't see it that way. I think it's a pretty great thing to be able to grow and develop into an adult when some of the people you love most are right there, growing along with you. It's not as if anyone became so different on the inside that their values and who they're drawn to changed. Plus, everyone comes back to Chicago. We all ventured out of state for school (I went to Miami of Ohio, Joy went to Vanderbilt, and the twins went to Purdue), but we all moved back as soon as we graduated. I mean, really, who wouldn't?

Joy has been my closest friend above all, ever since sixth-grade Spanish class. She's a vivacious, little power peanut packed into a hundred-pound Taiwanese body. For all her noise and bubbly personality, she's pretty damn brilliant, too. She's a gynecologist (not mine—that would be weird). And her husband is a litigator, but believe it or not, he's not even remotely an asshole. They're a great match, and have a condo in the West Loop that costs more than I'll probably make in the next ten years.

Oh yes, and me. Back then, I was a full-time, contracted editor for *Fixtures*, a business-to-business magazine for interior designers. Life could have been worse. I liked my boss, my co-workers didn't make me stabby most days, and I was two months away from a raise of an extra three dollars per hour. It probably would have made my two-hour-plus round-trip commute marginally worth it. I lived in a one-bedroom, garden apartment in Bucktown, just a few steps from the Blue Line. I kept thinking about getting a townhouse or something out in the suburbs closer to work, but I couldn't quite let go of "living the dream" of living in the city. As if I were the fifth *Sex & the City* character or something.)

Joy and Jonathan were perusing their menus, and I was surreptitiously scrolling through my Facebook page to see if I'd gotten any more birthday greetings in the past hour.

"I'm Eamonn, and I'll be helping you tonight. What can I getcha?"

I looked up and immediately thought, *Oh my*. Now I'll admit, ever since I saw the movie *Once*, I've had a soft spot in my heart (and other places) for Irish guys. This one was something else. He had dirty blond hair with just the right amount of bedhead, dark blue eyes with brown in the middle, and that sexy, lilting accent. Oh, that accent. I barely even noticed that he couldn't have been taller than me at 5'8" or so. I wondered if he knew how to play guitar.

"This girl here is celebrating a very special birthday tonight," Joy said, pointing at my head as I blushed. "So we need to make sure she's good and taken care of!"

"Oh, I'll take care of her," he said with a wink. "What would you like?"

"She'd like an Irish—"

"I'll just have a Guinness!" I said, cutting Joy off before she could embarrass the hell out of me.

"Us, too," said Jonathan.

"Three Guinnesses. Back in a minute," Eamonn said.

I made a face at Joy once he whirled away. "Really, Joy?"

She stuck her tongue out at me and grinned.

For better or for worse—okay, usually for worse—I did have a type, and a dirty-blonde waiter probably would fall within that category. That said, I've only actually dated three men in my adult life.

I met Jimmy on the Blue Line when I was twenty-two, just a few months out of school. I had been on my way to work, back when I wrote articles for a now-defunct health food website based in the Loop, and he had just gotten off of work—he worked an overnight shift as a cop in the Gold Coast area. He offered me his seat, which I found unbelievably sweet. Before I had gotten off the train we'd set up a dinner date for the following Saturday. He brought a bouquet of lilies and pulled out my chair for me. I couldn't believe my luck. I only saw him about once a week since he worked such crazy hours, but the time we did spend together felt like it was too good to be true. Turns out, that was quite the case. A month later, his wife called my cell phone and screamed at me until I hung up on her and started bawling. The last time I heard of him was when I saw his picture in the paper, some ongoing case about an off-duty police officer charged with assaulting a bartender.

Nick was a neighbor in the building I lived in when I was twenty-five. I was living in a sweet three-bedroom condo in River North with Leigh and Meg, owned by their aunt, a Loyola professor who was teaching in Rome for a year. He was a twenty-seven-year-old realtor who lived across the hall. He had the rumpled, sexy look I love (Did that all start with him? Shit, maybe), but what I didn't realize right away was that was because he usually slept in his clothes. Or rarely did laundry. He should have owned stock in Febreze. But, I guess that didn't make much of a difference. He was a realtor right when the housing market was starting to go south, and barely left the apartment. Most of our life consisted of sex once or twice a week, followed by me watching him play XBOX and yell at the screen over his headset. Our relationship was one of convenience, and when I moved out of the apartment after a year, I'm not sure he even noticed.

When I was twenty-eight, Leigh and I decided to sign up for an online dating site, which shall remain nameless. One of the first people to ping my profile was Marty, a guy who described himself as a "family-oriented Bears fan that loves life." What I found out that really meant was a “thirty-two-year-old guy who still lived at home because his mom did everything for him, and by the way, don't expect that he's saved any rent money to take you out, because he's blown it all on football shit and trips with his buddies to Vegas. What he will expect is to stay at your place all the time, and that you'll do all his laundry, and dishes too.” Not that I'm bitter about six wasted months.

"Hey, the twins are here! Oh, and Anthony's here too!" Joy stood up and waved them over to the table. I turned around and saw Meg and Leigh, my matching blonde friends who swear they're identical, although I've never had a hard time telling them apart. Trailing behind them was a tall gentleman with salt-and-pepper hair, pleated chinos, and a polo shirt, carrying a wine-sized gift bag. Wait. What the shit? Was that Anthony? My non-set-up set-up? I squinted as he started to make his way over. As he got closer, I saw that he wasn't quite as old as he originally appeared, but there was no way he was younger than forty. Maybe not younger than forty-five.

"Hi, honey!" said Meg, as Leigh wrapped me in a hug. "Happy twenty-ten!"

"Thanks," I said. “Henry couldn’t make it?”

“He’s dealing with bedtime hysterics. He should be here in a bit.”

Out of the corner of my eye, I saw Anthony had gone over first to greet Joy and then was formally shaking

Jonathan's hand.

"Everyone! This is Anthony," Joy said, as he gave an awkward half-smile. "And this is Amanda, our birthday girl!"

"Happy birthday, Amanda," he said. "Nice to meet you."

"It's nice to meet you, too," I said. "I've heard a lot of, ah, nice things about you from Joy."

"Please, take anything she says with a grain of salt," he said with a chuckle. "Here, this is for you." He proffered me the gift bag.

"Oh! Wow, you really shouldn't have. I'll open it later, if that's okay?" I didn't want the rest of my friends to feel like jerks. We hadn't exchanged birthday gifts since high school.

He held up a hand and shrugged. I tucked the bag under the confines of the table, as he sat down in the chair next to me and began studying a menu. I pulled one from the center of the table and did the same, half listening to Leigh on my other side regaling Meg with a story about her latest drunken text exchange with her off-again boyfriend, Brad. Nothing I hadn't heard before. I really hoped that Joy had a good plan for entertaining this Anthony guy, because I sure didn't know how to. Check that, I wasn't sure what she was even thinking inviting him. I mean, he wasn't unattractive—or short—but I could already tell this guy would be more at ease talking with my dad about his stock portfolio or watching golf than he'd ever be doing, well, anything with me.

"I'm gonna run to the ladies room," I said, swiftly nudging Joy's foot with my sandal before standing up.

"Me, too," she said. She gently touched Jonathan's hand and said, "Be right back, hon. Hey, Anthony, why don't you tell Jonathan about your fishing trip up in Door County?"

See, Joy has always been like that. She's always wanted to

make sure everyone's comfortable, everyone's included, everyone has someone to talk to. And I knew she wanted to set me up with someone because she wanted me to be happy, to be loved. But why this guy?

As soon as we were in the bathroom—one of those single bathrooms with just the toilet and sink, but I didn't particularly care if anyone saw both of us go in—I stared right at her and raised an accusatory eyebrow.

"What?" she said.

"What do you mean, 'what?' Joy, how old is he?"

"I don't know. He's probably forty...forty-two, maybe? He's been in his practice for a while. He's a really nice guy, don't you think?"

"He's perfectly nice. But this guy's practically my dad or something. What do you think we'll have in common? He's not my type at all."

"That's exactly why I brought him. Lady, you need a new type."

I punched her arm playfully. "Ha, ha."

She just raised her eyebrows back at me and shrugged. My smile fell.

"Oh, please," I said, crossing my arms over my chest. "What's so bad about my type?"

"You mean uneducated man-boys that spend more time playing *Call of Duty* than working?"

"That was only Nick," I said defensively.

"Or fantasy football addicts that still live at home?"

"Fine, that was Marty. But I get your point," I said with another eye roll.

We headed back to the table, and by then Meg's husband Henry had arrived. Their two-year-old son, Simon, was an adorable little dictator, so when both Meg and Henry could manage to come out at night, it was a pretty big deal to all of us. We politely ignored the fact that they spend half the time telling us how tired they are, and the other half reminding each other that they have to get back early to relieve the sitter.

Eamonn came back over with the three Guinnesses, and dropped coasters in front of the most recent additions to the table.

"Here's your Guinness, birthday girl," he said to me. I felt myself blush again. He took orders from the rest of the table, but I thought I caught him looking at me each time he raised his eyes from his notepad.

Anthony turned to me. “Amanda, you ever been fishing?”

“Can’t say that I have, other than in my subdivision’s retention pond as a kid.”

Just then, Eamonn returned with drinks for the rest of the table.

“Here you are,” he said, gently placing each drink on a coaster. “And, some Jameson for the birthday girl,” he said, directly handing me a little amber-filled shot glass. Our fingers accidentally on purpose brushed when I took it.

“What the hell,” I said, then downed the drink as my friends erupted in cheers. I was starting to feel it, along with the Guinness and the Riesling, in my legs just a little.

“I’ll take another,” I said.

“It’s on me, love,” Eamonn said with a grin and hightailed it back to the bar.

“Looks like you’re gonna have a happy birthday,” said Meg.

“More like a happy ending,” whispered Leigh.

I ignored them and watched Eamonn say something

unintelligible to the bartender, who shrugged. Eamonn surveyed the bottles of Jameson, then picked out the bottle of the Select Reserve Black Barrel on the highest shelf. He carefully poured a shot about half the size of the last and put it on the tray. We all watched as he returned and handed it to me.

"This one's me favorite, and only for a special occasion," he said. "You'll want to give it a little taste. Savor it before you throw it down, yeah?"

My friends all watched as I dutifully sniffed it and lapped at it with my tongue. Eamonn looked at me like a cat eyeballing a rogue mouse. I took a tiny sip and swished it around in my mouth.

"Delicious," I lied. I don't typically like whiskey, but my legs were feeling just that much tinglier, so I'd take it.

Eamonn smiled. "Let me know if there is anything else I can getcha," he said and headed back into the kitchen.

By now, Joy and Anthony were talking shop about work, Jonathan was playing on his phone, and Meg and Henry were arguing over whether they should bother ordering food. Leigh pounced.

"Did you see the way he looked at you?" whispered Leigh. "You should totally go for it."

"What about, um...." I slightly bent my head in the direction of Anthony.

"Meh," she said.

"That's not rude?" I whispered.

"Please," scoffed Leigh, all business. "I wouldn't worry about him. You just need to worry about how we're going to pull this off." Incidentally, she worked in event planning.

"Pull off what?"

"I'm gonna guess the bar doesn't close for another five hours, so he'll be working until then. You'll have to slow it down a bit if you're going to last that long," she confirmed.

"I'm not bringing him home with me!" I hissed. Probably a little too loudly, as Meg and Henry looked up.

"Wait, who?" mouthed Meg and gave an imperceptible nod toward Anthony, who was drawing a map of Door County for Joy on his cocktail napkin.

"Nobody," I mouthed back. Sheesh. This night was going from weird to worse.

Then, we all turned as we heard the sound of someone tapping a microphone.

"Can you hear me?" said a slight, wiry man with glasses and an authentic Irish brogue. I hadn't even noticed as a full band of six—no, seven—guys had assembled in the corner of the bar. And oh God, Eamonn was standing there holding a violin. (Is there an Irish word for violin? Would they call it a fiddle?) This was possibly better than a guitar.

"Without further ado, I'd like to introduce you to Failte," said the older man, and we all applauded. The band started out with a lively piece and some of the presumably regular patrons started clapping and cheering.

Over the next hour, I sat transfixed watching them (okay, him) as the rest of my group kept chattering away. It wasn't just his looks that made him sexy; it was the way his hands moved on the violin, how he put his whole body into the song, how he was so in tune with the rest of the group. There were so many more of them than you'd see in a typical bar band, and they all had to play off of each other, producing these amazing harmonies. There was another violinist (fiddler?) playing as well, but I could pick out Eamonn's the entire night.

It sounded sweeter. I had never appreciated Irish music at all before that night. In fact, I had thought it was kind of cheesy. There was nothing cheesy about the way Eamonn looked playing it.

Anthony, good sport that he had been, begged off at ten, citing an early call schedule starting the next day.

"Thank you for the wine," I said, giving him a pat on the hand as he left. He nodded and left. Meg and Henry soon followed, giving me quick hugs goodbye.

Just then, Eamonn took the microphone from its stand. "We've got time for just one more song tonight. I understand there's a lass here celebrating a birthday?" His eyes scanned the room for about half a second before landing on mine.

Oh, God. I managed a small wave as my friends started to clap and hoot in my direction.

"Any requests, love?" he asked, wiping a little sweat from his brow.

Crap. I didn't know any Irish songs.

"Er. Something by U2, maybe?" I squeaked out.

He conferred with his bandmates for a moment. They all then left the stage except for Eamonn. He pulled a stool up closer to the microphone and set it back in its stand, then adjusted it for height. He sat down, wiped his brow again, then smiled at me and started to play.

A hush fell over the bar as he alone proceeded to play the most extraordinary version of "All I Want Is You." Everyone was enraptured at this point, not just me. It was so melodious, so hauntingly beautiful and unlike anything I'd ever heard. I'd never been hugely into violin music before, but I knew I'd never listen to one the same way again.

When he played the last lines, it was like the end of a

massage. I felt so refreshed, so relaxed, but damned if I didn't wish it was longer. The bar erupted in applause, and Eamonn stood up to take a small bow. The wiry man returned to the stage and said, "How 'bout my nephew?" and gave Eamonn a large pat on the back.

Leigh turned to me after the cheers had died down.

"Seriously. If you don't sleep with that guy tonight, I will," Leigh whispered.

Let me just tell you that thirty-year-old me had never had a one-night stand before. And by definition, thirty-two-year-old me hasn't either, thank you very much. I just wanted to make that clear. Leigh, on the other hand, she was kind of slutty. A great friend, sure, but she would be the first to admit she had lost track of her magic number halfway through her twenties.

"I'm not sleeping with anyone tonight, all right?" I said. But that's not to say I was going to walk out that door and never see that guy again. Hell, no. I grabbed a coaster from the center of the table, and scribbled the words "Birthday Girl" and my cell phone number on it.

Joy looked at me. "Really, Amanda?"

"What?"

"A waiter?"

I rolled my eyes at her. A great friend, sure, but she's the first to admit she can be kind of an elitist.

"Guess I gotta stick with my type," I said.

Eamonn came by the table a few minutes later to give us our check. I immediately put my empty glass back over the coaster. Chicken shit.

"Thanks for the song," I blurted out.

"Anytime," he said. "Have a great night."

Jonathan pulled a wad of cash out of his wallet and stuffed it into the leather folder. "It's on me, ladies."

"Aww, thanks," we all said, then stood up and got our purses together. I slipped the coaster into the folder underneath the cash. No one noticed but Leigh, who gave an approving nod.

"Anywhere else we should go tonight, or...?" Leigh asked, as we stood in the entryway. The downpour outside had yet to let up.

Joy said, "It's up to you, Amanda."

"I think we can call it a night."

"You sure?" asked Leigh.

"Yeah, I'm pretty tired. I'm thirty, you know. Can't quite party like I used to," I half-joked. A small headache was starting to form behind my eyes.

"All right. It was so good to see you!" said Leigh. She gave me a hug, then looked out the window. "Ooh, taxis are at the light. Let's run for it!"

I glanced back at the bar and saw Eamonn taking an order. *Well, he'd be at least a nice memory*, I thought. We flagged down a minivan-sized taxi and piled in.

I was the first to be dropped off. About ten minutes after I got inside, I heard my phone start ringing. I spat out my toothpaste and ran for it. A 773 number I didn't recognize popped up on the screen.

"Hello?" I said.

"Is this the birthday girl?" asked an Irish voice. I heard the bustle of the bar behind him.

"It is," I said cautiously.

"You forgot your wine here," said Eamonn.

Believe it or not, this wasn't even intentional, although I

know it's the oldest trick in the book.

"Oh!" I said. "Thanks. Would the staff be able to hold onto it for me until tomorrow?"

"That'll be fine."

"What time do you open?"

He paused. "I believe four o' clock."

"Great, I'll be there at four."

"Grand. Good night," he said and hung up.

Grand. I guess. No offer to drop it by or meet me somewhere for it. And he probably wouldn't even be there, since he didn't know what time the bar opened. Fine. At least I didn't completely throw myself at him. I'd had a nasty habit of doing that back in college when I was wasted. Since then I'd reined in both my drinking and my desperation.

The last year or so, I'd been going through a dry spell. I won't lie, it had been a little lonely. I was really lucky that I had my family (my parents anyway—my brother had been teaching English in South Korea for the last decade) less than an hour drive away, and I could lean on them if I ever needed them. And I was grateful that I had loyal friends in my life that I saw on a regular basis. The married ones didn't act like my single status was contagious, and the single one was neither a man-hating feminazi nor someone who kept me around as the less attractive friend. Still though, there was something a little disappointing, a little twinge of "what's wrong with me," about being unmarried at thirty. And not anywhere in my life that I was even close to being married. Or to having kids. When I was younger, I'd thought I'd be like my mom and be done having kids by thirty. I could get a dog, but I was gone almost twelve hours a day. I could get a cat, but that would put me just one step closer to being the crazy cat lady. Those things multiply like tattoos—if you get one, you'll get two, and if you get three, you'll get ten.

But I didn't want to dwell on that. I really believed that happiness was dependent on appreciating what I did have, not bitching and moaning about what I didn't. And at any rate, I knew that tomorrow I was going to have a hangover (but only a tiny hangover!), an empty bed (but a lack of STDs and regrets!) and probably a fancy pants bottle of wine I'd pick up sometime around four. Ha. Little did I know what tomorrow would have in store.

2

I spent the morning puttering around the apartment, going through the mail, chatting with my mom, who was coming over for dinner with Dad the following weekend, once he was fully recovered from knee surgery, and generally just killing time. A little after 3:30, I left my apartment and walked a couple of blocks to Armitage and Western to flag down a taxi. The streets were pretty clear, and I got to Daly's just before four. The first thing I saw was a sign on the door that said, "Open 7 days a week at 11 AM," and immediately felt a little irritated.

The door jingled as I opened it, and the pub was nearly deserted. No hostess was manning the front, so I went to the bar. The bartender looked up from wiping glasses. It was the same wiry man from the night before.

"Can I help you?" he asked.

"I accidentally left a gift bag here last night. One of your waiters said you would hold it for me?"

"Oh, right, right. Eamonn!" he called into the kitchen.

Eamonn came out from the kitchen, unfastening his apron. He did a double-take when he saw me and smiled. So did I.

"Birthday Girl!" he said.

"That's me," I said, immediately glad I had taken the time to blow dry my hair and throw on a little lip gloss before coming here, just in case. "Do you have my wine?"

"It's upstairs."

"I didn't know this place had an upstairs," I said, puzzled. I'd been here probably twenty times and had never seen a staircase.

"In me apartment," said the wiry man, sticking out a hand to shake mine. "I'm Colin Daly, the owner. I live upstairs, with a never-ending supply of relatives from back home." He nodded his head in Eamonn's direction.

"Amanda Keane," I said. "Wonderful to meet you."

Colin threw a towel over his shoulder and picked up a few trays. "Likewise. Eamonn, thanks for handling the morning shift. I'll see you tonight," he said, and bustled into the kitchen.

"So does that make you a Daly, too?" I asked Eamonn.

"Nah, I'm a Shaughnessy. Second cousin once removed," said Eamonn. "Anyway, I'm sure you'd like to be on your way. I'll just run up and get your wine for you. Unless you'd fancy a cuppa?"

"Fancy a what?"

"A cup of tea," he annunciated in a faux American accent.

"Aye! I'd fancy a cuppa, that would be lovely," I retorted back in my best Irish accent.

"Well done!" he said. "Have a seat." He gestured at the booth in the corner. I did as he asked and watched him jog back into the kitchen. The way upstairs must be in the back. About five minutes later, he returned with the gift bag on his arm, and holding a tray with a teapot, two mugs and a box of teabags. He motioned for me to choose one, and I plucked out an Earl Grey. He did the same, then poured the boiling water into our mugs.

"So, Birthday Girl has a name. Amanda Keane, is it?"

"It is. Eamonn. Shaughnessy."

"Good memory," he said.

"It's not every birthday that I get serenaded."

He looked right at me with his penetrating blue-brown eyes. "It's not every birthday girl that does. Just the remarkable ones," he finally said, then looked down to blow on his tea.

The twenty-nine-year-old me might have blushed, but the thirty-year-old me was trying to be a little more objective. "I bet you say that to all the American girls," I said.

"You're the first American girl I've had a conversation with longer than the time it takes to write down her order."

"How long have you been here?"

"Just a week," he admitted.

"Did you move here or are you on a visitor visa?"

"I'll be here through the end of the summer. It's an ESTA, which is what you get instead of a visa. It's much easier. I can stay in the US for 90 days for business or pleasure."

"So which is it for you? Both, I hope?

"Absolutely. Technically I'm not 'working' for Colin, although I help out down here most nights when he's shorthanded, and I've been having a grand time playing in Failte. Colin will give me some money here and there out of the tips, and keeps a roof over my head for free. Can't complain," he said airily.

"Are you going to travel anywhere else outside of Chicago?"

"Not for a bit yet. But I'm hoping to make it down to Memphis if I can."

"No kidding! I was born in Memphis." It's true! I lived there until I was about four years old, when my parents moved back to Naperville, where they had grown up. "I don't remember much about it, though," I added. "Just the ducks swimming in the fountain at the Peabody."

He grinned. "Tell me more, Amanda."

And I did. Over the next two hours, I shared pretty much my entire life story with him, and he shared his. I learned he was twenty-five (Only twenty-five! Holy hell), the third of three boys, from Cork, and this was his first time outside of Ireland. He played in a few bands back home, had floundered from job to job, most recently working as a “lorry driver” when Colin had offered to house him in Chicago if he was interested. As soon as the ESTA was ready, he came straight here and began "helping" (can't say working) for Colin. He shared the guest room upstairs with two of his other cousins, one of whom spent the entire time Skyping with his girlfriend back in Galway, and the other had terrible body odor, and apparently Colin just had him helping in the kitchen. So far the pub kept him busy most of the evenings, but he spent his days wandering around the neighborhoods, taking pictures of the landmarks and in general just enjoying Chicago in the summer.

At six, the bar was starting to fill up with the evening crowd. Colin called out, "Eamonn! I need you in the front of the house."

Eamonn sighed and smiled an apology. "Duty calls," he said, but made no move to get up.

"I guess so," I said, picking up the gift bag of wine and putting it on my wrist. I never even checked to see what kind it was.

"So....what's next then? Can I see you again?" he asked.

The little Joy on my shoulder said, "I know he's hot. But

take away the fact that he's from Ireland, and you have an out of work truck driver-slash-musician who lives at home. Walk away *now*."

The Meg on my shoulder said, "Shut the fuck up, Joy! He's hot and he wants her." Leigh actually swung over to my other should to pin Joy down and gagged her with an Hermés scarf. "Amanda! Go for it!" she shouted while wrestling with Joy.

I was a smitten kitten, and there was no way around it. I stood up and grabbed my things. "I hope you do," I said, then leaned over to give him a peck on the cheek. I almost skipped to the door and jumped in the first cab I saw, not daring to look back, lest he saw that the twenty-nine-year-old, red-faced me was still alive and well.

I went home and tried to take my mind off Eamonn, but it was no use. I tried to eat some leftover macaroni and cheese for dinner, but my stomach was all butterflies. I couldn't remember the last time I'd felt like this. And how the hell was I supposed to go to sleep tonight? I'd taken today off, but I had to be up by six for work tomorrow.

Then, my phone rang just after nine. I recognized the unfamiliar number from the night before.

"Hello?" I said, probably a little more breathlessly than I would have liked.

"Hey, it's Eamonn," he said.

"Hi!" I said brightly. "What's up?"

"Well, I'm not needed at the pub anymore tonight, and I couldn't help but wonder what you're up to."

"Nothing, really," I said, heart pounding. "Just chilling here with some TV."

"Would you want to go out for a pint?"

I paused. "I don't know. I have to be up pretty early for work," I admitted.

"Ah."

I took a look, and the Joy on my shoulder was now hog-tied, and Meg and Leigh were sitting on top of her and laughing.

"Would you like to come over to my place for a drink?" I asked lightly.

"I'd love to."

I gave him my address and he said he'd be there in about fifteen minutes. I hung up and then ran for the bathroom, nearly tripping on the dirty towels on the floor on my way in. I threw all the bottles and tubes from the counter into the cabinet under the sink, and grabbed a tissue to wipe away all the loose hairs and make-up droppings left on the counter. I furiously brushed my teeth and my hair, and swiped on some mascara and lip balm. Then I surveyed the rest of the apartment. Okay, decently clean. The fridge had half a bottle of wine, and a couple of Amstel lights. I was still in my clothes from the day—a cute orange sundress and a short-sleeved white cardigan. Again, decently clean, and my underwear even matched my bra. No polish on my fingernails, but my toes looked okay. Five minutes to go. Leigh hopped over to my ear and whispered. I ran back into the bathroom and quickly shaved my bikini line. And checked the cabinet under the sink. Yep, there was still a dusty box half-filled with Trojans. I wiped off the dust.

Then, the door buzzer went off. I buzzed him into the building, and heard him go down the steps to my door. Before he could knock, I flung the door open.

"Hi!" I said. "Come on in."

"Thanks," he said. By the way, every time he said, "thanks," it sounds like "tanks." So endearing.

"Looks like you found the place okay," I said, walking over to the fridge. I opened the door and began scanning the contents. "What would you like? I have some wine, some beer...um, some apple juice if that's what you're into..."

I then felt his arm on my shoulder and I whirled around.

"I think you're what I'm into," he said, and then leaned in and kissed me.

To say this kiss was electric was an understatement. His lips first brushed mine, and then as he started to pull away, I leaned back in and went for it full on. He responded and pulled me into him, one arm around my back and the other in my hair. My arms took on a mind of their own and started pulling his Daly's polo off over his head. His chest, with the smallest amount of downy blond hair, wasn't chiseled, but toned, lanky and smooth. He tugged the cardigan off of me, then pulled the dress over my head in one fell swoop, barely breaking the kiss. He cupped my breasts in one hand, then deftly picked me up with the other, and I wrapped my legs around his waist.

"Bedroom?" he asked breathlessly, then began kissing my neck

"There," I pointed. We bounced into the darkened room and he rolled me onto the bed. He unclasped my bra and more gently relieved my body of it, then started stroking my right breast while lapping at my left with his tongue. Oh my God. This was really happening. I arched my back and whimpered. After a few minutes, I slithered down on the bed, moving his mouth to mine to kiss me and pull him on top of me. I felt his hardness through his jeans. It made me even more wet. I reached down and unbuttoned his jeans, pulling them down to his knees. He shook them off the rest of the way, and I felt the bulge even better under his boxer briefs.

"Wait a sec," I whispered. He rolled off of me, and I ran to the bathroom. I fished a Trojan out of the box and darted back into the bedroom.

"Should I or should you?" I asked, suddenly a little shy.

"I think you should," he said with a grin. He leaned back and peeled off the boxer briefs, then began kissing me on the neck as I fumbled with the wrapper. I clumsily rolled the condom onto him (distracted, I admit, by the tongue on my earlobe and hands on my breasts), then couldn't wait a second longer. I sat directly onto him and gasped as I felt him fill me. I rocked on him, pulsing on him in time and moaning as he responded likewise in sync. When I came, I screamed out a raucous yowl, louder and longer than I ever had before, throwing my head back. He looked at me in awe. I gave him a relaxed smile.

"Ladies first, I see," he said devilishly, then flipped me over to my back in one motion, never exiting my body. He grasped my wrought iron headboard with one hand and wrapped his other around my back. He moved in and out, back and forth with confident, full thrusts for a few more moments as I felt another wave coming on. I clenched him from the inside with all my might as I came and cried out again.

"Oh, God, Amanda," he groaned as he climaxed, then laid his head on my chest. We both lay still for a few minutes. Then he lifted up his head and kissed me gently on the lips. "What am I going to do with you?"

Ha. What *wouldn't* he do with me, it turned out. I called

in sick to work the next day and we had absolutely mind-blowing sex five more times in the next eighteen hours, only pausing for brief naps and breakfast (we skipped lunch). We finished off the box of Trojans, just in time for him to go back for the dinner shift at Daly's.

"I promise I'll come back here the second I get out for the night," he said in between kisses at the door.

"You'd better," I said, not wanting to let him go.

"Shall I stay over here tonight?"

"You'd better!" I repeated with a grin and spanked him. Yeah, that's right! I spanked him.

"Okay, I'll grab some things and I'll see you tonight." He gave me one more quick kiss, then headed out.

The day crawled by. He didn't have a cell phone in the States, he'd explained earlier, so unless he absolutely needed to call someone, he usually didn't bother with using the phone from work. But, he buzzed back into my building at a little past ten that night. I was already waiting for him in a long-neglected, black lace nightie, and we immediately tumbled into bed again. After this night's session, we kissed in bed for a good half an hour and snuggled. This was so foreign and exciting to me—a guy that seemed to want me as much as I wanted him, and who just clicked with me on every level. He'd stroke my arm while talking to me, kiss my eyelids whenever I started to drift off to sleep. It didn't matter anymore to me that I'd lived thirty years before this feeling. It was worth the wait.

"Do you want some water?" I asked, getting up.

"Please," he said.

"Be right back," I said and walked, naked (naked!) into the kitchen. I noticed that he had left his backpack on the floor by the door, one of those framed ones that you see people wearing when they're traveling around Europe. Or, duh, when they're from Europe and they backpack to America, I thought. It was actually bursting at the seams. It's probably the only piece of luggage he brought, I assumed. And he just brought over all his possessions to my apartment.

By the time I had filled the two glasses of water, it dawned on me: He'd moved in. Without asking. And I was completely fine with it.

I walked back into the bedroom with the waters and handed him a glass. He took a swig and then lustily stared at me. "Round two?"

I giggled and jumped onto his lap.

I could probably spend the next hour of your life entertaining you with all the different ways we fucked, but this isn't Fifty Shades of Irish. And it wasn't right away that I got knocked up, either. Quite a bit had happened in the meantime:

-Sex, sex, and more sex with Eamonn, true enough. I'd be jealous of me, too.

-I became a regular at the pub—something I hadn't done since senior year in college. I also developed a hankering for the Jameson shots Eamonn and I threw back with Colin after closing time. I loved feeling a lot younger than thirty again.

-We took a road trip—the first one I'd ever been on, and definitely my first vacation with a guy. We went to Memphis, St. Louis, Austin and Denver, staying in cheap motels and even camping out under the stars one night in Texas. I'll never forget it.

-For the first time in thirty years, I learned to cook. Never really wanted to before, but I had someone to take care of, kinda. I made him a traditional Irish breakfast every weekend and it was nothing to sneeze at.

And, then it was October, and Eamonn's ESTA was on the verge of expiring. The sixteenth, the date of his flight back, loomed like a black cloud over me that I kept trying to push away. So, for the week beforehand, I called in "sick" all week to work, and we spent all the time we could at our favorite places in the city. We wanted to make the most out of his last few days, and decided to not be completely miserable. So we went walking along the lakefront, had beers at The Map Room at midday, even went to one of the free evenings to putter around the Art Institute.

The sun was just setting as we left the museum, quietly strolling down Michigan Avenue hand-in-hand. We stopped when we got to the bridge so he could take a few last photos.

"God, it's so beautiful here," he eventually said with a groan. "I'd stay here forever if I could."

"With me, right?" I nudged.

He flashed me his best Eamonn-style grin. "Do you even have to ask, love?" he replied, wrapping his arms around me.

The night he left, I drove him to O'Hare's international terminal, and sadly, didn't even have enough time to go inside with him. Thanks to gawker traffic from an accident on I-90, we were cutting it close on time; his flight was going to board any minute. He had nothing but his backpack stuffed with clothes (a few less than he came with, since I'd snagged a few of his shirts to keep for myself), and a Dennis Lehane novel for the plane that he'd taken from my shelf.

"You'll Skype me as soon as you get home, right?" I said, unbuckling my seatbelt to hug him one last time.

"Of course," he said. He was going to have to reactivate

his cell phone once he got home in a few days, but we planned to mostly Skype, anyway. "I'm going to Skype you every afternoon."

"Okay. I love you," I blurted out, as he leaned in to kiss me. I'd never said that before—to Eamonn, or to any guy.

He just kissed me, long and sweet.

"We'll talk tomorrow, love," he said, stroking my chin.

I watched him as he slipped through the revolving door and jogged in the direction of security, then I finally forced myself to pull away. The void was back.

He did Skype me, just as promised, at 4 AM. I had woken up just about every hour on the hour before that. I spent the next hour alternating between tears and missives, and then once we signed off, I fell back into an exhausted sleep.

And after a couple of days, we fell into a rhythm. We'd Skype for about half an hour every morning for me (afternoon for him), and then around the time I got off of work (when he'd be ready to go to sleep). Sometimes we'd punctuate it with Skype sex. Okay, often.

After two weeks of this, my girlfriends dragged me out of my apartment to a Halloween party in order to rejoin the human race beyond my computer screen. I wasn't in the mood to go out—obviously—but Eamonn had made plans with his friends for that night as well, so I decided I wouldn't really be missing out on a night "together."

I wasn't about to dress up like a glorified skank in costume, though—I was still taken, or at least I viewed myself as such. I whipped up my favorite standby costume of an ancient Greek by fashioning a toga from a white sheet, using some fake leaves to make a wreath, and belting a rope around my waist.

I cabbed it over to ROOF with Joy, Meg and Leigh, and as soon as we got to the bar, I noticed something amiss.

"Does it smell like something's burning to you?" I asked, sniffing.

The twins frowned. "Nope," said Meg.

"What do you want to drink? First round's on me," said Leigh.

"How about a Long Island?" suggested Joy.

"Sure," I said.

We pushed our way to the bar, and got our drinks a few minutes later. I took a sip of mine and grimaced.

"Ugh," I said. "Are you sure this is a Long Island?"

"Yeah," said Leigh.

"I think they made mine wrong." I already felt my stomach slightly lurching.

"Mine's fine," said Joy. "Here, try a sip."

I did as told. It still tasted off. I ended up having an okay time with the girls, but called it a night by midnight. I was just wiped out.

I spent almost all of the next day, Sunday, in bed, feeling queasy and fluish. I only spent about ten minutes on Skype with Eamonn before I begged off.

The queasy feeling didn't go away on Monday, either, but I tried to work at home through it. I had fallen a little behind on my deadlines over the past few weeks since I'd been trying to spend every waking moment with Eamonn, both when he was here and in Ireland. Probably not a great idea career-wise, since in my company's perspective, I was a contractor and thus expendable. I took the garbage out twice, though. I didn't know what the hell it was that reeked in my apartment, but I couldn't seem to get rid of it. I sprayed Lysol and lit a few candles, but even that made my stomach turn.

Then after I finished up an advertorial on the upcoming lighting trade show in Vegas, and took out the bathroom trash, it hit me.

"No," I thought. “Probably not.”

I saw that old box of condoms still lurking at the back of the bathroom cabinet, though it was long empty; I’d made a trip to Walgreens to replenish my stock after Eamonn’s second night here. As I picked up the box, I saw the expiration date. It had been two months past.

I walked the three blocks to the closest Walgreens. I stopped at the shelf full of pregnancy tests and hesitated. The Joy on my shoulder gave me a small kick in the neck. I sighed and grabbed a cheap one. Not that I thought I'd really need it. I also grabbed some generic dish soap, Altoids and Baked Lays to toss in my basket, as if all of that would throw off the cashier.

At home, I ripped open the cardboard box, quickly scanned the instructions, and peed on the stick. I left it on the counter and went into the kitchen, bustling around to start on dinner and tried not to stare at the clock on the microwave for the prescribed three-minute wait period.

I came back into the bathroom and saw a very clear, very obvious, very pink plus sign. And started to cry.

But the thought of a baby—Eamonn’s baby—inside me, a piece of him he left behind, was unbelievably gratifying, After I pulled myself together a few minutes later, I called him on Skype.

"What's wrong, love?" he asked, seeing my blotchy face. "What happened?"

"Well...this happened!" I said, whipping the test out in

front of the camera.

He squinted to see what it was, then his eyes widened. "The fuck?" he said.

"Haha, yeah, the fuck. That's how these things happen!"

He screwed his eyes shut and started rubbing his temples. "There's no way."

All right, I'd let him be in shock for a few more minutes.

Finally he let out a huge sigh. "I guess that's how it goes, huh."

"That's all you're going to say?" I said.

He looked at me like I had two heads. "What am I supposed to say?"

"Oh, I don't know. Maybe, 'This is amazing! I love you so much! I will support you in any way I can! Let's figure this out!'"

He was quiet for a moment. "It's a lot to take in, love."

He was right about that.

"I know. I only just found out five minutes before I called you. It's still sinking in for me."

"Let's just think about this a little. Let's...let's sleep on it. I gotta run," he said, and he closed his laptop.

I was dumbfounded. My first instinct was to call him right back, but then I decided to hold off. This was shocking news. Huge. Earth-shattering. He was probably being a guy and going into panic/shut-down mode. I'd call him first thing in the morning.

I did, however, spend the next four hours Googling.

The next morning, I Skyped Eamonn at our regular time. He answered right away.

"You feeling a little better?" I asked timidly.

"I'm sorry about last night," he said. "You have to admit,

that news was a bit of a shock."

"I know," I said. "It was a shock, but I'm really excited about it."

"How are you feeling? Physically?"

"Ah, ok," I admitted. "A little queasy and pretty tired. But overall, not too terrible."

"I wish I could be there to massage your feet, and run out to get you gherkins and ice cream," he said.

"Who's to say you can't be here?"

"The U.S. government, for one."

"You don't think there's any other way you could be here?"

He scratched his chin. "Not off the top of my head."

I paused. "We could get married, you know," I said casually. After all, he *had once said* he wished he could stay with me in Chicago forever. More or less.

His eyes widened again. Slightly more than they had the night before. "Pardon?"

I laid it out: a no-frills civil ceremony over here in the next couple of months, then we'd start the paperwork for him to come over on a marriage visa. With any luck, that would go through a few months before the baby was born. I kept looking down, afraid by now of the looks on his face. When I was done, I peered up and saw him mulling it over...then he took a deep breath.

"Let's do it," he said.

Over the next week, we made plans for him to fly back from December third through sixth. He was pretty low on cash, not having found any work back home yet, so I sprung for his ticket. We'd go to the county building the next day, city hall the day after that, and we'd go out to dinner at Daly's with my parents and friends that night. My parents, as a gift, would put us up at the Omni's honeymoon suite for our wedding night, and then he'd fly back the next day. With any luck, he'd be able to return by March or April. Then we'd really focus on all things baby. And get him a job, probably at Daly's to start. I was glowing—not just from the baby, but from the promise of the life I'd always wanted finally beginning.

Of course, the lack of a huge wedding didn't stop my mom's excitement. She told everyone she knew that she was "finally" going to be a grandma (she was only sixty, but whatever) and insisted on shopping for a wedding dress. Immediately.

"It's just going to be at City Hall," I'd countered as she dragged me through Macy's.

"I don't care," she said. "It's your wedding day. You're wearing a wedding dress. End of story."

In the end, we found a tasteful, tea-length, champagne-colored sheath that hugged my slightly-expanding curves. With Eamonn's blessing, I picked out the rings from Overstock.com. They were stainless steel, slim bands that cost a total of $19.98 for the pair (plus $2.95 for shipping). In person, though, they looked platinum.

We had our last Skype date the night before his flight. He seemed a bit antsy, but I think we both were. I could barely wait for the next 24 hours to pass!

Just before signing off, he said, "I just wanted to tell you that I'll always have you in my heart, Amanda."

"Stop, you're going to make a pregnant woman all weepy."

"Well, I already made a weepy woman all pregnant. Might as well mix it up a little," he said and winked. "In all seriousness, love, goodnight."

I could barely make it through the workday. Finally, at two, I called it a day and headed for O'Hare. I didn't care that I'd be an hour early. I just had to be closer to Eamonn. I had already prepared a "welcome back" bag of some of his favorites—American Coca-Cola (somehow he preferred the high fructose corn syrup—weirdo), sesame rice crackers from Trader Joe's, Milky Way bars and Nyquil.

I took the Blue Line this time, since he'd be coming in around rush hour, and waited inside the gate where all the international flights came in, sandwiched among the state's emigrant population anxiously awaiting their family and friends to fly in. I kept checking the clock on my phone. It was almost five, when the arrival was scheduled. His flight looked to be on time. No bad weather between here and Shannon (I'd been checking all day).

5:30 rolled around. Must be a long line at customs.

5:45. I noticed some Irish accents as people came through the gates, and one of them definitely had an Irish flag patch sewn on her backpack.

6:00. Still no Eamonn. I was biting my nails by now.

6:15. I hopped back and forth between being frustrated at customs and annoyed by him. Why the hell hadn't he found a way to call me? I was getting slightly scared.

6:22. My phone pinged. I had an email. And it was from Eamonn.

Dear Amanda,

It's so hard for me to write this, and I'm sure even harder for you to read this. I want you to know how much I loved our time together in Chicago. But I know, and I am sure you know deep inside, that as much as we try, we'll never be able to recreate that perfect time we had, and getting married wouldn't do that. I know I have a lot of growing to do, and at this time in my life, I wouldn't be a great father. I'll support you financially however I can, but I know that you and the baby will be better off without me in your lives.

You deserve someone better than me. You deserve someone older, someone more established, someone who can take care of you and the baby properly. And I know you will find that person. I'm sorry it can't be me.

I'll be in touch. I promise, I won't disappear altogether. I'll do what I can for the baby. You have my word.

You'll always have a place in my heart.

Eamonn

P.S. I'll try to refund your ticket.

3

I ran into the bathroom, locked myself in the handicapped stall and sat in the corner for an hour straight, punctuated by several knocks and people asking me if I was okay. To which I replied, "Leave me the fuck alone!" and finally people did. I eventually pulled myself together enough to forward the email to Joy. She called me two minutes later.

"Where the fuck is he?" she hissed once I picked up. "I'm going to fucking kill him."

"Back in Ireland," I said, numb. "I don't know if he even went to the airport."

"Where are you? Are you still at O'Hare?"

"Yeah."

She sighed. "Oh, hon. I would come and get you, but I have two more patients. It's my late night."

"No, I can get home," I said.

"You shouldn't be alone. Hang on, I'll call the twins. They'll get you," she assured. "I'll come over as soon as I'm off of work."

"All right," I said sniffling and clicked off. Two minutes later, I got a text from Leigh: "ON MY WAY." She worked just a few miles from O'Hare in the convention center district.

Moments later, I was at the curb, and her Lexus screeched up to me. She ran out of the car and threw her arms around me.

"Oh, honey," she said as I started to shake with tears.

After a minute, she looked down.

"What's that?" She gestured to the gift bag in my hands.

"It was for Eam—"

"No, fuck that," she said, ripping it from my hands and throwing it on the ground behind me. "Here, get in the car. I'm taking you home." She ushered me into the car and buckled me in. We got on the road and she turned the radio down low.

After a few minutes, she said, "Do you want to talk about it? Joy didn't really tell me what happened."

"What did she say?"

"That he backed out of the wedding like a chicken shit, and decided to leave you and the baby high and dry."

"That's not how it is," I said, immediately defensive. "He loves me—us, he loves us. He just doesn't think he's good enough for us, and he's scared of failing us. So he panicked."

"Mmm," she said, noncommittally.

We were silent for the rest of the ride home.

"Do you want me to come in?" Leigh asked once we turned onto my street. "We don't have to talk or anything. But I think you should probably not be alone right now."

"I'm not going to harm myself." Okay, throwing myself off the Wrigley building *might* have crossed my mind.

"I didn't mean that. I just think you need some support. You know what, I'll make sure Joy and Meg are on their way. We'll take care of you," she offered.

Within the next hour, Joy and Meg came over bearing ice cream, hugs and a mix of rage and disbelief over Eamonn. We didn't talk much. We flipped on TBS and had old episodes of *The Big Bang Theory* on while everyone gave me sympathetic hugs and took turns getting me more Kleenex.

By the end of the night, I was all cried out. "He's really

not going to marry me," I said, matter-of-factly.

No one would say anything to that.

"Probably not ever," I added, resigned.

After a time, Joy said, "Probably not," and squeezed my hand.

"Do you think he always knew that?"

"No," they all said in unison.

"I don't know, though," I said. "I'm not sure I'll ever know. All I know is that I am going to be a single mom. And there's nothing I can do about that."

"You know what, though?" said Leigh. "You still get to *be* a mom."

I knew I should be comforted by that thought, but I wasn't. I cried almost nonstop for three days straight. When my parents came over the next day, I had to threaten my dad with disownment in order to convince him to not go over to Ireland to personally kick the shit out of Eamonn. And he was a pacifist.

And all that week, in between crying jags and the occasional nap, I found myself constantly reviewing all my old emails and texts from him, and flipping through the pictures on my phone, desperately looking for clues. We didn't have that many photos of ourselves together—just a few selfies from our road trip, and one that Eamonn's uncle Colin took of us outside the bar. In all the pictures, I was smiling like my life depended on it, or kissing Eamonn on the cheek; Eamonn was either making a goofy face, or purposely looking away from the camera. Did that mean something? Should it have been obvious that I was head over heels for him, and he was just kind of along for the ride? I didn't know. I'd never had to question it. It had always felt like he was just as into me as I was into him—and believe me, I know how it feels to date a guy with only lukewarm feelings for me at best. When you're around him, you feel inadequate somehow. You feel like you're unflavored oatmeal, or soggy cheerios. With Eamonn, I felt like I was pumpkin pancakes with cinnamon butter and a side of brown-sugared bacon.

And the smallest part of me, deep down started to slowly resent the part that was growing each day: the baby. I loved it—really, I did—but I was convinced that if *it* hadn't come along, then things would be different with Eamonn. Maybe if the pressures of becoming a dad weren't on him, we'd be chugging along merrily right now. He'd be making plans to use up the rest of his ESTA on a trip to see me for Christmas. Or I'd be on my way to Ireland and we'd tour around castles and breweries for a week. Either way, we'd be together.

I emailed my boss, Sandy, on Friday to give her the news that the wedding had been called off, and asked if she could somehow let my co-workers know in advance. The message must have gotten lost in the ether, because when I got to my cubicle on Monday morning, it had been draped with white streamers, tissue paper poms and silver dove confetti. Jesus. I sat down, swept the damn confetti off my desk and buried my face in my hands.

"Here comes the bride!" chirped a voice behind me. I spun around. It was the intern, proffering me a tray of white frosted cupcakes with little silver wedding bells on top.

I sighed and rubbed my temples. "The wedding was called off," I said through clenched teeth, looking down at my lap.

The intern froze, mid-grin. After a moment, her face fell into a sympathetic frown. She swayed from side to side for a second, then said, "Ummm....I'll just leave the cupcakes for you?" She gently laid the tray on my desk, then scampered off.

I took a look at the cupcakes. I chose one, picked the silver bell off, then crammed the entire thing in my mouth. I tried to work on my feature for the February issue, but for the next hour, all I could hear were hushed voices and gasps as my coworkers slowly learned what happened. I faked a headache and was out the door before ten.

Christmas soon rolled around. My parents had wanted me to come in on Christmas Eve and stay the night, but I demurred, insisting that it would be too crowded in their townhouse. My brother, Paul, had flown in from Seoul with his new girlfriend, Kai, who worked for Google. They'd met at the open-air market or some shit. I don't know, I didn't pay much attention when my mom gave me the rundown the week before.

On Christmas morning, I pulled into my parents' driveway a little before noon, took a deep breath and opened the front door.

"There she is!" my mom called from the kitchen. "Merry Christmas!"

"Hi, kiddo," my dad said, glancing up from *National Geographic*. He patted the empty seat next to him on the couch.

"Hey," I said, dropping my Target bag of gifts by the tree before joining him. "So where's Paul and the girlfriend?"

My dad nodded his head toward the door in the guest bedroom. "Still sleeping, I think. They're really jet lagged from the flight."

A moment later, the door from the guest bedroom opened and they tumbled out, pink-faced, disheveled and grinning. For fuck's sake. At our *parents'* house? On Christmas?

"Merry Christmas, sis," Paul said, wrapping me in a hug from behind. "Meet Kai." She was an adorable Korean pixie about half my size. She beamed and threw herself at me for a hug, burying her face in my chest.

"So nice to meet you, Amanda!" her muffled voice said. "And congratulations on the baby!"

"Thanks," I muttered, gently extricating myself. She and Paul then pulled back together like magnets and spent the remainder of the day that way: finishing each other's sentences, holding hands, and eating off each other's plates at brunch. It took every ounce of self-restraint I had to keep my eyes from rolling right out of my damn head. And looking back, I think they even tried to tone the lovey-dovey antics down a little for my sake, but my hurt from Eamonn was still so fresh that being around them was like lemon juice in a paper cut.

After brunch and presents, I went back to my own apartment (they'd gotten me a $100 gift card to Babies R Us, which was both thoughtful and a fantastic reminder that I was a pregnant, unmarried loser), and flopped on my own couch. I turned on the TV and it was about halfway through "A Christmas Story," a movie I'd never found to be particularly epic nor classic. I looked at the clock on my microwave. Only 4:18. God, I thought, how many more hours do I have to be awake before I can just go to sleep? I was starting to understand why suicides peaked in the holiday season.

It occurred to me, too, that this was the last time I'd ever be alone on Christmas night. No, I bitterly thought, I'll have plenty of company—the kid will probably be dealing with teething by this time next year. Or acid reflux. I probably won't have slept in six months, and I probably won't even be able to afford Christmas presents for the kid. It'll be fabulous. Much better than this!

I eventually shuffled over to the fridge and poked around. It was practically empty, except for some questionable eggs, orange juice, a few Greek yogurts and plenty of condiments on the door. I'd cooked quite a bit when Eamonn was around—I'd liked the new domesticity and having a reason to cook meals big enough for two—but since he'd left, I was left with a few half-used jars and bottles of various ingredients that went into recipes I'd tried: hoisin sauce for ribs I'd made in the crockpot; sriracha for pad thai; green chiles for enchiladas.

There was also an unopened bottle of sauvignon blanc that I'd bought in October.

I looked at the bottle. I looked down at my stomach.

"Fuck it," I said aloud, and grabbed the bottle off the shelf.

I drank straight from the bottle while watching "A Christmas Story" through tears and fell asleep on the couch before dark.

I woke up at dawn the next morning, wracked with guilt and a world-class splitting headache. I spent the next hour retching, hoping I didn't just give my baby fetal alcohol syndrome, and retching some more. I was on the couch with a washcloth on my forehead and a ginger ale when Joy called me at nine.

"I have a fun idea," she said.

"What's that?" I mumbled.

"I know your first OB appointment isn't supposed to be until next week, but Dr. Stevens had a cancellation for the noon slot. Why don't you come in and we'll do it now? We can even see if we can sneak in an ultrasound."

"What? Well, I don't know..." The implication that the lima bean inside me was really *real* was making me feel very uncomfortable.

"Come on. What else would you be doing that's more important today?"

Sigh. Why not. "Fine, I'll be there."

"Great. I'll make sure to pop in."

Three hours and two Tylenols later, I was lying on an examining table with my feet up in stirrups and a hand up my vag. I closed my eyes.

"Looks good," said Dr. Stevens. He brought out the doppler from the cabinet and lifted up the paper shirt just enough to expose my belly. First I'd hear the heartbeat, then they'd perform the ultrasound.

Just then, there was a knock on the door.

"Come in," Dr. Stevens said.

Joy came in, pushing the cart with the ultrasound machine.

"Hi, there," she said with a grin. "Did you the hear the heartbeat yet?" she said, eyeing the doppler.

"No, we're about to."

"Good," she replied.

Dr. Stevens turned it on, and pressed it lightly on my lower abdomen. I heard static, and then a rhythmic swish swish swish swish.

"That's it!" he said warmly.

"Wow!" I said.

"158," he said. "Very good. Very healthy."

Next, the ultrasound tech poked into the room, and she

and Dr. Stevens set me up for that as Joy and I looked on. The technician slathered the cool, lavender gel on my stomach, flipped some switches and the next thing I knew, my uterus and its contents were on the screen.

I was speechless.

It was not just a little lima bean. It was such a baby.

Distinguishable arms and legs, an oversized little head, knees, a stomach, visible bones. The tech took measurements as I watched in awe. *I can't believe Eamonn would miss this,* I thought. And then I suddenly felt very guilty. Guilty for last night—*what had I done?* In the midst of my own little pity party, I could have seriously hurt this baby—thank God it looks like I hadn't. How whole and healthy it looked, moving gently, breathing inside me.

But the guilt was for more than last night. That wine had only been the culmination of weeks of neglect, psychological if not physical. Since I'd found out about the baby, I hadn't focused on it, at all. Instead, I'd been thinking about the wedding, my future with Eamonn, and the faceless accessory we'd tote around in our Baby Bjorn as we loped around the city holding hands. We'd barely even talked about the baby. And since he'd ditched me, I hadn't actually tried to feel anything for it beyond fear, and that twinge of resentment. But this was very real. Eamonn had clearly understood this more than I had.

"Aww, it's so cute!" said Joy, abandoning her professional persona and giving my arm a squeeze.

After about ten minutes, I had to snap out of my reverie as the tech finished her job. She printed out some pictures for me to take home, and Dr. Stevens gave me a scrip to go to the lab and get my blood work done, preferably by the end of the week. I was also told that according to the ultrasound, my estimated due date was going to be July fourteenth, just under seven months away.

"I'll come by this weekend, okay, mamacita?" said Joy, giving me a quick hug before checking the clock. "Gotta go, I'm already running behind on my 12:30."

"Sounds good."

"You'll be ok 'til then?"

I smiled. "I'm more than ok."

And I was. I missed Eamonn terribly, but I was beginning to accept what he'd known, possibly all along: that we wouldn't have a future together. My future was this baby. This baby was going to be the love of my life, and I couldn't have had it without Eamonn, so I owed him thanks for that.

It's not like I felt like this all the time, though. Shit, I was pregnant—of course I was hormonal and had days where I wanted to fly over to Ireland just so I could throat-punch him. Unfortunately, there was no way for me to do that. He'd closed his Skype account, changed his email address and had more or less disappeared off the face of the earth, just like he promised he wouldn't. Every Google search I did on him turned out to be a dead end. It was almost as if he'd ceased to exist.

By the time February rolled around, when I was clearly showing and anxiously awaiting my "big ultrasound," I started to get a little panicky about the logistics of how this whole single mom thing was supposed to pan out. By now, at work I had gone from working five full days in the office to one morning a week for a staff meeting, with the rest of my writing and editing done at home and sent over email to the senior editor. So that at least meant flexibility in my schedule. I had told Sandy about the pregnancy just after Christmas, and especially in light of the Eamonn debacle, she'd been more than understanding.

"I don't care when or where you do your work, as long as it gets done on time," she said. "Same goes for after you have the baby, too. Working from home is fine. I don't want you to feel like you need to worry about finding a daycare on top of everything else."

That was a huge relief. Especially since I'd looked at my finances, which were going to be a joke in a very short time. The good news was that I'd always had private health insurance, so as long as this pregnancy continued to be easy and problem-free, I shouldn't have any major problems covering the cost of it. Once the baby was born, though, to add the kid to my policy was going to be....well, let's just say it was a little eye-opening.

My friends and family couldn't have been more supportive. Both my parents came with me to my big ultrasound when I was twenty weeks out, and all three of us had screamed in excitement once the ultrasound technician typed across the screen, "It's a Girl!!" I'd always had a little bit of a feeling that it would be, but the confirmation made it complete. I know I would have been just as happy with a boy, but I think finding out beforehand helped me shape my daydreams a little more and helped me mentally prepare a little more for the future with my daughter.

In early May, Joy threw me a baby shower. It was held in the party room in her condo building, a huge space with floor to ceiling windows, a view of the skyline, and a grandiose living room with plush, oversized leather couches. She and my mom had made a slideshow of baby and toddler pictures of me, and it played on the massive TV in the corner with background music. The songs were all featuring the word baby, including "Baby Got Back," "Baby, I Love Your Way," and "I'm Your Baby Tonight." Pretty cheesy, but everyone got a kick out of it. The appetizers included baby carrots, baby pigs in a blanket, baby quiches and cocktails—both baby-friendly and non-baby-friendly. Joy had more class than to offer any of the ridiculous shower games, so no one was tying any toilet paper around my stomach, but they were placing bets on when I'd deliver. I'm pretty sure the pool was up to over $200. Both Paul and I had been born more than two weeks early, so I put five dollars in for June thirtieth.

Maybe it was because they felt badly for me, I don't know, but everyone went overboard with the baby gifts. I had a coordinating teal and burnt orange mod print stroller with car seat attachment, deluxe playard (which I planned to use in lieu of a crib), high chair, bouncer seat, swing, and playmat. For clothes, I'd gotten about three dozen complete outfits ranging from newborn size to six months, and even shoes, a baby sleeping bag of sorts, pajamas, onesies; for feeding I got half a dozen nursing tanks, a nursing pillow, both glass and plastic bottles, and the piece de resistance, one of the top hands-free breast pumps on the market (again, thanks, Joy!). And not only that, I had more than 3,200 diapers and 2,400 wipes. Every guest had come with a Costco-sized box of one or the other in varying sizes 1-4. By the looks of it, I would hardly have to buy anything for the entire next year.

I was worried about money, though. More worried than I let on. My mom had offered a room in their house, if I wanted to move in. A few years ago, my parents had downsized from their home to a two-bedroom townhouse in a fifty-five and older community, not too far from the outlet mall in Aurora.

They loved the lack of yard work—especially with my dad's bad knees—but there wasn't a lot of space. The second bedroom functioned as a guest room/space for the NordicTrack/craft room for my mom's scrapbooking supplies and occasional Pinterest projects. And while my mom was going to be a fantastic grandmother, knowing her, I had a feeling that things could go one of two ways: she'd either take over completely and give me so much unsolicited advice that my head would spin; or, she'd politely bite her tongue, but watching her do so would grate on me and make me second guess everything I did anyway. I thought it was best to avoid either situation if I could. Plus, I was pretty sure that moving in there would violate the association laws, and my parents couldn't risk that. I knew that my dad wouldn't be retiring from the car dealership anytime soon; since the stock market had tanked, he'd lost most of his retirement savings. My mom was even working four days a week at a linen store in Wheaton now. They weren't living the golden retiree life. I didn't want to additionally burden them.

And when it came down to it, I just couldn't face the idea of moving back home unless I really, desperately had to. I hadn't lived at home since the summer I was twenty-one, and certainly didn't want to feel like a kid again when I was going to be raising my own. No, this is something I wanted to do on my own. Okay, if not with Eamonn, then on my own. I just hoped I could afford to hang on to my independence.

When I took the birthing class with Joy by my side (or actually, they had her sit behind me most of the time. It seemed a little sapphic), I felt even more ready for the big day. I certainly felt prepared to jump at the first mention of an epidural, after watching the video of an unmedicated birth—holy shit, no thank you. I felt prepared for changing diapers, I got the hang of the swaddle, and I was pretty excited about breastfeeding.

This part of the workshop was taught by a lactation consultant. She was firmly in favor of breastfeeding—obviously—but she made it a point to tell the class not to beat ourselves up if it didn't end up working out for our family.

"Breastfeeding is not going to be easy right off the bat," she had said, passing out a huge folder of worksheets and tips. "There are lots of different solutions to many common problems, but if it takes too much of a toll on you, only you can decide if you want to continue with breastfeeding. The most important thing is that you and your child are healthy."

June thirtieth came and went, so I lost the pool for the birth of my own child. No big deal. Then July fourteenth came and went as well. That was a slightly bigger deal. I was pretty uncomfortable by then, being forty weeks pregnant, not to mention *in July*. The only shoes I could wear were my flip flops since my feet were so swollen; I couldn't eat more than a few bites at meals because there was literally no room for the food to go; her sweet little butterfly flutters from the inside had turned into Muay-Thai force roundhouse kicks.

At Joy's practice, they had a firm guideline in place: in a low-risk pregnancy, no inductions until two weeks past the due date. Which, incidentally, would be my birthday.

"Can't you do something?" I whined to her on the fifteenth. "Strip my damn membranes or something?"

"No! A: You're not my patient. B: You're not high-risk. C: She'll probably come any day without any intervention." Joy did, however, ensure my induction was set up for me to come in the evening of the twenty-seventh, so the baby could come as early as possible on the twenty-eighth—if necessary.

And lo and behold, it was necessary. This kid. Did. Not. Want. To. Budge. I was jacked full of Pitocin, an epidural cocktail, and six hours later at the stroke of midnight, I was only at three centimeters. Six hours after that, I was at four. Six hours after that, I was back at three. I was exhausted from the painful contractions. The epidural had all but worn off. I was sick of the ice chips Joy and my mom kept feeding me. I was drained from throwing up so much from the pain. And oh, God, no one tells you what contractions are like at this point, and the awful, awful pressure. Just so you know, it's like having to take the worst shit ever, but you can't. You just can't.

I just wanted this baby out.

Dr. Stevens said, "At this point, we have two options. We can continue with the Pitocin and see if you progress; or, we can opt for a Caesarean."

I thought about it for about two seconds, then said, "C-section."

He nodded and said, "Okay. We'll be back shortly to take you to the OR."

After a short time, the team came back, moved me to a gurney and rolled me to an operating room. I was only allowed to have one person in the room with me, so I decided to keep Joy there.

"You're doing great," she whispered, as she held my hand and smoothed my brow. They set up the sheet so I couldn't see anything—thank goodness—and after feeling some brief tugging, I heard Dr. Stevens say, "It's a girl!"

They cleaned her off and toweled her up, my pink-faced little moppet with a healthy set of lungs and chubby cheeks.

My Madeline. Madeline Maeve.

"Happy birthday to us," I said softly. I tried to not think of it as the one-year anniversary of meeting Eamonn.

She was eight pounds, nine ounces and twenty inches of pure perfection. I was in love already.

4

Maddie was six months old, and already it felt like I'd known her all my life. It was a new, remarkable, kind of happiness, and so surreal to imagine she might not have existed; that I might have ever missed out on becoming a mother.

She was an easy baby overall, with a sweet temperament and curious nature. Once she could focus, she spent most of her time looking at the world around her, happily batting at the toys above her on the playmat, swinging in her swing, playing with her feet. When she was hungry, she quietly nommed on her hands, and I'd dart over to scoop her up and feed her right away. Even at night, I somehow developed some kind of mommy radar, and would wake up from the deepest sleep the moment she began to hunger. She ate seemingly all the time, but it was okay: I was producing way more than she needed, it was like my body was in overdrive. I continued to leak so much that after feeding her, I hooked myself up to the pump and expelled an additional ten to twelve ounces and stuck it in the freezer, in the hopes that one day soon, she actually *would* learn to tolerate a bottle. When she didn't, I started donating to the hospital's milk bank program, where donors provided the breast milk to babies in the NICU. I weighed about fifteen pounds less than I had before I got pregnant, and was a jeans size smaller. But still a double D in my bra. I would have felt sexy if I weren't so sleep-deprived.

But we were great, really great—except for one big problem. I was still mainly in denial over this, but I had a feeling that soon I would be finding myself in serious financial trouble. The c-section had made me hit my $10,000 deductible for my insurance and then some, and adding Maddie to my insurance plan cost an additional arm and a leg. Thankfully, she hadn't cost me much money since I still had everything from the baby shower, but between keeping a roof over my head and trying to pay off medical bills, I'd started using my only-for-emergencies credit card for my weekly trips for groceries and gas. Eamonn had yet to send me a dime. I wasn't even sure where he was living now, since his parents claimed he'd moved out since taking a job as a forklift operator at a cousin's construction company in Galway (Google had eventually provided me their address, and they wrote me a short, tersely-worded note after I'd sent seven, count them, seven letters).

I'd always paid attention to my finances, and sure, I'd worried about them from time to time, I guess, but I'd never known what it was like to feel this kind of anxiety. Because it wasn't just about me anymore. I could accept sacrifices for myself, but I couldn't live with inflicting those kind of sacrifices on Maddie. She deserved better than the dregs, and she had only me to count on. If anyone was going to make our lives more secure, it meant I'd be the one somehow instigating a change.

So, by April, I figured it was time for something to improve at my workplace. I'd been working for the company for close to seven years and I was good at my job; maybe I could finally leverage my contract position into a full-time one, with the benefits Maddie and I really needed. I spent hours rehearsing how I'd make my case to Sandy. I just needed *something* to change, I thought. And it did, but not the way I expected. The next morning when I went into work—Meg was great enough to let me drop Maddie off with her and Simon one morning a week so I could attend my department's weekly meeting and have actual adult conversations—I had barely turned my computer on for the morning when Sandy poked her head over my cubicle.

"There's going to be an all-staff meeting at nine," she said, looking grim.

"Do you know what it's about?"

She looked over her shoulder and lowered her voice. "Unfortunately."

My stomach started to churn. "Give it to me straight."

"I wish I could," she said, barely audible. "I'll see you in the lobby by nine."

Shit. I knew it. When I went to the lobby to join the rest of the forty-some employees, my head was swimming so fast that I could barely listen to the CEO when she announced that due to cutbacks and budgetary constraints, the company would be restructuring, and we'd be meeting within our individual teams for additional details. Half an hour later, Sandy numbly gave us a clearly rehearsed speech to inform us that *Fixtures* was folding into a once-a-year supplement to the parent magazine, and as a result, the last day for the entire staff would be April thirtieth—less than a month away. No severance.

I went back to my desk, pulled up my bank account online and grabbed my calculator from my drawer. I had just about enough money in my checking account for a month of rent. I had about $3,000 in my 401k that hadn't been touched yet or taxed. I hadn't hit the limit for my credit card—yet. I figured that Maddie and I would have about 2 more months of security. But after that, I had no idea what the hell I was going to do. The publishing industry was circling the drain seven years ago when I had first started at *Fixtures*; at this point in time, jobs in editing were so rare that the only people hired were new grads who'd take a salary that was half a step above minimum wage; or, the desperate and overqualified whose resume happened to stand out among the three hundred or so submitted for the position.

That night, I called Joy and broke down. After giving me the appropriate amount of sympathy, she got down to business.

"We have to find Eamonn," she said. "I mean, this is his daughter's livelihood we're talking about. He can't keep shirking his responsibility. "

"He shut down the email address he gave me," I said glumly. "And his parents claim that he moved out and don't have an address for him. They won't give up any info. I've tried and tried."

"Uh-huh," she said. "First, I think we should look into getting a private investigator. Second, we'll brush up your resume. And third, we'll start looking into jobs for you. Who knows, maybe you'll be able to find something in another field. Something where you can take the skills you already have, and kind of rework them into another job, you know?"

"I guess."

"Don't worry, we'll figure it out."

And just like that, it was over. Whenever I could get Maddie down to nap, I spent every moment I could desperately searching for jobs on Indeed, Monster, and

CareerBuilder. In the first week, I started a spreadsheet to track how many jobs I sent out, but then I stopped somewhere around week three / application eighty-five. It was getting too depressing to see the numbers of both the queries and the rejections escalating.

Maddie wasn't having a great time, either. She could tell something was up, and the more I tried to distract her with a movie or a toy so that I could fill out another forty-five-minute application, the clingier and whinier she got. At about nine months old, she was getting in her first tooth, too, so that didn't help matters much. I often let her sleep on me, as it made her fuss less. She started to nurse less then, as well. Instead she wanted to snack on frozen waffles or bagels, or whole carrots, anything large and hard that she could destroy. Still, I kept pumping during her normal feeding times, just in case. At least it made me feel useful; I just wished someone could pay me for it, seeing as it was about the only useful thing I was doing these days. I'd actually heard from Joy that there actually were these *for profit* milk banks popping up all over the country, where milk was sold, apparently, at around five dollars per ounce. They still didn't pay their donors, though: it all relied on volunteers. It seemed a little unfair. By my calculations, if I'd been selling *my* milk at $5 an ounce I'd have earned about $25,000 by now.

One day, not too long after the first tooth *finally* popped through at the end of May, I was drinking ice water through a straw, holding it in my left hand and holding her on my lap as we watched *The Pirates of the Caribbean* on WGN (I had just cancelled cable). I was daydreaming about Orlando Bloom when I suddenly looked down and saw her sucking the water down through my straw. The next day, I bought her a pair of pink straw sippy cups, and that was it for her. I kept pumping to keep up the supply she needed, and poured it straight into the cup.

It was bittersweet, seeing her grow up that little bit more—especially when I was still jobless. It got me waking up at night all over again, wondering how I was going to provide for the months and years ahead. I had all my friends primed to let me know of anything they heard of: corporate communications, copywriting, even if there was a small-time gig as a freelance sub-editor. I couldn't afford to be picky.

One day in mid-June, I was toting Maddie through the Lincoln Park Zoo (it's free!) when my phone rang.

"Hey, Joy," I said. "What's up?"

"I've got some really awesome news!" she said. "I think I've found you a job."

"For real?" I said. "What kind of job?"

"Okay," Joy said. "Now what I am about to tell you has to stay between you and me. Whether or not you decide to take the job."

"This doesn't sound good," I said.

"No, it is," she assured me. "But it has to do with doctor-patient confidentiality."

"Go on," I said, intrigued.

"You know how you have been donating milk to the milk bank for the NICU babies?"

"Yeah?"

"I have this patient who's very high-profile," she said, lowering her voice. "She came in for a routine exam last week, and then told me that she's expecting twins with a surrogate."

"How nice for her."

"Yeah. The *really* interesting thing to me was that she

consulted with me about getting a tubal a couple of years back, when she had flat-out told me she never wanted children. It was bizarre. But who the hell knows with people like her. Anyway, she was very direct, and asked me if I could put her in connection with a direct supply for milk for the twins."

"Why wouldn't she just get it from a milk bank?"

"Amanda, I'm telling you. She'd do anything to have them *nurse*," she insisted.

It dawned on me. "You want me to nurse other people's babies?!" I exploded. "What the fuck year do you think this is, Joy? This isn't goddamn Victorian England, and I'm not a goddamn governess. People don't do that."

"Oh, really? You want to place a bet?" she retorted. "You think that celebrities and models have multiple nannies just because they can afford it? Nope. Usually one of them is getting paid just for the breastfeeding service she provides, so the mom can go back to diet pills and cigarettes. And the actresses that work fourteen-hour-days on set, three weeks after delivering? Yeah, they're not nursing their kids. The ones that sign contracts with the magazines to post their 'back in shape two months after baby!' covers? They're not nursing, because it would make them too hungry. No, they're working out like crazy and living on broccoli and breath mints. It's not just they think their kids are above drinking formula. They want them to have the nursing *experience*. You know. Bonding. Make sure they don't grow up to be sociopaths just because they were bottle-fed the milk bank stuff.

"So they find the ultimate nanny—one who usually has been doing this for a long time, usually one from a third-world country where nursing your own kids and those of others is the norm—and they pay them a boatload of money for their services. And Amanda, to them, hiring you would be like hitting the jackpot. You're healthy, you're American, you speak English—you're a college graduate, for God's sake! You'd be making twice what your last job paid you. Easily."

"Joy," I said. "Come on. I can't do that!"

"What, like it's beneath you? It's just milk! Hundred-dollar milk! It's white *gold,* Amanda."

"But it's—I mean—it's like selling my body or something. You didn't give her my number, did you?"

"No, not yet." I could hear the tightness in Joy's voice; she was annoyed at me. "I'd heard some rumors about this kind of thing from the LCs, but this patient flat-out asked me if I knew of anyone..."

"Can you tell me who she is?"

"Only if you're going to consider it."

"I'll *consider* it." Not likely.

She took a deep breath. "Have you ever heard the name Alexandra Lang before?"

Holy shit. I knew exactly who she was. "Unfortunately, yes," I said. "So forget it."

"Amanda! You do know this could ensure a really secure life and future for you and Maddie."

"Uh huh. I'll call you tomorrow," I said.

"Don't take too long to decide," she said. "Who knows, they could ship in someone from Haiti to do the job before you know it."

Maddie and I made one last stop at the giraffes, then hopped on the bus to get home in time for her nap. As she started to doze off in my lap, I stroked her hair, and thought about my first encounter with Alexandra Lang. About five years before, when I had been vying for a permanent, senior editor position at *Fixtures*, I was assigned to write a profile on her. She ran one of the hottest new interior design firms in the city, specializing in restaurants. Their tagline was "Appearance is Everything," which would have made me snicker if her work wasn't so damn impressive. After the host of "Check, Please!" had hired her to provide the decor for her newest, Michelin-starred restaurant the year before, her business had exploded, and Alexandra was becoming a household name, not only among people in the industry, but in-the-know foodies as well.

I had tirelessly worked with her assistant to schedule an interview with her. Each time, the apologetic assistant would call me about five minutes beforehand, letting me know that she was "simply swamped" and wouldn't be able to make it. Once, the interview had even been scheduled at her office, rather than over the phone, and I sat in the lobby for two hours before the assistant sent me home. Finally, when I was a week past deadline, and Sandy was starting to breathe down my neck, the assistant sent me back a list of responses to the interview questions I had emailed in advance. Each response averaged a sentence in length—and I suspected were written by her assistant—and the picture they sent to go along with it was seventy-two dpi and looked like it was from the late 1990s. We had no choice but to run it.

Right after the issue came out, Sandy got an angry call from Alexandra's lawyer, spouting out about defamation of character and running unauthorized images. It took a retraction, written apology from our CEO and a year's worth of free advertising to pacify her. Our CEO also had my head on the chopping block, but Sandy stood up for me and somehow kept me on the payroll. However, the permanent staff job that had been just within my grasp? That went to the asshat in the next cube over who bathed in Drakkar Noir and clipped his nails at his desk. I was effectively demoted to covering basic departments and copy edits. Years later, and it still pissed me off.

No, I'd find another way to take care of Maddie. That was the resolution firm in my mind, until we got home, and I saw that my front door was ajar. Oh, shit.

"Hello," I called in, nudging the door open. Silence. Maddie was completely passed out in the Bjorn on my chest. Probably not one of my smarter moves, but I poked my head in, and gasped.

My entire apartment had been ransacked. My only TV, a 32-inch LG, was gone; my Bluray player, missing, with only the dust surrounding the perimeter of the electronics there to show for it. My Keurig had disappeared. I went into my bedroom and my jewelry box was empty, except for my sorority pin and a few pairs of long-unworn bangles. I had only had a pair of pearl drop earrings and my diamond studs from my parents that were of any value, but those were gone. The box from Overstock with Eamonn's and my wedding rings was empty and on the floor. I snorted. *Good luck getting any money off of those*, I thought.

I called the police, and they told me to stay outside, and they'd send an officer over to help me file a report. As I waited on the steps outside, I paced and kissed Maddie, who was still blissfully asleep. *I can't do this to you,* I thought. *I have to protect you. I have to be a better mom for you. I have to build you a better future.*

My parents picked us up and had us stay at their townhouse that night, as I was wary about being at home until we installed new locks and a deadbolt. Before I went to bed, I texted Joy: "Give her my number."

"Will do!" she replied.

PART TWO

5

The next morning, just after I put Maddie down for her nap, my phone started to chirp.

"Hello?"

"This is Alexandra Lang Interiors," said the assistant. This one was female, so it wasn't the same one who'd nearly ruined my career before. "I'd like to speak with Amanda Keane."

"Yes, this is Amanda Keane."

"Alexandra would like to meet with you regarding a childcare position. Would you be available tomorrow at 9 AM?"

"Sure," I said, heart pounding. "Should I come to the office?"

"Please do." The assistant rattled off the address and directions. It was the same place I had remembered as before, in River North.

My mom quickly agreed to watch Maddie the next morning so I could interview. I assumed I should dress up for the interview, but would a suit be the right way to go for a nanny job? I didn't have any designer-type clothes that would be on the same level as Alexandra Lang. *But she wouldn't expect that anyway,* thought my inner critic. *You're going to be the hired help.*

And the more I thought about that idea, the more I resented it. I graduated from Miami cum laude, I thought bitterly. I'm almost thirty-two years old. *Why the hell am I becoming a freaking nanny? No, not a nanny: a wet nurse.* I shushed my inner critic before she could say anything else snarky.

For my interview, I dressed myself in a black power suit—here's hoping she wouldn't realize it was from 2007—a Coach scarf that my grandma had gotten me for Christmas a few years ago, and black kitten heels. Not exactly nanny attire, but I didn't think it would serve me well to show up there in jeans and a hoodie.

I reviewed my resume as I took the train downtown, and chewed my bottom lip and frowned. Again, all I had on it was my professional work I'd done as a writer and editor. I'd never worked as a nanny before. But I wasn't supposed to put my year so far as a mom on there, was I? That seemed pretty unprofessional. I had listed the hospital's milk bank under "Professional Organizations," not really sure what else to do.

I got to the office about ten minutes beforehand, and once again, waited in the lobby for an inordinate amount of time. Around 10 AM, the assistant (slightly less apologetic than her previous one) let me into her office, where Alexandra sat. She was a tan, petite woman, with arms straddling the line between toned and muscular, and dark brown, close-cropped hair.

Alexandra didn't look at me; she was furiously scribbling with her stylus on her iPad. For as tastefully done as all her restaurants were, her office was actually quite minimalist. Not ugly at all, but just very bare, with white walls, dark hardwood floors, and a pervasive feeling of emptiness. No personal items or photos on her desk. A few large tables behind her, with plenty of space that I assume was for sketching.

"Take a seat," she ordered. As an afterthought, she added, "Please."

I did as I was told. She pulled a manila envelope out from her desk, opened it, and retrieved two identical copies of a contract. It looked to be close to twenty pages long.

"I'm going to get to the point," she said. "I'm in need of your services, starting in sixteen days, give or take a few in case of an early delivery. My surrogate is in Indiana, and I'll want you to provide care for the newborns once they are home. Can you do that?" she looked directly at me.

"I believe so," I said, trying my best to sound confident. "What are your expected hours?"

She laughed. "In my job, there aren't any expected hours," she said. "I might start my day at five and end it at ten PM. Maybe eleven. But you'll be working around my husband's schedule. He's a physics professor at Northwestern, and he's gone from eight to five or so most days."

"Will you need overnight or weekend assistance?"

"Possibly, but not frequently. I understand that you're lactating and must have a child of your own. And I can tell you're single and wouldn't have a lot of overnight care options."

How the hell could she tell that? Just because I didn't have a ring on my finger didn't automatically mean I was totally alone. Right?

"Yes, that's the case," I said. "How will the contract work? Will I be contracted for a set amount of time?"

"I'd prefer to leave it open-ended," she said. "They're twins, so quite frankly, I don't know that you'll be able to keep up with the demand. But I want for them to have at least tried the nursing route."

She did know that she could just buy milk from the bank, right? Well, I sure wasn't going to tell her in case there was something she didn't know.

"Shall we discuss compensation?" she asked. Not waiting for me to reply, she said, "Since there will be two babies requiring your time, I understand that you'd charge more. I'm prepared to pay you $1,500 per week, minus deductions for taxes and Social Security." She unclipped the contract packet and flipped through it until she found the W-9 form, which she slid across the desk to me. Just then, her phone buzzed. She glanced at it briefly, then stood up. I followed suit.

"Please be certain to fill this out before you leave," she said, slipping her iPad into its sleeve and tucking it in her case. "You can sit in the lobby and fill out the rest of it as well. Give it to my assistant, and we'll be in touch within the next few weeks."

Then she was gone.

This woman was cold, but there was no pretense with her. I realized there weren't going to be any fuzzy feelings on either side. I'd be there to do a job, and that would be it. I'll just be smart about it ahead of time, and never quit looking for jobs, I thought. In this field or otherwise.

I signed the forms, initialed where necessary, and promptly gave them to the assistant. I stopped in the restroom before leaving, and as I came out, I heard the assistant on the phone.

"Hello, is this Janine Payton? This is Kelly, the assistant to Alexandra Lang? Yes, you're welcome. I am sorry to inform you that as it turns out, Ms. Lang and Dr. Lang won't be needing your services as a nanny...yes, as it turns out, there has been a change of plans...no, I'm sorry, it doesn't. Take care now."

The next two weeks passed fairly quickly, with all the ducks I had to get in a row. I had two weeks to not only wean Maddie off of breast milk altogether, but also jack up my milk supply enough for two newborns. Maddie had tried some sips of whole milk in the past, but not many. I would have enough breast milk in my freezer stash to cover the next few weeks, but I wanted to have some backup for the twins in case this didn't go how I planned. I mean, what if my supply totally dropped? What if my body reacted to some strange kid trying to get all up in my body—would my hormones still respond the way they did with Maddie?

I decided I'd start off by mixing a splash of whole milk into Maddie's sippy of milk at breakfast the next morning. She didn't bat an eye. At her mid-morning snack, I splashed in an ounce or so more. Made no difference. It's probably TMI, but her poops were only slightly worse that day. By the end of the next day, she was drinking regular milk like it was her job. And for all intents and purposes, it was. I still kept pumping, and my body didn't notice anything different either.

By some amazing stroke of luck, the Bright Stars Children's Center, a two-block walk from my apartment and only steps from the L stop, had one last spot in the one-year-old room available, due to a child celebrating his second birthday earlier that week, and the last person on the wait list had just moved to the suburbs. I wrote my deposit check for—gulp—$628, which would cover Maddie's first and last week of care. About three weeks prior, my check might have bounced. However, I had just sold my 2003 Corolla to someone on Craigslist for $3,000, so I would be covered in rent for the month, plus daycare, food, electricity, water...but not much else.

Maddie had only spent the random afternoons every few weeks with my parents, or occasionally Meg and I would trade off sitting duties with each other, but the reality was that she had been with me almost twenty-four hours a day since she was born. I was starting to have major anxiety about leaving her at a daycare with unfamiliar people for eight-plus hours per day. What if she hated it? What if she got scared? Or what if there was a kid in her class that was a biter? She wasn't even walking yet, and the only words she could say were 'mama,' 'hi,' 'more' and 'ball.' What if she couldn't communicate what she needed to her teachers? What if they weren't watching and she rolled off the changing table one day?

I'd realized I'd put almost no thought or research into the type of place I'd be sending her to all day. I had no idea how this place compared to other daycares, or the way they used or didn't use discipline. I didn't even know what she'd be eating. All I knew was it was on the way to work, I could probably afford it, and it was going to be $314 per week. Oh, and I would have to provide the diapers and wipes.

When I wasn't stressing about Maddie, I was training for the new job by power-pumping as much as I could. I'd never had much of an issue before in terms of milk production, but I figured twins would be a new challenge. I followed every old wives' tale I'd heard of that could amp up my milk supply: I took fenugreek supplements religiously, ate a huge bowl of steelcut oatmeal every morning for breakfast, and drank a pint of Guinness every night, when I'd engage in another power pumping session for an hour. By the time the twins were born, I was up to about thirty-six ounces per day. Not bad.

Alexandra called me at 7 AM on the day they were born,

and actually sounded slightly excited about them. "Esther and Eunice were born at 5:15 and 5:17, respectively, this morning," she said. "6 pounds, and 5 pounds, 4 ounces."

"That's great," I said, stifling a yawn. "How are they? How is the birth mother?"

"The surrogate is fine. The babies held in there for so long that they made it to the c-section date, which is fantastic. She's in recovery at the moment."

"Good to hear," I said. "Congratulations!"

"Thank you. We'll be home in three days. I'll need you at 7:30 AM this coming Monday to start. Your normal start time will be 8, of course, but we'll need you in early to go over their schedule."

She wasn't planning to take any kind of maternity leave? And she thought newborns operated on schedules. Shit, maybe hers would, though, for fear of upsetting her if they did otherwise.

That was another thing. When I told my mom after my interview that I'd landed the job, she'd started actually jumping for joy. But once I explained to her that I'd be providing childcare for one of the most high-profile families in Chicago, she grew quiet.

"You're going to be a babysitter?"

"A child care provider, technically."

"I just don't understand. Why would you do that?"

"Joy got me in touch with the family. It was one of her patients, and they're having twins via surrogate. I'm just there to help out a little bit during the day, make it easier on the mom." I couldn't tell her I'd be nursing another person's babies. I just couldn't.

"What about Maddie? Will you be bringing her with

you?"

"No, she'll be in daycare."

"Daycare?!" she burst out. I then proceeded to tune her out as she lectured me about the evils of daycare, and how she wishes I would just move back to the suburbs so she could watch Maddie (not that she'd drive into the city on a daily basis to watch her—I was lucky if I could persuade Mom to make the drive once a season).

So all that was left to do was get over my mom's disappointment in me (ha, easier said than done), and prepare myself and Maddie for the first day of our new life. I admit, I couldn't even put her in her playard on Sunday night. I got her into her pajamas, flipped "Tangled" on to my Kindle, and let her watch in my bed with me until she fell asleep. Then I lay there, stroking her golden brown hair, watching her chest rise and fall as she softly snored away. I hoped I was strong enough for this.

6

When my alarm went off, I resolved to go in to this new routine with a brave face, at least for Maddie's sake. I made her pancakes and bacon for breakfast—both her favorite and mine—and sang our favorite Beatles' hits as I packed up all she needed—diapers for the week, two outfit changes, and a blanket to keep in her crib—and got her in the stroller by 6:30. I grabbed my purse and my pump, then locked the door behind us and wheeled to daycare. I was wearing a nursing tank under a loose cotton sundress, canvas flats and a light denim jacket. Again, I hoped I was dressed appropriately. The contract hadn't included anything about a dress code.

When we got to the daycare, I punched in my passcode and the system buzzed us in. A cute little boy of about three with short brown hair, ice blue eyes, and dimples was spinning around in a circle and almost knocked into Maddie's stroller.

"Whoa, buddy!" said presumably his dad, grabbing his arm before he tumbled into us. The dad was a carbon copy of the boy plus about thirty years, both dressed in loose-fitting jeans and a polo.

"Excuse us," he said with a half-grimace as he picked his boy up and put him into a fireman's carry over his shoulder.

Maddie and I walked into the one-year-old room, and her teacher greeted us.

"This must be Maddie! Hi, Maddie! I'm Miss Kelsie!" she bubbled.

Maddie looked at her blankly.

"Do you like Elmo?" she asked, pulling out an Elmo puppet from behind her back. "Because Elmo loves you!" She made the doll start munching on Maddie's neck. Maddie shrieked with laughter. She pulled away from my hold and reached toward Miss Kelsie. I let her go.

"Now wave bye-bye to Mommy!" Miss Kelsie said.

Maddie waved at me and laughed.

I reached in and gave her a kiss on the cheek. "Bye, honey. I love you so much." I gave her one more kiss on the nose for good measure. "I'll be back before six," I said to Miss Kelsie.

"We'll see you then!" she said, and whirled back into the room, where two little boys were playing with a pop-up toy, and two other little girls were eating Cheerios in their high chairs.

She's gonna be more okay than me, I thought.

I left without looking back again so I didn't lose my nerve, then got on the L.

Alexandra and her family lived in a gorgeous high-rise directly across from Millennium Park. I dodged a few tourists with fanny packs taking pictures of the lake on my way into the building, where I was greeted by a doorman.

“I'm Amanda Keane, here to see Alexandra Lang,” I said.

He picked up the phone and murmured into it. A moment later, he politely smiled and buzzed the door to the elevator entrance open. I headed to the fourteenth floor.

Alexandra greeted me at the door. "Come in," she ordered.

"Good morning," I said.

"And you," she said.

"How are the girls?" I asked.

"They're well," she said. "They've been sleeping for the past three hours, which is to be expected at this age."

Four days old and already having to meet expectations. Poor kids. A paunchy, grandfatherly man in a gunmetal gray sweater, trousers, and loafers walked into the room. This couldn't be...could it?

"You must be Amanda," he said, already about ten times more personable than his wife. "Nice to meet you. I'm Dr. Fred Lang."

"Nice to meet you, sir." Oh my God. I felt like I was back in high school meeting my friend's dad or something. He had to be in his early sixties. Was that a handkerchief sticking out of his pocket? "Congratulations on your little ones."

"Thank you," he said. "Would you like to see them?"

"Let's go over the schedule first," interjected Alexandra.

"Sure," I said. She motioned for me to sit down at their expansive, and doubtless expensive, bamboo dining room table. About half an hour later, my brain was hurting from trying to memorize all the specifications. And I hadn't known that dealing with cloth diapers was going to be part of the deal. After each diaper change (and there might be up to ten a day for each of them), I needed to rinse them out in the toilet, apply an organic stain remover, and take them to a special bin in the laundry area. So glad these babies' asses were too special for Pampers and a Diaper Genie.

She also went over all the specifications of exactly how she wanted me to feed them: simultaneously, as long as both were awake, held in football style, preferably on the daybed in their nursery, and no more than twenty-five minutes per feeding. Feedings were, for now, supposed to be only upon waking. But, I would have to do all the magic with the diapers first. Like a pair of twins waking up hungry were going to be thrilled to wait ten minutes for cloth diaper maintenance before getting a meal.

Alexandra looked at the clock on her phone. “I've got to run. Fred?" she called. "Will you show Amanda to the nursery?"

"No problem," he said, coming back into the dining room with a copy of *The New York Times* tucked under his arm. She gave him a peck on the cheek before dashing out the door.

"The nursery is this way," he said, shuffling down the hall. The apartment was a luxury version of Crate & Barrel, the irony being that Crate & Barrel was still more than I could afford. The place looked like a showroom. Not a trace of babies could be found, until we entered the nursery. Oh, for fuck's sake. It was all white. Did she think that her kids wouldn't puke, pee or poop, either? I seriously hoped they'd gotten all the meconium out while they were in the hospital.

The two of them were sleeping swaddled in blankets, cuddled together in the same crib, facing each other. They were such tiny, little red cherubs with downy blond hair and perfectly rounded little heads. My heart immediately melted. Maddie had never been this small. Being two weeks late, Joy joked that it looked like Maddie would be driving us home from the hospital instead of my mom.

"They are so perfect," I whispered.

"They should be," he chuckled," for what we paid for them." He gave me a wry smile.

"Alexandra told me you used a surrogate," I said, not sure what else to say. "I think it's wonderful that there are women out there who help people build their families."

"Mmmm," he said, shutting the door behind us. "Well, here's the monitor. I'll be leaving for the day soon. The list of emergency phone numbers is in the packet that Alexandra gave you."

"Great," I said. "We'll be fine. Have a good day."

"You do the same," he said, as he pulled on his trench coat and loafers, then closed the front door quietly behind him.

How in the world did those two get together? I wondered. *Hmm. Maybe better not to even think about it, because I'm sure the answer would thoroughly creep me out.*

I glanced at the monitor—the girls were still in dreamland, and I surveyed the main living space a bit more. Just like in Alexandra's office, the feeling was a bit minimalist, with no photos to be seen anywhere. The main decor was in the form of vases, a few plush throw pillows, a basket of fresh lemons on the counter, a clock on the wall. I didn't need to open the fridge to see what was inside, as the doors were see-through: one row of neatly lined bottles of Smartwater, and the other rows housed pre-packaged, labeled meals from what I assumed was their home meal service. I wondered for a moment, *did Dr. Lang really get with this program?* Maybe had his own fridge of snacks and a drawer full of Fiber One bars in his office. Looked like I'd be packing a lunch.

I started to hear a "neh neh neh" sound over the monitor. One of the girls was waking up. I jogged to the room, hoping to get to her before her sister woke up. Which girl was which, I realized I had no clue. I swiftly changed her diaper—luckily, the nuts and bolts were the same on these as they were for the disposables—and seeing that her sister was still asleep, tucked her into the crook of my elbow as I made my way to the laundry room. Sorry, lady, I'm not going to leave her in the nursery to cry and wake up the other one. There didn't seem to be any nanny cams in the laundry room that I could tell, so I just tossed it in the bin, washed my hands, and went back to the nursery.

By then, the other twin was mewling. I placed the first one back in the crib, changed the second one–she'd had a ginormous poop—ugh, I did not miss that part of the newborn stage–and for a moment I froze, not sure what to do next. Take the poopy diaper to rinse out and let them both scream? I was already dreading having to wash the poop that had gotten on the white chenille changing pad. (Again, who the fuck even makes a white changing pad?)

Instead, I laid them both on the daybed, unhooked my bra, set up the nursing pillow, took a deep breath...and let both of them go to town.

It was a little like ripping off a Band-Aid, and I felt the tears spring to my eyes right away as well. This had been *Maddie's* job, *Maddie's* role, *Maddie's* and my little bond, our little covenant, our little promise that I'd just broken by farming myself out to a pair of strangers.

As the minutes passed, though, it got easier. Looking at their sweet, golden heads as they quietly nommed away, they reminded me of what those first few weeks had been like. Going from taking care of only myself to having such responsibility for a tiny, dependent, perfect little creature. These babies needed me, too.

The feeding part itself was less difficult than one might think. My letdown came quick and like a current–no different than it had been with Maddie in that sense. Plus, it was nice to be able to experience the letdown from both sides at once, without fear of leaking or needing to pump on the other side simultaneously. I let them go for twenty-five minutes, as promised. I had to take times burping them—I hoped the other one waiting didn't feel too slighted—but other than that, it wasn't too bad. I laid them both back in their cribs, ran like hell for the bathroom to rinse out the diaper and get it in the laundry bin, and was back in under two minutes. And wouldn't you know it, they'd already fallen back asleep.

The rest of the day continued in more or less the same pattern. I quickly realized my best bet was to just stay in the nursery the entire day, so I could get to the first one before her sister was up. Some of the feedings were joint, others were staggered, but no more than an hour went by that I didn't have either one of them hooked up to a boob. My appreciation for the mothers of twins increased about tenfold by afternoon. I hadn't eaten lunch, since I didn't bring one for myself, and wasn't about to break into the Langs' meals; I'd barely had time to go to the bathroom; and I was a little on edge from being in the same white room the entire day, desperately trying to keep it clean and quiet.

Fred arrived shortly after five. I had just put the twins back down.

"How were they?" he asked with a paternal (grand-paternal) smile.

"Fantastic!" I said, almost bolting for the front door to get my shoes on. "I'll see you at eight!"

I ran into the 7-11 on the way home, buying a Big Grab of Cheetos and greedily shoveling them in my mouth on the L ride, not caring how gross I looked to the other commuters. I then made it to Maddie's daycare with about a minute to spare before six, when I'd be charged five dollars for every minute I arrived late to get her.

When I got to her room, Maddie was sitting at a table with two other tots, smearing pink fingerpaint onto construction paper. I came into the room, and she said, "Mama!" as soon as she saw me. The afternoon teacher quickly wiped off her wiggling fingers and took off her smock, and Maddie waddled into my embrace.

"How did she do today?"

"She couldn't have done better." The teacher handed me a report, complete with all of Maddie's meals, including how much she ate of each food; the time and consistency of each diaper change (anyone but a mom might be grossed out; I, of course, was intrigued) a list of activities in which she's participated, and the length of her afternoon nap. I took her stroller out from the kids' cubby room, sat her in it, and we cheerfully headed home. "Looks like we're both gonna make it," I said. My ass had been thoroughly kicked, but I had no doubt that both of us would settle into our new routines just fine.

The next day, we got to daycare at the same time as the Cute Daycare Dad and his little boy again.

"After you," he said, holding the door open for me and Maddie.

"Thanks," I said, squeezing the stroller past him. As I unhooked Maddie from her stroller, I watched with half an eye as I saw his tot tear down the hall squealing.

"I'm gonna get you!" said the dad, chasing after the boy and laughing before picking him up and dangling him upside down. I wondered if that little kid knew how good he had it, to have a dad like that. Doubtful.

I settled Maddie into her room, then headed out.

I got to work just before eight, and after the doorman buzzed me up, it was Fred who greeted me this time.

"Hello, Amanda," he said warmly.

"Good morning," I chirped back, entering the condo.

"Can I offer you some tea?" he asked.

Oh! That was nice. "Love some," I said.

"English Breakfast all right?" he called over his shoulder, opening the cupboard.

"Perfect."

He placed a teabag into a mug and poured some water in from the still-steaming kettle, yawning. I had a sneaking suspicion that he handled most of the overnight duties with the twins.

"I'm not much of a coffee drinker," he said apologetically, handing me the mug.

"Me, either," I admitted. "Funny, when I was a kid I always thought that drinking coffee was what made you an adult, so maybe I'm not there yet." And, my big mouth strikes again.

But he just chuckled. "If only," he said.

Just then, I heard a squawk from the nursery.

"I better get to work," I said.

"Me, too," Fred replied, transferring the tea from his Northwestern mug to a stainless steel Contigo carafe. "I'll see you this afternoon."

This day passed almost exactly as the first. I spent nearly nine hours trapped in that nursery just feeding, changing, transitioning to the nap. Feeding, changing, transitioning to the nap. Feeding, changing, transitioning to the nap. I had learned from my mistakes the day before and packed a liter-sized water bottle with me that morning, which I refilled twice throughout the day. I packed a sandwich for lunch as well, which I barely had time to scarf down, and ate a couple of granola bars just to keep up my energy. But the day flew by.

Around 4:30, when I was tossing the diapers into the laundry room, the Langs' house phone rang. I didn't think they'd want me to answer it, so I let the machine pick up.

"Hi, Mr. and Mrs. Lang?" said a nervous voice, with the slightly-southern twang you hear once you're about fifty miles from the lakefront. "Um, it's me. Emmalee. I just wanted to call and check in and see how the babies were doing. I, um...." Her voice trailed off and she started sniffling. "I just hope they're doing well. And all of you, too. Okay. Please call me if you can." She left a number and then hung up.

It had to have been the surrogate. I hadn't thought much about her until now. God, she sounded young. And lost.

Then, Fred came home just after five, so off I went.

Before I got on the L, I gave Joy a quick call to fill her in.

"How is your first week going?" she asked.

"Tough, but I'm surviving. Twins bring a whole new level of crazy to the baby equation. But Maddie seems to really like daycare, and it feels good to actually be working again."

"Sounds promising!"

"As long as the check clears," I said. "And Alexandra's husband is really nice. Did you know he's our dads' age?"

"We've met," she said. "So at any rate, what you mean to say is that your best friend hooked you up with an amazing, high-paying job," she prodded.

"Yes, yes," I said with an eye roll. "You were right, Joy."

"Can you teach Jonathan how to say that? It just sounds so good," she said.

We chatted for a couple more minutes, then I got on the

train.

I got to daycare and what do you know, Cute Daycare Dad was walking in right as I was again.

"We've got to stop meeting like this," I joked.

"Sorry?" he said, confused.

"Oh, nothing," I said, reddening. I punched in my code and hurried in.

That night, Maddie seemed a little more tired than usual, and was asleep only seconds after I put her down for the night. They must be wearing her out there, I thought. And the more I thought about it, the better I felt about Maddie being in daycare. She was getting so much more of an enriching life than I had been giving her, hanging out all day at home watching Sesame Street and occasionally futzing with her handful of Melissa and Doug toys. I sure as hell hadn't tried flashcards and finger painting with her before. She was practically in a preschool at this place! I patted myself on the back, thinking what good judgment I had in taking this job and getting Maddie one step closer to acceptance into MENSA.

Then, at 2 AM, I woke up to the sound of screaming.

7

I ran into Maddie's room and saw that she was drenched in sweat, red-faced and feverish. Shit. She'd never been sick before. I called the pediatrician's office, crossing my fingers that they had an overnight nurse on call.

"My daughter just woke up feeling really warm. I checked, and she has a fever of 102," I said. I did at least have a thermometer from the first aid kit I'd gotten at my baby shower. "What should I do?" *Please, please don't tell me I have to take her to the ER. Please, please, please.*

"How old is she?"

"She'll turn one later this month."

"I would recommend giving her a dose of concentrated infant's ibuprofen. The dose will last six to eight hours. You can also try giving her a lukewarm bath. But if it continues to climb over 104, I would recommend taking her to the ER."

"All right, I will. Thank you," I said, and hung up. I felt sick to my stomach. I didn't have any infant's ibuprofen on hand since she'd never been sick before. Dammit. And I didn't have an Eamonn on hand to go get it, either. Feeling like the worst mom ever, I gave Maddie a lukewarm bath, slipped her back into her pajamas, plopped her in her stroller, and headed down the street to the twenty-four-hour pharmacy.

A little over an hour later, I dosed a sweaty Maddie with her medicine, gave her another lukewarm bath, and placed her back in her pack and play to go to sleep. It was about six and light out when I had to wake Maddie up and get her ready for the day. Her fever had gone down to 99.8, so I decided I wouldn't even tell daycare. They had a rule about a child being out of there for twenty-four hours after a fever goes away, but there was no way I could call in sick on my third day of work. I'd just have to rely on adrenaline to get me through the day.

When I dropped Maddie off, she started sniffling and burst into tears.

"It's ok, honey," I murmured, feeling once again like the shittiest mom on the planet.

"I think she's coming down with the sniffles," I said to Miss Kelsie by means of explanation, as Maddie kept clinging to my leg and crying.

"Oh, they all do right now, pretty much now through the end of winter," said Miss Kelsie, wiping the nose of a rugrat behind her. I looked and she was right. All of the kids had boogers on their faces or watery eyes. How the hell had I missed this before? Jesus, I wasn't sending my kid to the preschool of the future. I was sending her into a plague-ridden death trap.

"Here's some ibuprofen. I brought it just in case she needs it," I said, and Miss Kelsie handed me a consent form to sign. I leaned down on the toddler size table to fill it out, and when I stood up, I felt a little dizzy. Oh no. I can't be getting sick too. Suddenly I felt overheated, as well. Shit.

I had no choice but to get going to work. Of course, it was already almost eighty degrees by 8 AM, and felt about twice as hot on the L train. I ran into the 7-11 to get a Gatorade out of the refrigerator to chug before going into the Langs' building. And prayed the twins would have an easy day.

Fred greeted me at the door, holding one of the girls.

"Morning," he said.

"Morning," I echoed, attempting my healthiest-looking smile.

"So, it's supposed to be beautiful out today," he said. "Alexandra left me a note this morning—she'd like you to be sure to take the girls out for some fresh air."

For fuck's sake. I think the heat index was supposed to reach one hundred. And the girls were barely a week old!

But I just smiled and said, "Of course."

He passed me the baby. "This one's Eunice—Esther's sleeping," he said. He showed me the Stokke double stroller in the closet and gave a brief tutorial on how to unfold it, then headed out the door.

Once the door latched solidly behind him, I held Eunice almost at arm's length, took her into her bedroom, laid a fleece blanket on the floor, and immediately gave her some tummy time. I felt like I shouldn't be holding either kid and spreading my germs. If the twins got the flu or whatever the hell I had, in my first week of work, I'd be screwed. Yes, I'd feel guilty about getting an infant sick, but I'd be screwed. I ran back to the living room, grabbed my purse, and fished through it until I found my little travel size bottle of Extra-Strength Tylenol, popped three in my mouth and swallowed them down with the last chug I had left of Gatorade. I also squirted hand sanitizer onto my hands and rubbed it in halfway to my elbows. I could barely hold my head up. I put Eunice back in her crib, turned on the mobile, crossed my fingers, and curled myself up on the daybed to sleep.

Two hours passed before either of the babies, or I, woke up. Feeling groggy, I tried my best to snap out of it, changed them, then simultaneously fed them. As my eyes wandered round the minimalist white space, I suddenly wondered if there was a nanny cam hidden here somewhere. Alexandra certainly seemed like the type to have one. Shit! What if I'd been caught sleeping on the job? But then again, where could she possibly hide one? This place was the emptiest, barest nursery I'd ever seen in my life. I found a baby pink bucket hat, light cotton onesies, lightweight linen pants and aden + anais blankets in the dresser. I hoped this would constitute proper lakefront stroll attire that wouldn't get them either too hot or sunburnt. I strapped them in, refilled my water bottle, and off we went.

We headed toward Millennium Park. I once again stopped in the 7-11, this time to get myself some sunscreen, since I hadn't banked on needing any when I left my home this morning. I felt ready to faint by the time we'd gone about a quarter of a mile. Sheesh. I hadn't gotten winded so quickly since I was pregnant.

I sat on a park bench under a shady tree, and pushed the stroller back and forth with my foot while gulping down the water. Eunice looked around at the trees and gurgled. A grandmotherly woman came shuffling by in a white sweatsuit and a bright blue visor, and started to smile as she approached the stroller. Here it comes, I thought.

"Twins! They're such little sweethearts," she said. Looking more closely at them, she furrowed her eyebrows and asked, "How old are they?"

"Just over a week."

"What a brave mother, taking them outside already!"

Thanks a lot, Judgy McJudgersons. "I'm actually the nanny."

She gave me a quizzical look. "Oh. How nice," she said,

and kept on shuffling.

A pair of little girls of about five and seven next jogged up. They were curiously eyeing my massive stroller, as their mom (or nanny, I suppose) trailed about twenty yards behind them.

"Are these your babies?" the older-looking one said.

"No," I said.

"Why do you have babies that aren't yours?" she asked as the littler one chewed on her thumb.

"Because I'm babysitting them."

"Oh. Okay." Satisfied, she wandered off. Man, people were nosy. That kid would be just like that little old lady in seventy years.

I pulled out my phone and pulled up WebMD to start looking up symptoms. After ascertaining that I probably did not have West Nile Virus, I slipped the phone back in my purse. I decided I'd done my part in this fresh air nonsense, so I headed back, taking my time to duck into a few air-conditioned stores, and stopping for a frozen yogurt that would constitute my lunch.

The twins went easy on me that afternoon, sleeping at the same time and affording me a chance to close my eyes while they did.

Around 4:30, I was awakened by the phone ringing again. After the beep, the same caller from yesterday left another message.

"Hi, it's me, Emmalee," she said. "I was really hoping to catch you. I just want to know how the girls are doing. I was thinking about them a lot today. Anyway, please call me back. Thanks."

A few minutes later, I heard the front door open and the

jangle of Fred's keys. I quickly wiped my eyes, smoothed down my hair and headed to the entryway.

"Did you have a good day?" he asked.

"Couldn't have been better," I said. "The girls are still sleeping. They enjoyed our walk. We stopped at Millennium Park, and they were a hit with all the grandmas out and about."

"I'm not surprised," he said. "I'll take it from here. See you tomorrow, Amanda."

I left for the L, and was even lucky enough to find a seat. When I picked up Maddie, she looked as pitiful as I felt. Luckily, she didn't have a fever any longer.

"She was really tired today," said Miss Kelsie sympathetically. "She just wanted extra cuddles."

"She'll get plenty," I promised, giving Maddie a huge hug as she wrapped herself around me. I plopped my purse into the seat of the stroller, and pushed it home with one hand as I carried Maddie. She had some apple juice and animal crackers for dinner, and was asleep about half an hour later. I popped some more Tylenol, drank some apple juice, took a cool shower and promptly fell asleep myself.

I felt marginally better the next day, which was an improvement over 'death warmed over.' My head was together enough so that I could figure out which twin was which. Esther had a small birthmark on her right foot, which I only discovered after having to strip her down for a post-blowout impromptu bath. Whenever I was hurriedly changing or feeding or transitioning them—so basically, all the time—I'd quickly slide the sock down so I could do a birthmark check. Luckily, the girls each had a few monogrammed items to mark their sides of the room, so I could put the right twin in the right crib. Mostly.

Once I was feeling back up to one hundred percent, I went home every night and ate a massive dinner, probably twice the amount that I used to, and nibbled on Maddie's leftovers when she was done. And I still lost about two unintentional pounds each week.

Whenever I felt my energy start to lag in those first weeks, I kept my eyes on the prize: that first paycheck. I had reviewed my contract again and still wasn't entirely sure where taxes would come into play, but that first paycheck should be in the neighborhood of $2,500 for my first pair of weeks here, and it would be coming in about a week and a half. And I knew exactly where I was going to put most of it: as the deposit for my new apartment.

It was about four blocks away—two blocks in the opposite direction from daycare—but closer to the definition of Bucktown than Humboldt Park. The building was newer, built around 2002 or 2003, and had laminate floors, granite countertops and stainless steel appliances, all standard issue from a decade ago, but infinitely better than what I had now. And the best part about it was that it was on the second floor. I'd checked it out and fallen in love with it from the Zillow posting, and I'd been emailing with the realtor. I just had to check it out next weekend, give them my deposit, and I could move in anytime after September first.

Now, due to the rest of the paycheck going to Maddie's daycare and my gas and water bill for the month, I knew I was going to be spending the remainder of the money left from the sale of my car on my rent for August in my current place. I hoped Maddie would develop a taste for Ramen noodles. Sure, I knew I could come to my parents for help if I was really desperate, but again, I didn't want to do that, especially because I knew they weren't rolling in cash themselves. I just hoped that for my upcoming birthday, when they took me out to dinner and gave me my gift, that it would be money.

And I couldn't help but feel a little jealous of my friends, and wondering what they knew that I didn't. I mean, all of us were reasonably intelligent, well-educated young women with similar upbringings. Why the hell was I the only one of them who was barely scraping by, while the rest of them had bought their own Volkswagens in cash, vacationed in Miami, and owned three-bedroom condos by the time they were thirty? I really can't blame it on having Maddie (or Eamonn, as much I'd like to). The publishing industry was going down the toilet whether I had a kid or not, and I'd have been out of a job sooner or later, no matter which news outlet employed me. The only thing that made me a valuable employee were the two feeding machines attached to my chest. Yippee. No doubt my parents would be thrilled to know that their eighty-thousand-dollar investment in my college education was making me hit the big time.

Then, Esther started blowing raspberries, which distracted me enough from my pity party to remember that I had a job to do. So, I took her out of the crib and fed her, feeling about as useful as a dairy cow.

The strangest part of my job was that daily, awkward moment when Emmalee called, nearly every day at 4:30. Sometimes she just hung up when the answering machine kicked on; other times, she left a message. Depending on the day, her voice could be teary, upbeat or flat-out pissed. I felt badly for her, because the Langs clearly weren't calling her back. Regardless, the whole thing was going from awkward to unfortunate to irritating to me. After several weeks of it, I couldn't help myself. When she called on the last Friday in July, I picked up. I hoped that if she at least talked to *someone* once, she'd bugger off.

"Lang residence," I said coolly.

There was a sharp intake of breath. "Um. Hello?" Emmalee squeaked.

"Can I help you?"

"Yeah....can I talk to Mr. or Mrs. Lang?"

"They're unavailable at the moment...Emmalee. Can I take a message?"

"How do you know my name?" she asked suspiciously.

"I've been hearing you leave messages every day," I said. "I'm Amanda, their nanny."

"Figures," she grumbled. "You know, they told me that Alexandra was going to take a year off to be at home with the twins."

I didn't say anything for a moment. "They're both busy professionals," I finally said. "But I can assure you that Esther and Eunice are in a great home."

She mulled it over for a second. "They promised me they'd love them like their own," she said.

"Well, they *are* their own," I said, a little defensively. She seemed to be overstepping her boundaries a bit for a surrogate. "At any rate, is there a message I can pass along?"

"I guess not. Thanks."

"Sure. Take care," I said and hung up.

When Fred showed up at the end of the day, I practically zoomed out of the condo in anticipation of getting to spend the entire two days straight with my best girl. On Sunday, I'd be going to brunch at Sweet Maple Cafe with all my friends to celebrate my birthday and Maddie's, which was next week. I had thought briefly about holding a party for her, but my place was too small, I couldn't afford to rent out any location, and the only other kid she knew was Simon. He mostly ignored her, anyway.

Leigh greeted me and Maddie with huge hugs when we got to the restaurant on Sunday. I had been impressed that she made it there by nine. I had made it there by the skin of my teeth after spending an hour on public transportation.

"It's been forever since we've seen you!" she said. It truly had been. I thought for a minute and realized that it had been at least two months. God, what had I been doing in that time? Other than feeling sorry for myself, sending out resumes, nonstop taking care of Maddie and working for the Langs...not much.

"I know," I said, handing Maddie some Baby Mum-Mums to crunch on while we waited outside until a table was ready—it was always worth the wait here, but a wait it was. "What have you been up to?" I asked.

She started chattering away animatedly. She and a couple of her girlfriends from work had gone to Vegas last month and stayed at the Venetian. They had gone to a trade show for work, but spent all the evenings partying like bachelorettes. She told me about the guys from Los Angeles that they had met at Tao, and how they hooked up with them in their limo, but then totally avoided them at the pool the next day when they realized they were all paunchy and balding.

I wanted to care. I really, really did. I wanted to feel even a little jealous about it, and wish that I had gotten to have a one-nighter with some random guys who would buy me drinks all night and take me around in their limo. I wanted to want to feel young. But I didn't. And I wasn't. Not anymore, not on the inside. I much preferred my life with Maddie, lounging in my pajamas and watching "Curious George" over breakfast. I barely even drank anymore, other than the Guinness for work, but I wasn't one to get sloshed alone.

But, I'd be lying if I said that Maddie's and my little existence was all I wanted from life. I still missed Eamonn so much more than I wished I did. I didn't know what the hell was wrong with me. Why would I miss an asshole who ditched his pregnant fiancee a few days before the wedding, never contributed a dime toward his own child, who he'd never made an effort to meet? I tried to avoid the topic of him as much as I could with all my friends, because I knew that my feelings for him defied logic, and they all thought he was totally worthless. But he was the only guy who had ever made me feel worthy of love.

Did I still picture Eamonn and myself walking around the city with Maddie in the Baby Bjorn? Sometimes. I would daydream that I'd hear a knock on my door and it would be him, jet-lagged and sweaty from having hopped the first flight over from Shannon when he realized the error of his ways, and couldn't live one more day without us, and, with tears in his eyes, begged me to give him a second chance. Of course, I'd think about it for about a nanosecond, then I'd wrap my arms around him, and then he'd pick up Maddie, who had crawled over, and boom, we were a perfect nuclear family.

Deep down, I knew that was never going to happen. Still, I couldn't let myself think about a future with anyone else. It almost felt like cheating. And besides, I didn't *know* anyone else. I had always worked with all women. I didn't have any guy friends, other than my friends' husbands, and they certainly weren't prospects. And we saw how well it worked out the last time one of my friends had tried to set me up. I doubted that anyone would do that again, especially because I had a kid. It takes a special kind of guy to accept someone else's child; when I was single, I certainly wasn't about to date any single dads. I always liked kids and all, but dealing with someone else's kids is a whole 'nother ball game, not to mention dealing with ex-wives. Why would I expect someone would not only love me, but love my child enough to want to parent her? It wouldn't matter that Maddie was the sweetest, most easygoing, lovable child in the city; she was still some other guy's child, and always would be.

I snapped out of it when Joy and Jonathan came in, momentarily scanning the room for our table. I waved them over, and they greeted me with hugs. A few minutes later, Meg and Henry came in, pulling the arm of a red-faced Simon behind them, pouting.

"Happy birthday, girls!" said Meg, putting a wrapped pink box in front of Maddie.

"Aw, you shouldn't have," I said. Maddie grabbed the box and started examining it.

"Let her open it," said Henry.

"Okay," I said, and tore at the corner of the paper to start her off. Maddie finished the job a few minutes later.

The box showed a child-sized tablet that looked infinitely more sophisticated than my Kindle.

"Coooooool!" exclaimed Simon, perking up immediately. "I know how to use this." He took it out of the box and started setting it up. Was he turning five or twenty-five? Maddie looked on, intrigued.

Meg winked at me. "All part of the master plan to get

them to sit at a restaurant for an hour," she said. She tugged on the shirt sleeve of a waitress walking by. "Can I get a mimosa?" she asked.

"Sure," the waitress said, pulling out her pad and counting how many adults sat around our table. "Mimosas for everyone? Six?"

"Ah...actually, make that just five," said Joy, smiling. Her hands were cradling her stomach.

I stared at her, openmouthed. "Shut the front door," I said. "For real?"

"I didn't want to steal your birthday thunder or anything, but I wanted to tell you all in person though..." she trailed off, looking a little embarrassed. Jonathan gave her a kiss on the hand and patted her tummy.

"That's awesome, Joy!" Leigh said.

"Haha, sucker...oh, I mean, congratulations," Henry said. Meg elbowed him hard in the ribs.

"Congrats, you guys!" I said. "When did you find out? When are you due?"

"I'm only five weeks along, so we aren't telling the rest of the world yet. We just found out. I'm due in April," she said.

"Were you trying?" asked Leigh. *Ha,* I thought, *leave it to a non-mom to say that.* To a parent, that question might as well be, “Hey, did you actually want your baby?”

"We're totally ready for a baby," said Joy. *Ha,* I thought again, *leave it to a non-mom to say that, too.* Even a gyno can't be fully prepared for a baby. Meg and I exchanged knowing looks across the table.

Regardless, I knew she was going to be a fantastic mom, and even in utero, that kid was already one of the luckiest babies around. It couldn't have asked for a greater pair of parents, and it was never going to lack for anything in its entire life.

I chewed my lip and looked down at Maddie, who was squeaking away excitedly at the Beauty and the Beast game that Meg had thoughtfully pre-loaded onto the iLeap or whatever the heck that thing was.

You know what? I thought. *My little girl isn't going to lack for anything, either. I've got a good job. We're moving to a better place in a month. She's in a daycare that is going to practically guarantee her a slot in AP classes by the time she's five (ok, maybe not, and maybe she would going to get cholera or typhoid or another Oregon Trail illness, but at least she could fingerpaint with the best of them). She's growing up in the best city on the planet. She has a great support system around her, and charms every person she meets. She is the definition of love.*

And I took a deep breath. *And she is going to have love in her life, and so will I. We both deserve it.*

The next morning, I pushed her stroller to daycare with one hand, the other holding the cupcake carrier of treats I'd made for her to share with the class. I'd dug out my Wilton cupcake pans from the back of my cabinet and prepared about two dozen funfetti cupcakes—only the best for my little girl! I figured there would be enough to share with the preschoolers as well, unless the tots in her room wanted seconds, which would have been fine by me.

I was trying unsuccessfully to maneuver the doorknob, the cupcake carrier, the stroller, and my pump, which fell off my shoulder and thudded to the ground, when as luck would have it, CDD (Cute Daycare Dad) swooped in and opened the door for me. He was looking extra handsome today, with his just showered hair and requisite polo shirt.

"Thanks," I said, embarrassed, reaching down to get my pump and the collection bottles, which were now rolling on the sidewalk.

"I take payment in cupcakes," he said with a smile, eyeing the treats. He had killer dimples, too.

"I want cupcake!" shrieked his little boy. "Cupcake! Cupcake!"

Maddie gave him the side-eye. Of course, she hadn't ever had cupcakes yet, so what did she know.

"Lucas, settle down," he said calmly. Lucas started to wail and flopped facedown on the carpet.

"Hey, Lucas," I said, crouching down. "It's Maddie's birthday today. She's going to share her treats a little later today. Will you sing happy birthday to her and have a cupcake with her at lunchtime?"

He thought for a second and nodded.

"Thank you, Lucas," I said. His dad used the touchpad to scan them inside and mouthed "thank you" to me before walking in. I smiled back, scanned us in, and took Maddie to her room. A few minutes later, once she was all settled in, I walked back toward the door, and CDD was standing there.

"Just wanted to say sorry about that," he said. "Lucas is in the throes of the terrible threes."

"It's no big deal," I said. "I'm sure Maddie will have days like that, too. I'm just playing it by ear."

"I think we all are," he admitted. "By the way, I'm Dan." He stuck out his hand to shake mine.

"Amanda," I said, shaking his hand. Nice. Firm. Not sweaty. And as I looked down, I saw the other hand was nice as well. And ringless.

"Nice to meet you," he said. "Anyway, I better go, but happy birthday to your little girl."

"Thanks," I said. "It's nice to meet you, too."

"Have a good one," he said, and turned to the right. Unfortunately, I was turning left. But this birthday was already turning out just fine.

So, maybe I started timing my daycare drop offs just a little bit more precisely to try and ensure that I'd get there at the same time as Dan and Lucas. Usually three days out of five, I succeeded. He'd always give me a smile and a "Hey, Amanda," and I could usually get Lucas to give me a high five. Maddie had just started to take her first steps after her birthday, and often wanted to practice waddling in the hallway before going into her classroom. I just about died of cute overload the one morning that she took a few steps toward Lucas, who was darting around like usual, and when she fell, he stopped, took her hands and helped her up.

"You're okay, baby," he said.

"Lucas! That was so nice of you," said Dan, patting him on the shoulder.

"Thank you, Lucas," I said. I turned to Dan and said, "He's probably a great brother."

He laughed. "No! No, Prince Lucas is an only child. Not getting any siblings anytime soon. Probably ever."

"Oh, sorry! I didn't mean to be nosy—-or bring up a sore subject or anything—“

"No, that's not it," said Dan. "No, I'm divorced. I have full custody. His mom's not really the maternal type."

"Again, I'm sorry. I wasn't trying to pry." (But I'd be lying if I said I wasn't thrilled!)

"Don't worry about it. Anyway, all I meant was it's just us

dudes."

"Well, at our home it's only Maddie and me. Just us girls," I added.

"Ah," he said.

"I gotta get to work," I said, before I had to admit that no, I wasn't divorced as well; rather, I had been knocked up by a twenty-five-year-old deadbeat Irish tourist on the lam.

"See you around," he said. I hoped I would.

That day was uncharacteristically gorgeous for late August—sunny, about eighty degrees and a cool breeze coming off the lake—so soon after the twins woke up, I fed and changed them, then loaded them into the stroller for a walk. I was fumbling inside my purse for my sunglasses once we stepped outside the building when I felt a tap on my shoulder.

"Excuse me, are you Amanda?" asked a twangy voice.

8

I whirled around to see a short, stocky blonde of about nineteen, dressed in a gray cotton tube maxidress and carrying a backpack. Her face looked a little weathered for such a young girl, and tattoos of paw prints on her chest peeked out from underneath her dress. Emmalee.

"Yes?" I asked, playing dumb.

"Hi, I'm Emmalee. The girls' mom," she added.

I decided it wasn't my place to correct her regarding her title, and instead said, "Are the Langs expecting you?"

"No, no," she said, shaking her head. "I was wondering if I could talk to you. Please."

"I don't know," I said. "I'm not really comfortable with this."

She blew up at her bangs. "I took the train in from Portage this morning, and I'll be taking it right back in about an hour," she said. "I only want a couple minutes."

I glanced inside the building to evaluate the doorman. He was pretty built and could help in an emergency. Still, though...

"Let's go sit in the lobby," I eventually said.

We headed back inside, and I parked the stroller. We took a seat on the bench.

Emmalee gazed adoringly at the girls, who were peering around at the surroundings.

"God, they're beautiful," she said wistfully. "Aren't they

the most perfect babies you've ever seen?"

"Close to it," I admitted. "You said you wanted to talk to me about something?"

"Right," she said, wiping her eyes with the back of her hand. "I just...I just want to know how the girls are. What they're like. How they're doing. When I gave them up to the Langs, they promised me they'd update me weekly, but I haven't heard a word from them."

I felt for her, really I did, but something *had* to be said.

"Emmalee, look," I started. "I can't even imagine what it must be like to be a surrogate, and to know that the babies you carried belong to someone else, but—"

"Wait, what?" she said, cutting me off. "'Surrogate?' What are you talking about?"

I narrowed my eyes. "The Langs told me that they had their babies via surrogate."

She snorted. "Uh, no. They found me online when I was about seven months along. These were *my* babies I gave up for adoption. And I was really on the fence about them until I saw what kind of an amazing life they could give them, and Alexandra swore up and down that she'd be a hands on mom—and 'love them like they were her own.'"

Oh.

Neither of us spoke for a few minutes as the reality of the Langs' deception sunk in.

Then I carefully asked Emmalee, "Would you like to hold them?"

She gave a small laugh. "Yes, yes, of course," she said, her eyes glistening.

I carefully unbuckled each girl from the stroller, and gently placed one into each of Emmalee's cradled, thick arms.

She grinned down at each of them, rocking from side to side and humming "Daisy Bell." Even I started tearing up.

"You know, this is only the second time I've gotten to hold them," she said quietly. "Do you hold them a lot?"

"As much as I can," I said. "They're so little, they still sleep a lot of the time."

"Do you think the Langs—do you think they—" she started choking up again.

"Shhh," I said, patting her on the shoulder. "They're both really involved, loving parents," I lied.

She gave me a doubtful look.

"These girls are going to have a fantastic life, and it's all because you were so selfless and giving, and put their needs first," I added. I hoped all of that would turn out to be true.

A few more minutes passed, and the girls' little burbles turned into snores.

"I better put them back down for a nap," I said.

Emmalee nodded and slowly handed Esther, then Eunice back to me as I reinserted them into the stroller.

"Can you let the Langs know I'd really like to hear from them?" she asked.

I paused, weighing my words. "I think it's probably best for everyone if they never know that this morning ever happened," I ultimately said.

She looked down and nodded. "Yeah, you're probably right."

I gave her a sympathetic look. "It'll be all right. Take care now, Emmalee," I said, giving her hand a squeeze.

"You, too," she said, slinging her backpack over her shoulder and heading out the revolving door.

God. That poor girl. I couldn't even imagine what it

would be like to give up your own babies. And I wondered if the Langs were truly giving Esther and Eunice a “better” life than the one Emmalee would have provided.

The more uncomfortable thought nagged at me: What if I’d been a decade younger when I’d had Maddie—what would I have done? Would I have made the same choice as Emmalee? There’s basically three things you can do when you find out you’re pregnant. Had I been a teenager instead of thirty, I don’t know that I could have ruled out any of the options.

I hoped I had done the right thing this morning. And I really hoped, for the sake of my job, that the Langs would never find out.

After that morning, I threw myself into the job even more when I was on the clock—not just taking care of the twins, but making sure I was consciously *caring* for them as well. And as a result, I felt the best I had in, well, years. I finally felt like I was where I was supposed to be. Nannying with benefits wasn’t where I’d pictured my career ever going, but it was preferable to sitting in a cube. The twins were extending both their naps and alert times, so I had little breaks in between the times when I changed and fed them, where I’d cuddle them extra, sit them on my lap when I read Eric Carle books, practice some of the baby yoga moves I’d playfully done with Maddie. I actually didn’t mind the cloth diapers much at this point—luckily, I wasn’t responsible for washing them, and guessed they had an invisible or off-hours cleaning lady who took care of that—the only real pain in the ass was annotating every diaper change, the consistency, color, type, along with the length of each feeding, who ate from which side. And yes, I realized the irony that Maddie’s daycare provided nearly identical information for me, which I found to be crucial. At any rate, it felt good to enjoy my job, cash my paycheck, and not worry about money anymore.

Then before I knew it, August came and went, and I was moving in to my new place. My parents both came to help me move. Most of my furniture was, embarrassingly enough, from IKEA, and wasn't too heavy, so we were able to pack everything in with just two trips in my dad's Explorer. With the extra bedroom and bigger living room, I had about an extra 200 square feet of space, and the wood flooring made it seem to echo. I planned to buy a little bit more furniture, a piece at a time, and slowly turn the room for Maddie into not exactly a nursery, but a toddler-aged room with teal and purple stripes. I had already Pinned a bunch of ideas I couldn't wait to execute.

Joy and Jonathan came over that night to help me unpack, and gave me my first housewarming gift: a mini Weber grill to put on my balcony. It was the first time I'd ever had one of those before, but it was practically a law that anyone living in Chicago with a balcony needed one. I felt very grown up. I guessed I would also need to learn how to grill. My view was of the back of the building behind us, and the balconies facing mine from maybe twenty feet away. But it made for a quieter atmosphere than the apartments that faced the street, and I couldn't wait to sit out here and relax at the end of a long day, maybe read with a glass of wine as Maddie slept inside. It already was starting to feel like home.

For me, at least. Maddie apparently wasn't so thrilled about the change, and woke up three times a night for the first week, seemingly confused about where she was. I'd eventually get her back down to sleep each time after much coaxing and consoling, but damn, it was like having a newborn all over again.

When I picked her up from daycare on Wednesday, she had a note taped to her diaper bag with my name on it. Puzzled, I plucked it off and unfolded it:

Dear Ms. Keane,

This is a letter to inform you of an incident that occurred during circle time today. While Ms. Kelsie was teaching the children a new song, Maddie climbed over to another child and bit him, unprovoked, on the shoulder. The attack did not break skin, but we are taking all precautionary measures. We'd also like to meet with you tomorrow morning to go over our Policy of Peace. Please arrive by 7 AM if possible.

Regards,

Sloan Ansel

Director of Programs

I was stunned. Maddie *bit* another kid? On purpose? I looked down at her and she was happily babbling away and playing with the straps on her stroller. She had never seemed like the kind of kid who'd lash out at another one (even if he had it coming).

After much googling that night, I determined that she was probably not destined to become a serial killer—rather, she was just expressing herself in a nonverbal way; or adjusting to the change in her environment; or, maybe even just teething. Regardless, I ordered her about fifty dollars worth of teething toys from Target.com and swore I'd hit up Home Depot this weekend to paint her room in the exact same shade as my old apartment.

The next morning, I dropped Maddie off in her room, shot a death stare at Miss Kelsie the snitch, and knocked on Sloan Ansel's door.

"Do come in," she said, waving me inside. She was about fifty, with curly, gray-streaked hair, large glasses and a batik-patterned sundress.

"I'm really sorry about yesterday," I hurriedly said. "We just moved, and I think Maddie's still adjusting to the new place. Plus, she's getting in her one-year-molars, and—"

Sloan closed her eyes and put up a hand to stop me. "We understand that children do go through periods of upheaval," she said. "The only constant in our lives is change."

"Whew," I said. "Thanks. I'm sure it won't happen again. I just ordered her a Sophie and we're working on expressing feelings. She's a good kid, you know?"

"Mmm," said Sloan. "I do have to inform you, though, that in accordance with our Policy of Peace, we cannot allow for this to happen again. We cannot tolerate violence, and should this happen again, Maddie will no longer be able to attend our program."

Are you fucking kidding me?

"I see," I said tightly. "Well, I need to be going now. I have to get to work."

"Before you go, we'll need you to sign off on the incident report from yesterday," she said, sliding a form to me across her desk.

I skimmed it, only briefly stopping at the words "unprovoked" and "attack." I thought for a moment about telling her what I really thought about this bullshit, but I just quickly signed it and left.

That kind of thing has a way of seriously fucking with your entire day. I fumed all the way to work, replaying the conversation in my mind and imagining all the things I should have said to her. First, I should have told her where she could stick her ridiculous Policy of Peace. Second, I'd have s-l-o-w-l-y clarified to her that a teething one-year-old girl wasn't violent, and that her use of the word "attack" was grossly offensive. Third, I would have scooped Maddie out of there and put her in a daycare that wasn't run by a bunch of dimwits. Fourth, I would have thrown a frigging hair straightener at her head, and lastly, I would have cold-cocked Miss Kelsie on my way out of the building.

And the worst part of it was, I could never do any of those things, because I relied on this place for daycare, and I'd be utterly screwed without it.

It was one of those weird late summer days, where it feels too humid, too stormy and foreboding for its own good. And of course, it was the day that I had to get the twins packed up and ready by 8:30 to stroll about a mile down State Street to get to their new Little Tumblers class by nine. (Let me assure you that no actual tumbling occurs in this class. It's mostly for nannies to bounce the infants on their laps and practice rolling them over on semi-sanitary mats, just so the parents can have something new to brag about to their equally rich comrades.)

By the time the class finished, the sky had already started to considerably darken, but I had no choice but to leave as quickly as possible. The downpour started like it does in the movies, when you feel only a few drops before it starts coming down like a monsoon. I darted into Starbucks and ordered myself an iced chai latte, hoping the storm would pass quickly.

After a few minutes, Eunice started to complain. I knew they'd be getting hungry, but I was under strict orders to never feed them in public. I always had a nursing cover in my tote, although I'd never actually used it since my first day on the job. Part of me didn't see why it would be a big deal to feed either baby if we were out and about—after all, who would connect the dots between me, the twins, and Alexandra?

Luckily, the rain only lasted another ten minutes or so. By now, her fussing had started to become a wail. I gave her a pacifier and shushed her as best I could, and raced toward the Langs' building. When I got there, I was in for a worse surprise than the storm.

"The storm knocked the power out," apologized the doorman. "I've been on the phone with Com Ed, and they've promised to send someone as quickly as possible, but it may be at least an hour."

"So the elevator's out, too?" I asked, growing increasingly anxious as her cries became more frantic.

"I'm afraid so," he said. "I'm terribly sorry. We're working to fix everything as quickly as we can."

Eunice was up to a shrill scream, and now Esther was starting to look anxious. Ugh. Maybe it was because I was already stressed out from that morning and my patience tank was on empty, but I was just *done*. I had no choice but to make do and feed her.

I strolled them to the suede couch in the back corner of the lobby, as far away from the windows as I could. I quickly tied on the nursing cover, unsnapped my tank top, pulled Eunice out of the stroller and tucked her under the cover. She immediately began to eat like there was no tomorrow.

Unfortunately, the lobby wasn't as quiet as it could have been. Other residents of the building were complaining to the doorman about the power outage, demanding to know how they were supposed to get back upstairs without the elevator. None of these people looked incapable of walking, nor did they have a massive stroller, so I had a hard time feeling any sympathy. Still, I kept my head down and willed her to eat as quickly as possible, meanwhile positioning a binky into Esther's mouth.

A stylish, angry woman about my age with silky, jet black hair and a chartreuse romper was pacing the lobby, barking into her phone. Seeing only me in the quieter corner of the room, she started coming closer and stuck her hand over her un-phoned ear to block out the complaints of her neighbors.

"Well, I can't get to the interview right now because these fuckwads at Com Ed have their heads up their asses....no, it's on the goddamn 22nd floor....they're just going to have to wait. Fine." She hung up and groaned. "I hate people," she said to no one in particular. I wasn't sure what to do, so I just shrugged.

She looked my way, saw Eunice's bare feet sticking out of the nursing cover and raised an eyebrow. Then she turned around and started dialing again. I peeked down at Eunice, and she had slowed her nursing to a crawl, and had very nearly passed out. I deftly unlatched her, pulled her over my shoulder, burped her and settled her back in the stroller to nap. Then I re-hooked my tank top and stuffed the nursing cover back in my purse. I really, really hoped that woman wasn't an interior design aficionado fan. Or a friend of Alexandra's. Of course, as far as I could tell, Alexandra didn't have any friends, but I crossed my fingers and prayed that I wouldn't cross paths with the fuming woman again.

I couldn't wait for the next day to pass—I was so ready to just get to hang out with Maddie for a weekend and forget about the crap that had gone down all week long.

"So what are your plans for Labor Day?" I cordially asked Fred on my way out the next day, Friday.

"We trade off families each year, so this year we'll be going to my daughter's house," he said.

"Oh!" I said. "I'm sorry, I didn't realize you had other children." I should have. He was probably older than my dad.

"I have two," he said. "Well, two other than the twins. A son and a daughter. Craig is an architect living in Boston. And Clara is an interior designer. She and her husband have a three-year-old, Preston. They live in Glencoe." He pulled out his phone and scrolled to show me a picture of his daughter holding a little red-haired boy.

"What a beautiful family," I said. "And such creative types. I'm sure your daughter and Alexandra must have a lot in common, being in the same field."

"Well, that's how I met Alexandra—they were in grad school together—" he cut himself off before he said anything else incriminating. "Regardless, it's a long story."

Probably a juicy one, too, but I decided it was best not to pry.

"Understood," I said. "Well, have a great weekend!"

"You, too," he said, and I did.

Maddie and I took the train to the suburbs to spend the weekend with my parents, where we went swimming at their clubhouse and napped as much as possible. When Monday night came, I was packing up Maddie's diapers and spare outfits for the week to take to daycare, and my phone rang.

"Hello?" I said, not recognizing the number.

"Hello, is this Amanda Keane?"

"Yes, speaking."

"This is Kelly, the assistant to Alexandra Lang? I am sorry to inform you that as it turns out, Ms. Lang and Dr. Lang won't be needing your services as a nanny any longer."

"What?" I exploded. "Why not?"

"As it turns out, there has been a change of plans. Take care now."

PART THREE

9

Click.

Screw that. I was not about to take that for an answer. The next morning, I packed Maddie up, took her to daycare, and made my way to the Langs' condo. I was there a few minutes early—thank God—and I waited in the lobby.

The doorman eyed me nervously.

"I know I'm not on the list anymore, okay?" I snapped. "I'm just waiting for Mr. Lang to come downstairs so I can have a discussion with him."

He was visibly relieved. "No problem," he said. "Just take it outside, okay?"

I chewed on my thumbnail and continued to stew. About ten minutes later, I saw Fred get off the elevator.

"Morning," I said calmly as he went through the revolving door.

He was startled. "Amanda," he said with a sigh.

"What happened?" I asked, trying to keep composure. "Was it something I did?"

"No, no, it was nothing like that," he assured me. "Come on, why don't we sit a minute. Or maybe we can go get a tea?"

I nodded, and we went to the Starbucks on the corner. He got us two Grande Tazos and met me at the table.

"I just don't understand what happened," I said earnestly. "I thought things were going really well. I did everything Alexandra wanted, the twins were well taken care of, I recorded every single feeding and every poop—"

"I know," said Fred gently. "You were—are—a wonderful caregiver. We couldn't have asked for anyone better. But as you know, Alexandra's job can be very demanding, and quite frankly, I'm getting too old to take care of infant twins five times per night."

My first thought was that they gave the twins back to Emmalee, but I quickly pushed it away. "Babies aren't for the faint of heart," I said eventually.

"That's an understatement," he said. "Alexandra—we—realized that what we needed was around the clock care. We'd been searching for a while, and we were finally able to sponsor a nanny from the Dominican Republic who could fill all our needs." He took a sip of his tea.

"'All of your needs?'" I asked. "So does that mean she's a wet nurse, too?"

"Yes, it does," he admitted.

"Where's her kid, then? Back in the Dominican Republic?" I pressed.

He didn't answer. Which was my answer.

"Is she here already?"

"She flew in on Saturday."

Neither of us said anything for a few moments. I took a deep breath. I had to at least appeal to his human nature.

"I think it's a little cold to let me go without cause, and without providing any kind of severance," I said. "You know I have a daughter to provide for."

He cleared his throat and coughed. "Alexandra made sure the terms of the contract were ironclad. I, personally, am so sorry to let you go." He looked as though he meant it. "I'll be happy to serve as a reference for you."

As my last-ditch attempt, I said coolly, "I know Emmalee wasn't a surrogate."

He looked startled. "Beg pardon?"

"About a month ago, she came to Chicago, looking to see the girls, and told me how it all really happened."

"She's out?" He looked bewildered.

"'Out?'" I repeated. "You mean out of Indiana? She said she only took the train in for the morning."

"That's—that's not—oh, for pete's sake." He took off his glasses and rubbed his face.

"I still don't understand why you weren't honest about the babies," I continued, jogging on my moral high ground. "There's nothing wrong with adoption."

He put his glasses back on and took a long sip of his tea. "No, but there's certainly a stigma with adopting from a mother living in a juvenile detention center," he said.

Shit. It all made a little more sense now—why Emmalee had called at the same time every day; why they'd chosen someone who, at least at the time, had next to no other options. I wondered what the alternative would have been for Esther and Eunice—would they have gone into foster care? Argh. Who could tell? And who knew why Emmalee had been jailed in the first place? Maybe the twins were better off with the Langs in the long run. It was hard to say.

He stared down at his tea as he quietly added, "Plus, you know Alexandra Lang Interiors: 'Appearance is Everything.'"

I then saw Fred for what he was: a decent man, but in the end, he was nothing more than Alexandra's doormat, and a threadbare one at that. I knew Fred wouldn't have told me the truth if he didn't trust me with it. Moreover, *he* knew as well as

I did that it wasn't in my nature to blackmail them over this. That wasn't me.

"Guess that's all there is to say, then," I finally said, gathering up my purse. "Take care."

As soon as I stepped out of the coffee shop and onto the sidewalk, I was suddenly aware of how busy it was. Thousands of people purposefully striding, weaving in and out of the human traffic, on their way, and in a hurry to get there. But not me. I didn't know where I was going to go. I got on the L and made my way toward home.

I had only been a wet nurse for two short months, but it felt like a lifetime. I could hardly remember what my previous career life had been like. Maddie had changed everything. I was working now for her—it didn't matter what I had to do for a living, as long as I could provide for her. I knew that. But, I had no clue what the hell I was going to do now. No one had yet to respond to the hundred-plus resumes I'd sent out over the summer. I quickly did some mental math and realized I'd be set financially until the end of the month, but after that, I was toast.

I got off the Blue Line at my stop, but I didn't have it in me to go pick up Maddie just yet, and attend to anyone's needs but my own. Instead, I called Joy and rehashed the whole morning for her.

"Oh, man. I'm sorry, that sucks," she said.

"I'm going to need another job, stat. Do you know of anyone else who would need me?"

She lowered her voice. "No. I really don't. Alexandra's the only person who'd ever approached me about it."

"Could you, you know, mention it to any of your other patients?" I pleaded.

Joy’s voice took on an uncharacteristically harsh tone. "Can I be your pimp? No."

"You're the one who got me to do this job in the first place!" I retorted. "Now, all of a sudden, it's beneath you?"

"I totally went out on a limb for you," she hissed. "I could have lost my job if anyone had found out. Or if you ever tell anyone that I'm the one who connected the two of you. Or if it hadn't worked out. But you're my best friend, and you were desperate, and I wanted to help you. And Maddie."

"I wasn't desperate."

"Please," she said. "You're too proud, or lovelorn, or who knows what to demand that Eamonn grow a pair and take responsibility for his daughter, but you're perfectly willing to let other people jeopardize their lives so you don't have to stand up for yourself. Do you not see the problem here?"

"I can’t *find* Eamonn! Anyway, I can take care of my daughter myself," I said through gritted teeth.

"Then do it, and find yourself another client. Seriously, I could get screwed over if I did this again. Getting you two in touch was a huge risk for me. You get that, right? Look, I've got to get back. I have to do a c-section in twenty minutes." She clicked off before I could say anything.

Dammit.

By now, I was at my building. I went inside, grabbed a Guinness out of the fridge and cracked it open (go ahead, judge away) and thought about what Joy said. Sure, so I could go and file child support paperwork for Eamonn. But how was that even to work when the father was a citizen of, and living in, another country, and so obviously didn’t want to be found? I took a long pull of my beer.

I then allowed myself about an hour for an ugly cry, and

decided, screw it. Screw Joy. Screw Eamonn. Screw the goddamn baby-stealing Langs and their Dominican nanny. Screw everyone who is going to avoid helping me and Maddie. I'll find another job by my damn self. Before it was time to pick up Maddie, I'd already posted my profile on a childcare-search website, and hoped for the best.

By the end of the week, I'd had two phone interviews for traditional nannying jobs, neither of which went well. I'd been upfront in my profile, stating that I was looking for a position paying a minimum of twenty dollars an hour, knowing that I couldn't afford to keep a roof over my head and pay for Maddie's daycare for any less than that. One caller had tried to get me down to twelve dollars an hour, and the other had insisted on eleven dollars. I'd declined at that point, not wanting to waste anyone's time.

I only put so much effort toward obtaining a nannying job, though. I was no idiot—I knew I couldn't compete with all the fresh-faced twenty-one-year-olds who lived at home, could work fifty-plus hour weeks for barely more than minimum wage, and didn't come home to children of their own. Granted, I hadn't mentioned in my profile that I was a wet nurse—I wasn't sure actually where I could advertise that kind of thing (well, other than fetish websites, but I wasn't about to go there).

My mom called me to ask how the job search was going.

"Horribly," I replied. "And you should probably just assume it stays that way until I call you and tell you I got offered a job."

"It's going to happen," she assured me. "You're smart. You've been working for over ten years now. Someone is going to recognize that."

"Not likely," I sniffed. "As far as I see it, the recession's still in full force. I don't know who's going to hire me."

"Well, if it's any consolation, *I'd* hire you if I could. And so would anyone who knew you."

"Thanks, Mom."

After I clicked off, it hit me. She was right! Maybe if people just knew a little more about me—who I really was, and what I could really do—they *would* hire me! And I did have a shitload of experience, so I might as well put my editorial skills to use. After Maddie went to bed each night for a week, I worked on my new website for my fledgling business: mothersmilkconsultants.com. "*Your 'breast friends' to guide you through the transition to motherhood. One-on-one consultations to assist you and your growing baby.*"

I thought it gave enough info to hint at what I might do, and just vague enough to hide what I really do. In other words, I sounded like a real consultant. I whipped up some corresponding fliers in Publisher and printed them on glossy cardstock as well.

That Friday, I dressed myself in my best pre-layoff Seven for All Mankind jeans, Frye boots, thin sweater, and full makeup. I dropped Maddie off at daycare, took the L down to the loop, then went to the closest Garrett's to pick up a four-gallon-sized tin of popcorn. My next stop would be my most important one: the milk donor depot at the hospital.

I carefully slid my file of fliers inside my oversized purse, slung my cooler of milk over my shoulder, and tucked the tin of popcorn under my other arm. I was starting to wish I had a luggage cart.

I huffed down the hall to the elevator and went to the fourth floor, same as I had done nearly every week this year, with the exception of my two-month stint working for the Langs.

"Hi, Lindsey!" I said as brightly as possible, upon seeing the receptionist (I guess that's what you'd call her? I don't know, she's the recent college grad that works at the desk and takes my milk). She's always been pleasant. I heaved the cooler onto the counter.

"Hi, Amanda!" she said, slightly taken aback. "You're back! I haven't seen you in a while."

"Yeah, well, I just wanted to stop in and say hi. Had to make sure my favorite...milk bank staffers knew how much I appreciated them. This is for you," I said, proffering her the tin.

"No way!" she said, examining it. "I love Garrett's. Thanks!"

"You're welcome," I said, smiling. "Did you have a good summer?"

"Oh, it was great," she said, and started chattering about spending Labor Day at her new boyfriend's parents' home in Hinsdale. I kept smiling, and whenever she looked away, my eyes darted around the room. Hmmm. There was a small bulletin board in the office behind her, but that was no good. The door to the milk depot was always bare, and anything adorning it would probably be too obvious. Then I saw a nearly empty plastic rack of fliers advertising the hospital-sponsored moms' group. *Bingo.*

After Lindsey finished talking about the fantastic Vera Bradley bag her possible-mother-in-law got her, she asked me, "So what have you been up to?"

"Oh, not much, just family stuff," I said. "But I'm really excited for what I have going on starting this fall."

"What's that?"

"I'm finally starting my own business!" I said excitedly. "It's a consultancy for new moms who might be having feeding difficulties with their newborns. I'm sure you see lots of that here," I added.

"For sure," she said. "Basically all of them."

"I know," I nodded sympathetically. "I feel so lucky to have had a great feeding experience, and I just want to help struggling new moms in any way I can."

"That's so awesome of you," she said sincerely.

"Hey! I have an idea," I said. "What if I leave some brochures about my business here? I think maybe some of the moms might be interested in my services. What if I just put them in this rack right here?" I asked, gesturing toward the Lucite rack on the right.

"Hmm, I don't know," she said, chewing a thumbnail. "I'm pretty sure it's just supposed to be hospital-sponsored stuff here. I think there's a, like, 'no solicitors' policy."

"Oh," I said, my face falling. "Okay. I wouldn't want you to get into trouble or anything." With my hand at my side, I quickly dug my index fingernail as hard as I could into the pressure point in my palm until the smallest of tears welled up in my eyes. "Guess I'll be back next week with my milk donation." I started to gather up my now empty cooler and purse.

"Wait," she said, lowering her voice. "You know, no one who works here would even notice. I'll put a few out when I know the regular clients are coming."

"Really?" I said, wiping my eye with the corner of my palm. "You'd do that?"

"Sure," she said. "It's no problem."

"That would be amazing!" I said, and pulled out about 50 from my folder. She tucked them into her drawer.

Then I decided to go for it. "Hey, just out of curiosity," I said. "When are your busiest times here?"

"Monday mornings," she said automatically. "Always. Why?"

"Oh, just wondering....so I know when not to come. I hate lines," I added.

"Me too," she said, opening up the tin of popcorn. "Well, thanks again!"

"No, thank you," I said. I knew where I'd be on Monday.

After I left, I made a few more stops at places I knew with bulletin boards and a rich mom clientele: the gourmet grocery store by the Langs' place; a cloth diaper store in the Gold Coast; a few Starbucks locations in Lincoln Park. By the time I was done, it was nearly four.

I incessantly checked my email to see if anyone had hit the "Contact Us" button from the website. Nothing that day. Or the next.

On Monday morning, I dropped Maddie off at daycare and made a beeline for the milk depot. When I got there, just as Lindsey had noted, it was busier than I'd ever seen it. There was a line about nine women deep waiting to purchase the milk that had already been processed and perfected. It didn't take long to realize that, of all the women waiting in line, only two of them looked like they were the mothers. The rest were household help—a few seemed to be nannies, as they had the strollers or babies in the carriers (I'm guessing they weren't all twenty-two-year-olds with money to burn on breast milk)—but the rest were older, servants who could be spared an hour for errands. One was even in a uniform.

It occurred to me that I was starting to have serious qualms about this place now. When I donated thousands of ounces of milk a year to this milk bank, it originally was for newborns in the ICU. I hadn't really thought about the milk since it started going to a bunch of rich assholes that were paying top dollar for it. And paying it to the hospital—instead of to me.

Well, no time like the present to start marketing. The girl in line in front of me was the one with the infant in a sling. The baby looked to be about a month old and was fast asleep. Here goes nothing, I thought.

"What a cutie," I said, smiling at the baby. "How old?"

The girl did a double take. "Six weeks," she said curtly, then turned her back to me.

Great.

About five more minutes passed before anyone got in line behind me. Then, an elderly woman with a babushka hobbled in. A few minutes later, I turned around and said, "Some line, huh?"

She gave me a quizzical look. "English not so good," she said, with an apologetic smile.

Strike two. Somehow, I'd had it in my mind that I'd serendipitously strike up a conversation with a wealthy mom in need of a wet nurse, we'd hit it off, and boom! Hired. However, I failed to remember two key things: 1, I am absolutely not a salesperson; 2, I'm usually afraid of talking to new people without the assistance of alcohol.

After what felt like half the morning, I finally made it to the counter to drop off my milk. Lindsey was taking a phone call, so it was some other staffer I'd never met who helped me. I looked at the counter and the fliers were gone, replaced by the original ones about the hospital-sponsored moms' group.

"Thanks for your donation!" said the stranger at the desk. "Have a good week."

"You, too," I said, trying not to sound as glum as I felt. I wasn't so sure it would be. That morning, I had just mailed my check to my landlord and had $197.22 left in my bank account. I had contacted my financial advisor last week—really, he was my dad's financial advisor, but he set up an account for my 401K to go into after I was laid off—to cancel said account, and could he please mail me the check for the total, minus the taxes. I was also really kicking myself for not setting up that account until I was twenty-eight, and doubly kicking myself for only putting in about forty dollars per month. I wasn't sure how much the check would be since I tended to ignore most stock market news, but I was hoping it was going to be at least $1,500 or so to pay most of my rent. I wasn't sure how I was going to pay for Maddie's daycare next week, and hoped to God they'd take credit. I couldn't afford to keep her in daycare, but I couldn't afford the risk of pulling her out of it, and having to potentially scramble to find a new one in case a new job popped up, either. It's not like I could rely on Eamonn to watch her in the meantime.

Despite the many fliers I'd posted and my marketing-speak-filled website, I had a grand total of four people who had contacted me to ask about my services that week. Once I explained that I was really a wet nurse, two of them responded with awkward pauses before they found an excuse to get off the line; one hung up on me; and the fourth asked exactly what a wet nurse was. When I explained it, she told me that she used formula and was *very* happy with her choice, and I should stop being so judgmental, because it's people like me that make mothers feel horrible about themselves. In this case, I was the one with the awkward pause and making a quick excuse to bolt.

And what further irritated me was the way that the little Leigh on my shoulder cheered me on as I persevered. "Work it, hooker!" she hooted, raising the roof. "Get them dolla-dolla bills!" Because I was *not* a prostitute, either, thank you. I wasn't!

Was I?

The thought kept me up until after 2 AM one night. After tossing and turning, I finally grabbed my Kindle from my nightstand and looked up the official definition.

"Prostitute: to offer indiscriminately for sexual intercourse, especially for money," I said aloud. *Ha.* If anyone did that, it was Leigh.

"How about you keep reading," said the Joy on my other shoulder.

I rolled my eyes and went to the next line. Definition two was a little harder to swallow.

"To devote to corrupt or unworthy purposes: debase, as in *prostitute* one's talents."

Huh.

After a moment, I decided the Joy on my shoulder could shut her pie hole, too—she's the one who got me into this in the first place.

Still took me another couple of hours to fall asleep.

The 401k check came on Saturday. The stock market—not that I'd ever paid attention—had been having a crappy run of it the last few months. The check was for $828.04. I knew as soon as I deposited it that I'd be heading back to the milk bank line on Monday.

When I got there, there were only two people in line ahead of me: a maid in uniform that I recognized from last week; and... a guy who looked to be about twenty-four. He was shorter than me, impeccably dressed in skinny jeans and skinnier tie, rocking a Bieber-esque haircut and 80s-style glasses, playing on his iPhone.

Interesting.

I got in line behind him. After a few seconds, I tapped him on the shoulder, and he whirled around, looking expectantly at me.

I flashed him a smile. "Just had to say, this is the first time I've ever seen a dad here," I said, knowing full well that couldn't be his backstory.

He laughed. "Far from it," he said in a British accent. "I'm on an errand for my boss."

"No kidding! Does that fall under 'other duties as assigned?'"

"More or less. I'm a PA."

"Nice."

"You must be a mum?"

"I am. I actually donate milk here, now that my daughter is weaned," I explained, motioning toward my Trader Joe's bag of milk I'd placed on the floor. After a second, I added. "I'm Amanda."

"Pierce," he said with a nod.

"Nice to meet you," I said.

"Likewise."

The maid in front of us appeared to be finishing up at the counter, so we shuffled forward. The receptionist—the stranger who wasn't Lindsey—greeted Pierce and went to the back room to fill his order. It was now or never.

"You know, Pierce," I murmured, passing him my flier, "I'm actually a wet nurse as well, and I'm looking for a new family to offer my services. If you'd like, you can pass this along to your boss, see if she'd be interested in cutting out the middleman."

He looked at me quizzically for a second, then his eyes widened. "Oh! I see. Well, I'll, ah, I'll run it past."

"Great," I said, as cheerfully as possible. *Please, please, please let me not have sounded creepy and desperate.*

The receptionist returned with his cooler. He grabbed it from her, gave a quick nod to both of us and fled.

Shit.

I sighed, and heaved my milk onto the counter.

I could scarcely believe it when I checked my email that night.

10

Dear Ms. Keane,

Thank you for your interest in the position of child caregiver for the Tyson family. Mrs. Tyson would like to meet you for an in-person interview to discuss the opportunity. Would you be available at 10 AM on Wednesday? Please let me know, and I will send you additional information.

Best regards,

Pierce James

Personal Assistant to Mariela Tyson

Mariela Tyson, Mariela Tyson...shoot, why did I know that name? I did a quick Google search on her and gasped. She was the wife of Eddie Tyson, Chicago's star point guard.

According to Wikipedia, Mariela Tyson nee Gomez was twenty-five, and had been high school sweethearts with Eddie since their days of growing up in Queens. Her mother was Puerto Rican and her father was from the Dominican Republic, now deceased. She had two younger brothers in high school. She had married Eddie when she was nineteen, not long after he was drafted into the NBA after his freshman year at University of North Carolina. He'd played for Los Angeles for three years, then was traded to Chicago, where he'd spent the last three seasons and was going into his fourth.

And, that was just about all there was on her. She didn't have a scandalous life; she wasn't on any of those ridiculous reality shows about baller wives; she didn't start any clothing lines or stores where she did two percent of the work and took one hundred percent of the credit. No, I just saw a couple of Getty images of her and Eddie at the opening of a retired player's restaurant, and there was a link to an article in *Celebs* that announced Oliver's birth. It appeared that she wanted to keep a low profile. Good for her.

I quickly called Leigh to ask if she'd be able to babysit Maddie that morning. Once she agreed, I typed my response back.

Dear Pierce,

Thank you for your e-mail! Please let Mrs. Tyson know I'd be happy to meet her at that time.

Sincerely,

Amanda Keane.

His reply came less than five minutes later.

Dear Ms. Keane,

Great! The interview will take place at the Tysons' residence at 747 N. Wabash. Please let the doorman know you are here to see them, and I will collect you upon your arrival. Please bring your resume and a list of three personal and/or professional references. Also, please fast that morning, as you will be required to have blood drawn.

We'll see you soon.

Best regards,

Pierce James

Personal Assistant to Mariela Tyson

And that was that.

For my interview, I decided on a black maxi dress with flats, a chunky necklace, a white cropped blazer, and flats. I figured I looked dressy, but appropriate for the position. I hoped.

When I arrived at the building, a beautiful, modern tower with all green glass and atrium-style walls, Pierce was waiting for me in the lobby by a fountain of hopping water.

“Morning, Amanda," he said warmly.

"Yes, hi," I said, reaching out my hand to shake his. He instead gave me a kiss on each cheek. "Am I late?"

"No, you're early," he said, nodding me toward the elevator bank. "We'll head on up. Mariela is upstairs. Oliver is probably just getting up from his first nap right now."

"Great," I said. I noticed as he pushed the button for the 36th floor: the top floor of the building.

A moment later, we arrived. He unlocked the door, and we stepped into an immense apartment with bamboo floors and floor-to-ceiling windows overlooking the city and the vastness of Lake Michigan. I tried my best to seem unimpressed, but I was a little giddy. The furniture around the place was mainly teak end tables, brown leather ottomans, and oversized white couches—I'm assuming it would have to be for a resident nearly seven feet tall—but the Fisher Price playmats, half-empty box of Huggies, and foam alphabet letters told the true story of who ruled the roost here.

"Mariela?" Pierce called out.

"Coming," she said.

I heard the telltale flip-flop of sandals padding down the hall, and in walked Mariela. She looked a few years younger than me, but I couldn't say how old for sure. She was about my height, with glossy black hair in a casual bun on her head, flawless cappuccino skin setting off her tight white tank top and yoga pants. She didn't have a drop of makeup on, but was stunning without it. Over her shoulder was a linen baby blanket doubling as a burp cloth, and an adorable little seven-week-old still not fully awake.

"Hi, I'm Mariela," she said, rolling the r. "It's nice to meet you."

"Likewise," I said. "Your son is such a sweetheart."

"Thank you," she said, rubbing his back and smiling. "Please, sit down." She took a seat on one of the couches and laid Oliver down on it. He rubbed his eyes as she played with his foot. I sank into the couch opposite them.

"Would you like anything to drink?" she asked.

"I'm fine, thanks."

"Can you get me a Pellegrino, please?" she asked Pierce.

"Sure," he said and headed down the corridor, presumably to a restaurant-grade kitchen.

"So, Amanda, umm..." she stumbled. "Tell me about yourself and um, how you decided to get into nannying."

"I worked for the past decade in publishing," I started, "but due to the corporate climate and downsizing at my previous company, my position was recently eliminated. So I decided to look for a change in careers."

She looked at me, urging me to go on. Well, I guess this wasn't going to be the kind of interview where you avoid talking about your kids, I thought.

"So, I, ah, I have a daughter. She just turned one in July. She's the light of my life—you understand, being a mom," I said. Mariela smiled at this.

I continued, "She decided to stop nursing a couple of months ago, once she started to get in teeth and that bothered her, and she preferred to drink from a straw. I hadn't really cut down on pumping, though. I'm still producing more than enough for her to drink that way, and then some."

"How many ounces per day?"

I looked up and thought. "Ehh, thirty, give or take."

She let out a low whistle and gave me a look that was a mix of awe and jealousy. "Lucky," she said with a trace of bitterness. “I’ve been having major issues with feeding. He's had latching issues since the beginning, and never seemed satisfied after eating. The doctor said he had a tongue-tie, so she clipped him, but it still didn't get any better."

"Poor little guy," I clucked.

"We've tried everything that we could think of. Nipple shields, no luck. Extra pumping, fenugreek, Guinness—no luck. A few weeks ago, I threw in the towel and switched him to formula. Then he was projectile vomiting after almost every meal."

"Oh, my gosh.” Stories like this made me glad Maddie never had any problems like that.

“Yeah, so I heard about that milk bank. It’s been a little better for the last day or two, but I don’t know. He still hates the bottle on top of everything else, so...I thought maybe you’d be worth a shot.”

"I'm very lucky," I said. "I know that not everyone is as lucky with my, um, gift, and I don't take it for granted.”

"Everyone acts like it’s supposed to be *so* easy," she continued. "My mom was here until last week. She kept giving me all these suggestions and making me try different positions. It only made me feel like shit and like I was some kind of failure." She picked up Oliver and wiped away the start of a tear with the back of her perfectly manicured hand. He started to fuss.

This was definitely unlike any interview I'd ever been to before. I wasn't sure what to say.

"Can I hold him?" I asked.

"Sure," she said, picking him up off the couch. I held out my arms as she transferred him to me. I maneuvered him so my left arm was scooped underneath his butt, and my right arm was across his chest as he faced out. I stood up and pulled him close into me, rocking from side to side. He was immediately quiet.

"How did you do that?" she asked.

"Oh, it's my 'patented' baby-quieting move," I said with a chuckle. "I call it 'the dip.'"

"Really?"

"It's just something that Maddie always liked," I said. "I figure most babies probably do." I started humming "Yellow Submarine," and he craned his head up to look at me, smiling.

Mariela gave a satisfied sigh. "You're hired," she said.

"Wait, really?" I said, startled. "Shouldn't we talk about, ah, specifics? And didn't the e-mail say I need to get a blood test?"

"Oh, right, right, right," she said, remembering. "Yeah, the nurse will be here soon to do it. But as long as you don't have any crazy diseases, I'm sure it'll be fine. I'll have Pierce email you the contract once it's ready. It'll have everything in there about salary and hours and whatever."

If their apartment gave any idea as to what the salary was going to be like, it wasn't going to suck. Still, I couldn't be an idiot about this—not after the last time.

"I'll have my lawyer take a look at it, and I'll contact you as soon as possible," I said.

"No problem," she said. And on cue, the doorbell rang. Pierce darted out of nowhere to get it, Pellegrino in hand. An ice-blond nurse entered, carrying what looked to be a leather medical kit.

About twenty minutes and half a dozen vials of blood later, I'd been quizzed by the nurse on my sexual history, family health background, personal habits, criminal history (of which there was none, thank you) and philosophy toward child-rearing. Again, definitely unlike any job interview I'd ever had—at least the one for Alexandra had taken place in an office. When it was done, Mariela gave my hand a squeeze and said, "You'll be hearing from me soon." Pierce escorted me back down the elevator.

"Keep an eye on your email," he said as he held the front door open for me.

"I will," I said.

The contract came around dinnertime. I read it and frowned. I'd been under too much duress to even read the one I signed with the Langs, but now that I scanned this one, it seemed a bit suspect—like it had been written by an amateur. I decided to forward it to Jonathan to ask what he thought about it. He called me about an hour later.

"So is this something I should sign?" I asked nervously. "There weren't any tax forms to go along with it. It doesn't seem legit."

"Honestly, I wouldn't really worry about it," he said. "First of all, there's no way in hell an actual lawyer drafted this. If one had, it would have had a lot more stipulations. It also would have had an actual confidentiality clause, if not a nondisclosure agreement."

"You think I have anything to worry about?"

"Meh." I could almost hear him shrug. "It's a three-month contract. And no offense, I don't know that you're going to get a better offer than this anytime soon for this, uh, line of work."

He had me there. I don't know that I'd get a better offer than that in *any* line of work—not in this economy. And their offer, at $1,000 per week, was certainly livable. I signed the agreement, scanned it and emailed it back to Pierce. Pierce called me once it was in, and I was good to go. I'd be starting the following week.

Joy texted me later that night: Congrats!

I was about to type: Thanks! (No thanks to you.)

In the end I just responded with: Thx.

When I got to the building on my first day, Pierce was waiting for me in the lobby again.

"Morning, love," he said. I tried not to cringe. The accent was different enough, but it still reminded me of Eamonn.

Oh yes, Eamonn. For the record, I did try to get in touch with him again, right after the Langs let me go, but I still hadn't any luck. He did open up a Facebook account, and my friend request was now pending. Once the Tysons had hired me, I decided I wasn't going to hassle Eamonn about money since I had a job again and everything. Truthfully, one of the main reasons I wanted to be his Friend was to see if he was in a relationship or not, since I couldn't tell by his profile picture—it was one of him playing the fiddle. Sad, huh? That was my main concern: I wanted to know exactly how far he'd moved on.

"Hi, Pierce," I said warmly.

He introduced me to Wade, the doorman. He instructed him that my name was now on the list for the Tysons, so I'd be able to check in and take the elevator on my own without any problem.

We zoomed up to the top floor and walked into the

apartment. Mariela was bouncing Oliver in her lap and trying to calm him as he fussed.

"He's been having a bit of a tough morning," she said apologetically. "I've been trying to hold him off until you got here."

"Oh! Do you want me to feed him right now?" I asked, dropping my bags to the floor.

"That's what you're here for," she said, passing him to me.

Couldn't argue with that. Pierce excused himself to go make a phone call. Mariela looked at me expectantly. So I sat on the couch, grabbed a suede throw pillow with my spare hand, held him in the cradle position and set up shop.

"Shhh, shhh," I said to Oliver, who took a few seconds to find my nipple. As soon as he did, I felt my letdown go and he began to feed. Mariela peered at him curiously, cocking her head, as if to see if I'd managed success by using a different angle or position or something. I just smoothed my fingers along his hair. This felt weird. It didn't feel so very different to nurse someone else's child at this point, but it certainly felt different to have said child's paying mother staring at me.

"Least he's eating," she said, resigned.

I wasn't sure how to respond. The last thing I wanted was to be insensitive to my new employer.

"Would you mind passing me that pump?" I asked.

"Sure."

Without moving Oliver, who continued to eat like there was no tomorrow, I quickly hooked up half the pump so that I could pump my right breast while Oliver was eating from the left. I attached a collection bottle, propped it up to me and turned on the machine. It started to make the familiar dairy-machine sound. I always felt kind of like a cow when I was hooked up to it.

"I figured it would make more sense for me to do one side while he eats, so that as long as I had the letdown going, I could make sure you had enough milk for evenings and overnight," I explained.

"Is he going to get enough from just the one side?" Mariela asked, sounding skeptical.

"For my last job, I nursed newborn twins simultaneously, so this should work out." In the span of this conversation, I'd pumped almost two ounces already. A few minutes later, I was up to six ounces, and Oliver had passed out.

"Want me to put him in his crib?" I asked.

"I'll take you there," said Mariela.

We walked through the long corridor to the wing with the bedrooms. His was the third on the right. It was larger than my entire apartment, and tastefully decorated, too. A mural had been painted on the wall of a tree with a flock of owls of different sizes and colors perched on the branches (no Etsy wall decals here). A cherry wood bookcase held a larger library than I owned, housing all sorts of hardcover children's books, and the thick, sturdy crib, changing table, and glider all matched it. This room was gorgeous. And thank God, it wasn't another all-white room, in case I found myself trapped in there for hours on end.

I gently laid Oliver in the crib. He was softly snoring by now.

"That's the first time he's ever done that," said Mariela. "Conked out from eating, that is."

"Ah, I don't know that it's the best thing in the world," I said. "My daughter made a bad habit out of it. She still doesn't sleep through the night—she often needs to eat in order to fall back asleep."

"Must make you pretty tired in the mornings?"

"Oh, no, I'm fine!" I said, with my best perky smile.

Mariela smiled back, relieved. "Here, I'll show you the rest of the apartment," she said.

She pointed out the double-doored entrance to the master bedroom, but we didn't go in.

"Eddie's sleeping—he's off today," she said. She showed me the two guest rooms, and the one which I would use if I'd ever be working overnight.

"But that probably won't happen much, if it all," she said. I definitely didn't remember seeing anything about working overnight in the contract, but I just nodded.

We passed back through the living room and dining room, then around the corner to what was a massive, restaurant style kitchen. I tried not to let my jaw drop too much when I saw the eight-burner Viking range.

"The fridge is stocked, so you can make whatever you want for lunch," said Mariela. "Or, if Pierce is going out for food, he'd be happy to pick something up for you, too." She opened the brushed steel doors, and she wasn't kidding. The fridge was fully stocked with just about every fruit and vegetable in season, gourmet cheeses and over a dozen butcher packages marked steak, chicken, tilapia, salmon...wow.

"Great, thank you." I was getting more used to this job by the minute. This was never an option at any job I'd had before! Of course, Oliver might keep me just as busy and I'd be asking Pierce to pick me up Chipotle every day. I could get used to that, too.

"Do you do a lot of cooking?" I asked.

"Edna does. She's the housekeeper, part-time. She comes in at three to clean, and she makes us dinner, too."

She then showed me the half bathroom off the hall, and we went through the man cave. Apparently penthouses can have man caves.

"Here's where Eddie spends most of his time during the off-season," she said.

"And the on-season," joked Pierce, coming into the room, clutching his ever present iPad.

"Ha, ha," said Mariela, rolling her eyes. "Yeah, this is pretty much his domain. He's usually playing PS3 online or something. Usually some Call of Duty shit."

"Oh. Yeah, that can be pretty addictive," I said, remembering what it was like to date Nick.

"Anyway, moving on. Here's the office," she said, walking us into a room with three huge L-shaped glass desks, executive chairs, a large saltwater fish tank with a nurse shark pacing anxiously, and a sixty-inch flatscreen TV up on the wall tuned to HGTV. Looked like *House Hunters International* was having a marathon. "This is where Pierce and I usually hang out when Oliver is napping," she explained. "If you ever want to use a computer or anything, that one is free. We consider that the public iPad."

"Thanks!" I said, sincerely. That could be nice. Maddie's daycare had a webcam for parents, so maybe I'd pop on from time to time and peek in on her.

"And that's pretty much it," she said. "So, here's the monitor. When Oliver gets up, just change his diaper, play with him, and then feed him. You're a mom; you know what to do."

"Absolutely," I said. "How long does he usually nap?"

"It's hard to say. He might sleep about an hour if I'm lucky. That's kinda how he's been. Up an hour, down an hour. All day. And all night." She yawned.

"That must be tough," I said.

She gave a wry smile. "Let's be honest, it fucking sucks," she said. "He gets up all the damn time overnight. It's like, get up, try to eat, scream, maybe puke, throw a fit, get rocked to sleep. Repeat an hour later."

"Well, if there's anything I can do to help..."

"Trust me, you already are," she said. "I'm off to take a nap. I'll be up...I don't know. Sometime before you leave."

"Okay!" I said. "Have a nice rest."

She waved and headed back down the hall. Pierce's phone pinged and he started typing away. I placed the monitor on the desk, sank into the free chair and started watching *House Hunters*. Was I supposed to make small talk with Pierce? Place a lunch order? I wasn't sure.

"So...any advice on working for the Tysons?" I asked him. "What's your experience been?"

"You won't exactly need a manual, love," he said without looking up from his phone. "Not much you need to know. Just show up on time, do what Mariela asks—and she'll ask, she's not one to order people around—and stay out of Eddie's way."

"Really?" I asked. "What do you mean 'stay out of his way?'"

"Say hello, goodbye, and leave it at that. He's not one to make friends. Mariela is, though. You'll like her a lot. She's changed a bit since becoming a mum, but that's only because she's knackered all the time, especially once her mum left town. Eddie's not one for babies, so she's been on her own."

"Ah, I see." Not like I had anyone there to change diapers or warm bottles for me either, but luckily the eating and sleeping issues weren't quite as bad with Maddie. Or maybe she did wake up that often as a newborn. I don't remember. I may have blocked that from memory. "So what do you do as her assistant?"

"It's not a terribly difficult job," he said. "I'll fetch her lunch, pick up the dry cleaning, make sure her haircut is scheduled, things like that. Order a car service if she and Eddie ever have to go to an event, or make their dinner reservations. But she's a homebody when it comes down to it. She's very normal."

"She seems great," I said.

"Best boss I've ever had," he said. "Anyway, I think I'm going to get some lunch. How's Chipotle?"

I could tell I was going to get along with Pierce just fine. After I gave him my order and tried to give him a ten dollar bill, which he refused, he left with a promise to return in twenty minutes. I hoped he would, since I'd like to eat before Oliver woke up. I just ordered a vegetarian fajita burrito bowl, with guacamole and light cheese. I didn't want to get anything spicy in case it would irritate Oliver, just to be on the safe side. Plus, I wasn't sure how often I was going to get to relax during his naps, if they were going to be so short.

Pierce came back with lunch, and we ate in the kitchen. I flipped the monitor's camera back on to watch Oliver in case he started to stir, but he was peacefully snoozing away.

"So, how did you start working for the Tysons?" I asked.

"I sort of fell into it, really," he said. "After graduating from NYU, I'd moved out to L.A., and I landed a gig as a PA for Daniel Hartwell."

"Wait, *the* Daniel Hartwell? Doesn't he have at least two or three Oscars for Best Director?"

"The one and the same. I worked for him for about a year, and it was grueling. Nineteen-hour days were the norm, since he'd edit well into the night, and I'd constantly be running out to fetch him dinner, or get one of the producers on the line for him, or we'd be doing reshoots at all hours."

"Wow. I bet you learned a lot, though?" I offered.

"Yeah. I learned that film, TV, Los Angeles overall, weren't for me. I really wanted to get back to theater, which was my true passion. So I decided to sign up for an acting workshop, just to keep my skills fresh. And that's where I met Mariela."

"She was an actress?"

"Everyone in L.A. aspires to be at some point. Anyhow, we hit it off straight away. She hadn't made many friends out there among the wives—cows, the lot of them," he said with a sneer. "Eddie was happy about it, since she was in a better mood and had a friend who he could trust—obviously. And then when he got traded to Chicago a few months later, she begged me to come with them and hired me as her PA."

"That's amazing," I said. Has it been worth the move?"

"Absolutely. It was a good experience in L.A., sure, but it wasn't a life. I can have one working for Mariela. You will, too. Just steer clear of Eddie. I mean that." He tossed his empty tinfoil in the recycling bin.

Just then, I heard a squeak over the monitor. I looked and saw Oliver stretching his little arm behind his head and yawning. I looked at the clock on my phone. It was just after 12:35.

"Two-hour-nap, not too bad," I said, sliding off the stool.

"Longest I've ever seen," said Pierce. "Get him to do it again today, and you'll probably get a raise." He padded back off toward the office.

I opened the room to the nursery and saw Oliver smiling up at the birds on his mobile.

"Hello, handsome," I said, nuzzling his neck once I lifted him up. I loved the new baby smell. If I could bottle it and sell it, I'd be rich. I changed his diaper and came back to the living room, and set him on his playmat, watching him try to bat at the jungle animals dangling from above it. After a while, I read to him from his extensive Sandra Boynton collection, played with some of his finger puppets, and gave him a little tummy time. Mariela still hadn't reappeared. I hadn't seen Pierce again, or Eddie, for that matter.

At around 2, Oliver started to fuss again. I grabbed my pump and my nursing cover, and went to work. Fifteen minutes later, Oliver had a drunken grin on his face, gave a huge belch, and snuggled back into my arms. I put him back down in his crib, just before he fell asleep, and shut the door behind me. I went back to the living room, grabbed the milk collection bottle and put it in the fridge with the other one, and fixed myself a snack of grapes and iced tea.

Not sure what else to do, I wandered back into the office, where Pierce was flipping through the Netflix menu on the TV.

"Hey, Amanda," he said. "Oliver's down for another nap?"

"Yeah," I said. "Have you seen Mariela?"

He looked at me quizzically. "I thought she left?"

"I didn't see anyone come or go. Is the only entrance the front door?"

"That's the only one. She must be sleeping."

"Is that normal for her?"

He chuckled. "No, normal for her these days is walking around like a zombie trying to take care of a screaming infant. She's probably slept more today than she did all weekend."

"Glad I can help, then."

He turned his eyes back to the screen. "How about 'Anchorman?'"

We heard Edna, the housekeeper, poke in a few minutes later to introduce herself. She looked to be in her forties and spoke with a thick Polish accent. She only stayed in for a moment, then went to start her own routine.

Before I knew it, the clock said 4:30. I heard a few voices down the hallway, and then the front door closed. Mariela came into the room, rubbing her eyes and still in her sweats and tank top.

"The bear emerges from her winter's-long hibernation," says Pierce in a Discovery-channel style voiceover.

"Dude, that was amazing," she said, stretching her arms over her head. "How's Oliver?"

"He's had a great day," I said. "He slept from 10 to 12:30, and then we played a little this afternoon. Then he ate, and went back down to sleep around 2:15."

Mariela looked at me uncomprehendingly. "He's still asleep?"

"Sleeping like a baby." I turned the video feed on the monitor for her.

She watched him and smiled like only a mother can at her own child. "I can't believe how much he's sleeping. You must know something I don't."

"Oh, no, just probably a fluke," I waved her off. But I thought, *Yes, keep thinking this. Please. I need the money.* "So, Mariela, I left the milk in the fridge for you. I labeled it with the date, and I'll just keep using my own collection bottles, unless you want me to do something else. I have plenty."

"Yeah, yeah, whatever's fine," she said, still watching Oliver.

"Is there anything else I can do while I'm here? I mean, I can wash bottles, or straighten up toys, anything you need." Seeing as how I spent only 2 hours today "working."

"Don't worry about it. That's Edna's job." She looked at the clock on the wall. "Actually, if you want to go home for the day, that's fine."

"Are you sure? It's still a little early."

"Yeah, it's fine. We'll see you tomorrow morning. Have a good night, Amanda. And thank you."

"Okay. See you tomorrow," I said, and gathered up my things. "Have a great night!"

I let myself out the door and took the elevator down to the lobby. As I exited, I nearly bumped into Eddie, who had a bag from Subway in his hand and was in sweaty workout clothes. Or for an NBA player, I guess those constitute work clothes.

"Excuse me," I said, as he muttered something unintelligible and continued on toward the elevator. Shoot. Do I say something or introduce myself? I hadn't actually met him yet.

I cleared my throat slightly. "Mr. Tyson?"

He turned and gave me an exasperated look. "Look, when I'm at my home, I don't do autographs."

"N-no!" I stammered. "Um, I'm Amanda Keane. I'm helping out with your son. We haven't met yet?" I added.

"Oh, no shit!" he said. "Aw, I'm sorry." He walked over

and shook my hand. "I'm Eddie. It's nice to meet you."

"Nice to meet you too," I said, still probably beet-red.

"Hey, I gotta thank you," he said. "Baby's been quieter today than he's been since he was on the inside. For real."

"He slept a lot. He had a great nap this morning, and I think he's still taking his afternoon one."

He whistled. "Damn! You're like the damn baby whisperer or some shit."

I blushed. "I'm probably just some shit."

Did I really just say that? Dear God.

"Anyway, I better get going. Have a good night, Mr. Tyson."

"Take care now, Amanda," he said with a wink, and got into the elevator.

Well. That didn't go too terribly. I wasn't sure what all Pierce's warnings were about staying away from him. He seemed pleasant enough to me. Right?

11

The next morning, I arrived at the Tysons' just a little before ten, and a beaming Mariela answered the door.

"Hi, Amanda!" she said.

"Good morning," I said. "And good morning to you, too," I said to Oliver with a wave, who was happily examining his hands while sitting in the vibrating bouncer seat.

"You won't believe this," said Mariela. "He slept from ten at night until three in the morning. Then after he ate, he slept all the way until seven!"

"That's great! Much better than my daughter did at his age," I said.

"Until last night he woke up an average of three, maybe four times a night. This was beyond amazing."

"I hope you got some sleep, too."

"Ha, kind of. I kept waking up every hour like I normally do. Then I'd check the monitor just to make sure he was okay. A couple of times, I even went into his room just to make sure he was still breathing."

"Been there." I remembered when Maddie was born. I don't think I slept the entire first two weeks she was at home for that very reason.

"So I didn't get the greatest night of sleep. I think I might go lie down for a bit again. I just fed him the last of the milk when he woke up. I think he'll be ready for another nap soon."

"Great. Anything else I can do for you once he's down for

a nap?"

She looked up and thought. "Nothing I can think of. I guess put his toys back in the box?"

There were two stuffed animals and a handful of soft blocks on the near-spotless floor. "Okay, will do."

"Thanks," she said. She gave Oliver a kiss on the nose. "Mommy go night-night, okay?" She then went back down the hall.

About half an hour later, Oliver started showing his tired cues, so I took him into his nursery. I figured I may as well rock him and enjoy that plush Land of Nod glider the Tysons had. Within about ten minutes, he was on the verge of falling asleep, so I gently laid him in his crib, grabbed the monitor and closed the door. I went down to the entertainment room and office corridor, where I found Pierce.

"Morning, Amanda," he said, sipping an iced latte.

"Morning," I said. "So, you think I passed my first day?"

"I think she'll probably ask you to move in at this rate."

Wait, wait, wait. That thought hadn't crossed my mind....but holy crap. That could be the answer to everything. I could be the live-in wet nurse slash au pair. I'd be living in a swank penthouse in the Gold Coast. I wouldn't even have to commute...maybe I wouldn't even have to send Maddie to daycare! Maybe they'd like the idea of Oliver having a playmate.

Or maybe you'd be up nursing him all night, said my inner critic. *And how would Maddie respond to seeing her mom having to choose caring for someone else's baby instead of her all the time?* My inner critic had a point. Best not to even think about it until Mariela offered it.

"She's taking a nap," I said.

"Right on," said Pierce. "I've got to pick up their mail and take Mariela's car for an oil change. I'll be back sometime around lunch."

"Okay, see you later," I said as he left. I spent the next two hours nibbling on an apple and brie sandwich I'd made from the huge selection in the fridge, and reading the latest Janet Evanovich novel on my Kindle. I also checked in on Maddie once on the daycare cam. She had been in circle time, and Miss Kelsie was showing the kids flashcards of different shapes. I could have watched it all day, but I didn't want to get into that habit. I'd once been hooked on the Shiba Inu puppy cam, and missed a few editorial deadlines because of it.

The rest of the day passed almost exactly as the day before had. Oliver woke up, ate, played, then went back to sleep around two. His afternoon nap was a little shorter—he woke up around four—but this worked out fine, as I was able to feed him and pump, so the Tysons would be set on milk until the next morning. I'd started feeding and pumping in his room—it was more comfortable to be in there with the door closed than risking someone wandering into the living room when I had my shirt up.

Mariela walked in not long after I finished feeding Oliver.

"Hi, pumpkin," she said, taking him from me. He gave a squeal and nuzzled into her.

"I'll tell you, I feel like a new woman," she said to me.

"Sleep will do that," I said. "I remember the first time I got more than a four-hour stretch. I think I was ready to take on the world."

"The sleep deprivation with a newborn—it's no joke. People can warn you, but you don't really understand until you're there."

"You aren't kidding. There's a reason war criminals use sleep deprivation as a form of torture."

"Amen," she said.

This was nice, connecting with another mom. I didn't really have a lot of that. Meg, I sort of could relate to her, but Simon was so much older than Maddie, and she didn't always want to rehash those early days when her main issue right now was preparing him for kindergarten. Also, he regularly slept through the night at three months. I kind of hated him for that.

Joy didn't really count among a "mom friend" yet—not only because she only had an inside baby, but because I was still a little annoyed at her, and I hadn't talked much to her in the last month. But, now that things looked to be going well at my new job, maybe it was time to get over it. I was thinking earlier that day that I should have an official housewarming party this weekend, so I'd message her tonight to invite her.

"You can get going if you like," Mariela said. "I think I've got it from here."

"You sure? I want to make sure you get your money's worth from me."

"Honey, Oliver has slept more, eaten more, and smiled more in the past two days than he has in the past two months. Believe me, you're earning your keep."

"If you're sure," I said. "Same time tomorrow then?"

"See you then," she said, and pulled a book off the shelf to read to Oliver.

The next morning, Mariela and Oliver greeted me at the door again, all smiles and energy.

"Hi, Amanda," she said in a baby voice, making Oliver wave to me. "I want to play today!"

"I want to play with you too, Oliver!" I said, mustering up as much excitement as I could.

"He slept ahhh-maaaaazing again last night!" said Mariela. "And so did I!"

"What a good boy," I said.

"So now that I finally feel like a human being again, I'm going to start acting like one. I have an appointment with my personal trainer at eleven, and then I think I'm going to get some shopping done," she said.

"Sounds like a good plan," I said.

"And since it's supposed to be gorgeous out, you should take Oliver out today in between his naps. Maybe go for a walk along the lakefront? Get him some sunshine and fresh air."

"Of course," I said.

"Great. I'm going to get changed and then be on my way." She kissed Oliver on the cheek, handed him off to me, and practically skipped toward her master suite.

I kind of wondered where Eddie was all the time. Other than the first day I worked there, which he'd spent entirely in his room, I had not seen him at all. I didn't want to ask Mariela, since Pierce had explicitly warned me to stay away from him and I wasn't sure how she'd react at the question. It was still technically the off-season, so it would surprise me if he had to be at the gym or conditioning all day long. He hadn't made any appearance in his man cave that I'd noticed, either. I then reminded myself that it was none of my business, and as long as the check cleared, that was the only thing I needed to worry about.

The rest of the week flew by, and then on Saturday at six, my friends all came over for a housewarming barbecue: Leigh; Meg, Henry and little Simon too; and Jonathan and Joy.

After the grand tour, and helping the guys set up the beer brats on the grill, the conversation turned to my new job.

"How do you like the new job?" asked Leigh. "I heard you're nannying for Eddie Tyson's baby."

I gave a slightly smug smile in Joy's direction.

"It's true. Believe it or not, it's pretty much a dream job. I'm only there from ten to five, and the baby sleeps almost the whole time. I just mostly hang out in their penthouse all day and watch movies or read in the meantime. It's *way* better than my last job."

While it had crossed my mind that I had been monumentally lucky to bump into Pierce in line that day, I was glad I didn't have to really go through with the whole consultant thing, or take a job via that childcare website. Pshh. I wouldn't need their chump change if this gig with the Tysons kept up.

"Really?" Meg wrinkled her nose. "That's fantastic...but that seems kind of odd. Don't celebrity nannies usually work crazy hours?"

"This is what they had in my contract. And honestly, I am not sure that Mariela—Mrs. Tyson—even wanted a nanny. I get the feeling that she was really looking forward to being a mom and wanted to do it all, but...a few things ended up being harder than she thought. So I'm just there to help out a little during the day so she can rest, catch up on whatever else she needs to do."

Meg took a sip of her mimosa. "I'm still confused. If the baby's napping the whole time you're there, why doesn't she just nap then? Is there anything else special they have you do?"

I just shrugged and tried to appear as blasé as possible.

"Celebrities with too much money and time on their hands. What can I say?"

Leigh chimed in, "No, we know you're really there as a side piece for Eddie," she said with a sly grin.

I narrowed my eyes at her. "Hardly. I've only seen him once, and that was just outside the elevator. Trust me, I'm not that kind of hired help."

"It's not like he doesn't have that kind of track record," Meg pointed out.

"What do you mean?" I asked.

"Don't you remember?" said Leigh. "It was about two or three years ago, when it was all in the news. He was getting sued by someone—maybe his personal chef or something—for sexual assault."

"No, no," said Meg. "I think it was his housekeeper. Some young chick from Belarus."

"No, you're mixing up the two different cases," corrected Henry, from out of nowhere. "It was the personal chef who he had sexually assaulted, maybe four years ago. Then a year ago, there was a girl from Belarus, who was *maybe* eighteen, that had an affair with him. She sold her story to *Celebs*. And Eddie never admitted guilt to either."

"Shit, even I remember that story," said Jonathan.

I sure as hell didn't. I was also pretty busy with a newborn at the time, so keeping up with celebrity gossip wasn't high on my priority list. Suddenly, Pierce's warnings were starting to make a lot more sense. Well, whatever. I wasn't quitting on account of this news flash.

"Better keep an eye out for that boss of yours," said Leigh. "I don't want to see you in the tabloids!"

"Unless you sell your story for a boatload of money; then

that's cool," said Meg.

"Pretty sure I can handle myself," I said. "And anyway, he's not my type. He's too short," I deadpanned.

After everyone left, and I put Maddie to bed, I went to my desk and re-read my contract just to make sure I didn't give up my right to sue at any point. Then, after I had a quick tutorial on Eddie's legal dramas via Google, my next thought was, *how the hell did he not have a badass legal team prepare my contract?* It was almost as if it had been prepared by Pierce or something.

Then it dawned on me. The contract *absolutely* had been prepared by Pierce—or maybe by him and Mariela—and they did this specifically to circumvent Eddie. I bet Eddie hadn't even seen it. Maybe he didn't even realize I was part of his staff, since he was never there when I was—that probably accounts for why I only worked a few hours a day, and why Mariela just had me provide the milk for overnight. It probably would be a lot harder to explain my constant presence if he was under the impression that I was a one-time baby sleep consultant or something. Then again, Pierce had said he was a really hands-off dad. Did he know that Mariela had feeding problems with Oliver? Did he still think she was breastfeeding Oliver?

I didn't know what the hell was going on with that marriage dynamic. All I knew was I was going to stay the fuck out of it.

The next two weeks of work passed mostly like the beginning had. Every day, I'd get there and Mariela would quickly leave to go to the gym, followed by a round of shopping on the Mag Mile. I was guessing Eddie might not have been aware of as much shopping as she did, as I noticed that part of the housekeeper's job was grinding the shopping bags into the large-scale paper shredder in the office, and putting them in sealed garbage bags before sending them down the garbage chute. Either that or the Tysons just had something against being eco-friendly and recycling. And maybe he wasn't even aware of how much working out she did, either. I mean, she was looking fantastic—she'd probably lost at least five pounds in the past few weeks, and had a gorgeous glow about her—but maybe he thought she dropped all the weight from nursing. Or magic. Who knows what Eddie thought?

There was only one real downside to the job at the Tysons: due to the different schedule from my job at the Langs', I never got to accidentally on purpose bump into Dan at daycare anymore. So after three weeks on the job, I was pretty excited when I saw him and Lucas in the produce section at Trader Joe's on Saturday morning.

I was debating for a minute if I should say hello, or if I should pretend not to have noticed him and let him notice me first, when Lucas tugged on Dan's arm and said, "Daddy, look! It's Maddie! Hi, Maddie!"

Dan looked up from the red peppers and gave me a smile of recognition.

"Hey, Amanda!" he said. "Long time, no see."

"Hey," I said. "I got a new job, and my hours are different, so I drop Maddie off around 9:15 now."

"Oh, no kidding," he said. "Congrats! What line of work are you in?"

My mind raced for a minute of possible answers: child care provider, lactation consultant....nah. Better to just be honest-ish. "I'm a nanny," I admitted.

"No kidding?"

"Well, I used to be a magazine editor," I quickly explained, "but, the recession...you know how it goes. I kind of fell into this line of work."

"I hear that," he said, feeding Lucas a grape. Maddie started to whine a little, so I pulled my phone out of my purse to give to her.

"What is it you do?" I asked.

"I'm a graphic designer. Self-employed," he added. "I mostly work with small businesses, help them get their logos and websites going, things like that."

"That's cool," I said. Too bad, his skills could have come in handy for me a couple of months ago.

There was a moment of awkward silence, which was broken by Maddie giving a shrill cry.

"She's just about ready for her nap," I said. "I probably should check out and get her home."

"Right on," he said. "It was nice seeing you."

"You, too," I said truthfully. I wheeled us back toward the cashier when a few seconds later, he said, "Wait, Amanda?"

I turned around.

"Do you like Thai food?"

I grinned. "I love Thai food."

"There's a new Mexican-Thai fusion restaurant nearby that just opened—it's called Muy Thai. Would you want to check it out?"

We agreed tentatively on next Saturday, as Lucas would be with his mom that weekend. I'd have to check with my parents or see if maybe Meg would watch her. We exchanged numbers, and I promised I would let him know as soon as my babysitting was set.

As it turned out, my parents were going up to their friends' cabin near Lake Geneva for the weekend, and Meg was going to be hosting her in-laws, so they were out. I debated for a minute, but decided it was time to get over myself, and just ask Joy.

'Sure, I'll do it," she said. "Good practice for taking care of my little one, right?"

"Something like that," I said.

"Any chance of you getting laid?"

"Joy!"

'Well?"

"Last time I slept with a guy on a first date, it didn't end up so well in the relationship department," I said. "I'm not into collecting pregnancies like snow globes."

"Fair enough," she said. "What's this guy like?"

"I really don't know that much about him," I said. "He's divorced and has the primary custody of his three-year-old, so that shows to me that he's responsible and a good parent. He owns his own graphic design business, so he's probably creative. He has really gorgeous ice-blue eyes and long lashes, and he smiles every time he sees me. He seems like he would be...very normal."

"You could use some normal."

"Agreed."

I texted him to let him know I was set for babysitting, and we agreed to meet at the restaurant at seven the following Saturday. The week dragged on and on. I felt like I was about fourteen and counting the days until Homecoming.

Joy came at six on Saturday to help me get ready, and I greeted her with a huge hug. It felt nice to be back to normal with her.

"So what kind of look are you going for?" she asked, hands on her hips and scanning my closet.

"Not too mom-ish, but not trashy, either."

We settled on a loose black sweater with skinny jeans, plus my black knee-high flat boots, and she helped me with my hair so I had a curly, wavy look going on. Some berry-colored lipstick and diamond studs completed my look.

Maddie had seemed a little cranky that day—could have been the molars that were making their way in—so I had her distracted by a DVD of *Kung Fu Panda* while Joy got me ready.

"She usually goes to bed at about seven, but you can play it by ear," I said. "She can finish her movie, then give her a bath, and she'll drink maybe half a cup of milk before bed. Brush her teeth, read her a story or two, and she'll be out like a light a few minutes after you put her down."

"Got it," said Joy. "Good luck tonight!"

"Thanks," I said, feeling a little nervous. "Okay, Maddie, Mommy's going bye-bye! I love you!" I kissed her on the forehead as she moved out of the way to better view the DVD.

"I feel so loved," I said, with an eye roll. "All right, later."

I belted on my coat. For late October, it was still warm enough that I could walk, as long as the rain held off, but I was thinking about taking a cab anyway. I didn't see any, so I just started walking in the direction of the restaurant. It was only a few blocks away. I got there about five minutes early, and Dan was already there waiting in the loud, crowded entry. He was in a cranberry merino wool sweater with gray pants that were tailored just right. He looked hotter than usual—kind of like he stepped out of a Banana Republic catalog.

"Hey," he said, greeting me with a chaste peck on the

cheek.

"Sorry I'm late," I said. I wasn't late. Why do I always say that if I get there anytime after the person I'm meeting?

"You're fine," he said. He turned to the hostess. "Dan, party of two is here."

"This way," said the bored-looking hostess, and led us to the table. I shrugged off my coat and Dan pulled my chair out for me. He was scoring points already.

The hostess gave us our menus and departed.

"You look great," he said.

"Thanks. You clean up nicely, too."

"Working at home, it doesn't happen too often."

"Working as a nanny, I don't either," I said. "I'm actually taking care of a two-month-old right now. Between him and Maddie, it's a miracle when I don't end the day covered in some kind of body fluid."

"Doesn't get much better when they're three," he said.

"Oh, no?"

"Ugh, God. Just wait until you have to start potty training." He launched into a story about his failed attempts at potty training Lucas, which included everything from a weekend of naked time (disastrous, even more so for the furniture), a sticker chart (useless) and bribery (useful until he started puking up all the candy he'd been rewarded).

"So what finally did work?"

"Nothing, really. Until one day he just decided, 'I'm done with diapers,' and threw them in the trash. He hasn't had an accident since."

"That's amazing."

"Lucas works on Lucas time, and not a nanosecond faster. He's like that with everything."

"He seems like a really sweet kid."

"He is," he said, his face warming with pride. "He's a lover, not a fighter."

"Maddie is, too," I agreed. "I feel like I got really lucky with having her—she's so easygoing about everything, and just content. It's like I hit the baby lottery."

Just then, our waitress came by. We ordered drinks—a Sapporo for him, and I decided to try their Muy-Thai-rita, their house special for the night.

"This is nice," he said, once the waitress had left. "It's not too often I can talk with a woman so openly about my kid right off the bat."

"Have you dated much since your divorce?" I asked. (Well, he practically begged the question!)

"Not a lot—no serious relationships," he said. "What about since your divorce?"

I hesitated. "I'm not divorced," I said. His eyes widened for a second. "I was never married. Maddie's father and I were engaged—kind of—but it didn't work out. He's from Ireland, and lives there."

"That must be kind of tough for Maddie. She must not get to see him much."

The waitress reappeared with our drinks. I took a quick sip from mine.

"He's never even met her," I admitted. "He's never even tried. So, he's pretty much a useless waste of space." I was surprised how much I meant that when I said it.

I took another sip.

"What's your back story?" I asked.

He also took a swig. "Guess we may as well just lay our cards on the table," he said. "Ex-wife and I were married for five years. We divorced when Lucas was 1. She works as a flight attendant and she finally admitted to screwing a pilot, or six."

"That's shady," I said. "Sorry."

"It's okay. I honestly don't think she even wanted kids. She loves Lucas, of course, but we're much better off. She gets him every other weekend. I got our condo out of the divorce, and she has a townhouse in Rosemont."

"Really?" I said, wrinkling my nose. "People live in Rosemont? I thought it was just the airport and the convention center and stuff."

"No, Rosemont's all mobbed up." He started telling me all about the reputation and background of the mafia in Rosemont, which led to a story about Capone, and how some of his guys had lived near his great-grandmother's home in Riverside. I didn't even have to pretend to be interested—he had some seriously cool stories about Chicago history.

About an hour and a half later, we were both enjoying a healthy buzz and about to dig into our carne asada lard nar (me) and pollo pad thai (Dan) when my phone rang. It was Joy.

"Excuse me, it's my sitter," I said, standing up. "I'll be right back."

I dashed outside so I could have a chance at hearing her over the din in the restaurant. Turns out, I probably didn't need to.

"Hello?" I said. I heard Maddie wailing at the top of her lungs in the background.

"I don't know what the fuck to do," Joy said, completely frantic. "She is just freaking the fuck out! I did everything you said, and then at bedtime, I turned off the light behind me and a few minutes later she went nuts! She's been screaming at the top of her lungs for almost an hour now. I mean, she sounds possessed."

"Did you go check on her?"

"Yes, I fucking checked on her! I tried rocking and soothing her, I changed her diaper, I tried to read her another story but she just keeps screaming," Joy said, sounding on the verge of screaming as well. "I just don't—I mean—are you gonna be back soon?"

I sighed. "I'll be there in 20 minutes."

I went back into the restaurant, frowning.

"Is Maddie okay?" asked Dan, sounding concerned.

"I'm sure she'll be okay, but I think she might just be freaking out about someone other than me putting her to bed," I said. "Plus, she's got some teeth coming in, and had a short nap today—you know how it goes."

"Sure," he said, waving it off.

"But my friend Joy, who's watching her, is having a meltdown over it. Any chance we could pack up our food and head back to my place to finish dinner?" I asked.

"Waitress!" he called, flagging her down. Five minutes later we were out the door. He grabbed the first cab we saw and opened the door for me.

"After you," he said. I slid in, but not quite all the way over. The collar of his wool jacket felt nice against my cheek, and I could smell his faint fresh laundry scent.

I directed the cabbie where to and we were there in moments.

"I'm really sorry about this," I said to Dan as we took the elevator up. "I'll get her to sleep—it shouldn't take too long."

"Trust me, I get it," he said. "Lucas had the worst

separation anxiety when he was little. I used to have to put him to bed and follow the exact same routine until...well, I pretty much still do that. Chances are, he's giving his mom hell right now. I can wait in the hall if you think it might be easier."

I heard Maddie's cries from the hallway. "That might not be such a bad idea."

I turned the key in the lock, and found both Joy and Maddie in tears on the couch. Joy was attempting to read Maddie *The Very Hungry Caterpillar*, and Maddie struck the book out of her hands, bawling.

"Maddie! That's not nice," I said. She whirled around and froze mid-whine. She then got off of Joy's lap and padded over to me.

"Uppy!" she insisted.

I picked her up and she nestled into my shoulder.

Joy looked utterly exhausted. "Guess my work here is done," she said, wiping her eye with the back of her hand.

"You okay, hon?" I asked.

She sighed. "Please tell me it's not always this hard," she said, looking down woefully at her slightly bulging bump.

"Course not," I teased. "Sometimes it's *really* hard."

She threw a pillow at my knee. "Thanks a lot," she said. "Your date go okay?"

"It's still going on," I whispered. "He's in the hall. I'm going to put Maddie to sleep first, and then we're going to finish dinner."

"Hope you've got something good planned to make him for breakfast."

"Hey, now," I said, mock covering Maddie's ears.

"I'll scoot then," she said, grabbing her coat and purse. "Talk to you soon."

"Thanks for watching Maddie," I said, already taking my sleepy girl into her bedroom. Maddie was sucking her thumb and playing with her hair. I laid her in her crib, sang "Yellow Submarine" to her, and she was asleep before she learned about everything that someone on a submarine needed. I tucked her plush bunny under her arm, tiptoed out and shut the door behind me. I opened the front door, keeping my fingers crossed that Dan would still be in the hallway.

He was.

"That was quick," he whispered as he stepped inside.

"She's out like a light," I replied, taking his coat.

We fixed our plates, nuked them and I got us a couple of Guinnesses from the fridge, quickly, so he wouldn't notice the half a dozen Medela milk collection bottles I had sitting in there.

"Guinness, huh?" he said. "I like a woman who can handle her beverages."

I just smiled and nodded. I wasn't about to tell him that I drank these nightly for milk production. Especially now that Oliver was getting bigger. I was starting to have a hard time keeping up with the demand, and I kept getting painful milk blisters. What's a milk blister, you ask? It's an actual blister, on your nipple, from overuse. I basically pop them in the shower, and then try to rub breast milk and nipple cream on them to heal them. But, when you're nursing and pumping four times apiece every damn day—they pretty much never heal. I never had any of these with Maddie, and they hurt like a bitch.

They were also really obvious-looking, too. So regardless of how well things went with Dan tonight, I was keeping the bra on. I was also really hoping he wouldn't notice the nursing pads at any point.

The microwave dinged, and we moved to the couch. I flipped on the TV, and we watched the second half of an old *Friends* episode while we finished eating. After a while though, I realized he wasn't looking at the TV anymore. He was looking at me.

"What?" I said, with a nervous laugh.

"I think you're one of those girls who became hotter after becoming a mom," he said appreciatively.

"Is that right?" I said coyly.

"I'm guessing you were always pretty, but you really came into your own after having Maddie. I think it might have given you some more confidence, and you wear it well."

"Confidence isn't exactly my strong suit," I admitted. "But some days I have more than others." And with that, I leaned over and kissed him.

It started out slowly, deeply, lusciously. He ran his fingers through my hair, stroking my cheek, then pulled away so that he could kiss my neck. He started to slowly suck on my earlobe. I gave a slow moan. He then laid me back on the couch and pulled on top of me.

I felt him harden as I sensed myself becoming wet. Oh, God, it had been so long since I'd felt this way. Don't get me wrong, I'd had more than a few visions of this happening with Dan, but it had never been so real before. He moved his lips back to my mouth and hungrily kissed me, sucking on my lip and moving his hand down to my shirt. I let him keep it on my bra for a second, then decided I didn't want to quite risk him feeling something amiss. So I moved his hand down to my jeans.

He stopped kissing me for a second to look at me with a

raised eyebrow. I gave him a lascivious grin back.

"Naughty," he said, then unbuttoned my jeans, He slowly pulled them off, kissing my knees as he raised each leg to take them out. I was wearing a pair of silky black bikinis. Not exactly porn-star worthy, but I hoped it wasn't disappointing.

He didn't seem disappointed. He regarded me for a second.

"I'm deciding what exactly I should do with you," he said, answering my unspoken question. "I think I have the answer."

He crouched down, and peeled my underwear off. With his teeth. I giggled as he flung them from his mouth across the room.

"That'll be the last time I hear you laugh," he said, mock-sternly. He then leaned in and began to slowly, quietly kiss me down there. He lightly flicked his tongue back and forth, from left to right, and then, like the kisses on my mouth, became hungrier, more wanting, more urgent. More. More. More. My back arched and I gasped. He grasped my hips with both hands and held me firmly down, not missing a beat. Oh God. I wanted him. So. Badly.

His tongue pressed harder and harder into me as I rose to meet him every time. In the last second, I grabbed the pillow from behind my head and pushed it onto my face as I screamed into it, long and low and guttural. When I had finished, he finished by kissing me lightly on my thighs. Still slightly panting, I removed the pillow from my face and saw him looking at me, apparently satisfied by a job well done.

"You are something else," he said.

"Still. Recovering," I said, slowly sitting up. I looked down at his lap. He was still very, very hard. "Can I, ah, return the favor?" I asked.

He gave me a sly grin. "If you insist," he said.

Normally, this isn't something I offer to do. Normally, this isn't something I particularly like to do. And normally, I'm not dating a guy with a tongue that puts a vibrator to shame. But there you have it. And by the way he moaned and screamed my name into a pillow, I'm pretty sure I didn't disappoint him, either.

At any rate, I was even more sure that I was going to keep the true nature of my job under wraps around Dan—he was *not* someone I wanted to scare off anytime soon.

Afterwards, we both dozed off a little bit, wrapped in each others' arms on the couch, waking around twelve to the closing credits of *Saturday Night Live*.

"I should probably go," he yawned. "It'd be weird for Maddie to see me here in the morning."

"You're right," I said, frowning. "This was nice, though."

"I'd say it was better than nice," he said. "Can I call you?"

"Of course," I said.

He paused. "Can I see you tomorrow? Both you and Maddie?"

A smile crept on my face. "Really?"

"Yeah. I get Lucas back around lunchtime. Maybe in the afternoon we can all go to Navy Pier or something."

"I'd love that," I said. "As long as you don't think it's moving too fast, though."

He shrugged. "You're a parent. You know as well as I do that we can't afford to screw around," he said. "And I wouldn't just screw around with you."

He then added, "No pun intended," as he slid into his coat. He wrapped me into a big bear hug and kissed me on the neck some more.

"I'll call you in the morning," he said.

"Good night," I said, opening the door for him. "And thanks again for dinner."

"Thank you for dessert."

When he was gone, I just stood at the door for a moment, grinning and hugging myself. God. It had been so long since I had felt this way. And somehow, it was even better than I had felt with Eamonn. With him, it was truly just animal lust overpowering us, not to mention his accent rendering me illogical and impulsive. I had fun with him in and out of bed, but when push came to shove, that was all he wanted out of the relationship. But with Dan...I saw how things could be different. He was really intelligent, fun, sexy, and what made him even sexier to me in a way was the fact that he was already a parent. Yep. It was really attractive to me that he was so responsible and loving, that he was the number one person that his kid would rely on. Maybe he found me attractive because of that, too.

Or maybe it was just the huge boobs I had going on. Either way.

12

I woke up to a call from Pierce around 7 AM.

"Hello?" I said groggily.

"Amanda. Mariela needs you. Oliver is apparently going through a growth spurt and ran out of milk around 4 AM. Can you get over here—immediately?" he asked. By the sound of his voice, I was on speakerphone.

Ugh. Dammit.

"I can be there in about an hour. I'll have to bring my daughter with me, too. I hope that's all right."

I heard Oliver shrieking in the background. "What if we came to her place?" I heard Mariela call out in the background.

"That's fine by me," I said. I gave them my address.

"We'll be right over," he said.

Right away, I started picking up the living room, tossing all the dishes into the dishwasher and throwing all of Maddie's toys into the closet. Pierce, Mariela, and Oliver were at my door a record-breaking fifteen minutes later. Oliver was howling, tears streaming down his face.

"Come in, come in," I said, and quickly ushered them inside.

I offered them a seat on the couch, and I grabbed my Boppy from the recliner and began to feed Oliver. He quieted immediately.

"I'm really sorry," said Mariela, rubbing her temples.

"It's fine," I assured her, lightly stroking Oliver's hair.

Pierce, clearly uncomfortable, said, "I'm double-parked, so I'll go move the car. Mariela, just come on down when you're done, and I'll be waiting in front." He quickly left.

Both Mariela and I gazed at Oliver as he fed. He was such a sweet baby, a lot like Maddie was. I loved seeing the world through his eyes as he started to discover his hands, his feet, started to recognize me and smile to greet me each morning. I liked to think that I was helping bring out the best in him, and that Mariela was getting to know the real Oliver because of the effect that I (and my boobs) had on him. There were then a few minutes of relaxed quiet, which was soon broken by the sound of Maddie whining. I tried to ignore her and gave Mariela a weak smile.

"Do you want me to go get her?" Mariela asked.

"Please," I said. "She's the first door on the left."

Mariela rose and returned a moment later with Maddie, who to her credit, wasn't crying anymore. She gave me a huge smile, but started screaming the second she looked down and realized I was feeding Oliver. She wrestled herself free of Mariela and landed on the floor, darting toward me and throwing herself toward my lap.

"Shh, shh, it's okay," I said, quickly unlatching Oliver before Maddie could get to him. I handed him to Mariela and scooped Maddie into my lap. We both started to pat our respective child's back and soothe them.

"I'm so sorry," I apologized to Mariela. "She's never seen me with another baby before."

"Really, don't worry about it—you just completely saved me," she said. "Anyway, we'll get going."

"Let me get you some milk to last until tomorrow," I said.

I carried a whimpering Maddie toward the fridge and opened the door with my spare hand. I filled an empty Trader Joe's bag for Mariela with the four filled collection bottles I had.

"You're the best," she said. "I'll see you tomorrow." She and Oliver were swiftly out the door. Maddie still clung to me like her life depended on it. I kissed her on the head.

Ok, so I clearly didn't have a future as a live-in au pair; but, I did just save the day for my employer, and I hoped that counted for something. Recently, I'd started to think a little more about my job with the Tysons, and I realized it was possibly the best job I'd ever had. Laid back corporate culture, plenty of perks, great coworkers—and the job was really getting easier by the day as Oliver got older. I hoped they'd keep me on after he was weaned. Who knows, maybe I could even work in some extra freelance writing or editing during his naps! I'd been able to do it with Maddie, and Oliver was even mellower than she was. Plus, I still had my debt from the c-section and my lapses in employment hanging over my head, and any extra work would help. Now, I felt like I finally had a chance again at the life I was supposed to have: a steady job and an employer who appreciated me; a roof over our heads in a great neighborhood; possibly even Mr. Right.

And, speak of the devil, Dan called shortly after my visitors had left.

"So what do you think about Navy Pier?" he asked.

"Love it!" I said. "Do you want us to meet you there?"

"No, I'll pick you up. I'll call you when we're on the way around noon. Just have the carseat handy and we'll get Maddie set up."

See what I mean? Only a dad would think of that. Sexy!

And, just after twelve, he pulled his Forester up to my

building where Maddie and I were waiting just inside the door, carseat and stroller in tow. He put on his hazards, jumped out, and gave me a quick kiss on the cheek.

"Hey, beautiful," he said.

"Hey, yourself."

As I held Maddie, he snapped the carseat in place, then as I buckled Maddie into her seat, he folded up the stroller and stuck it in the back. He then opened the passenger door for me. I was pretty sure that no guy had done me that favor since prom.

"Have you girls eaten?" he asked, as we headed east on Armitage.

"She mostly grazes on the weekends," I said. "She'll be fine either way. Have you?"

"Yeah, we're good. Let's just go right to the Children's Museum. Have you been recently?"

"We've actually never been," I said.

"What?!" he said. "That's a travesty. Good thing we're remedying that."

And it was. Maddie had the time of her life when we were there. She was getting to be a professional walker by now, and toddled from room to room, trailing after Lucas, who knew the place inside out. She followed him everywhere he went, imitating him as he splashed with the toy ducks and boats at the water table, climbed in the cardboard box exhibits, shopped for food in the pretend grocery store. And Lucas was all too happy to have a groupie, saying, "Come on, baby!" each time he departed for a new room.

"I think someone has a new best friend," I said to Dan, watching them in adoration. I might have spoken too soon, as Maddie was about to go down a slide and Lucas pushed her out of the way to go first.

"Lucas!" chided Dan, walking over to the play structure. "Don't do that to Maddie." Lucas started to wail in protest.

Another mom walking by with a double stroller saw Lucas' ruckus and clucked her tongue. "Siblings," she said to me and shrugged. "What're ya gonna do?"

I didn't correct her. I didn't want to, either. It struck me that this was the first time ever that I had looked like I was part of a family. When I was out and about with Maddie, it's not like I had a sign above my head that said "Single Mom," but I'd never been in a situation that would suggest otherwise, either. It was so quickly starting to feel like we *could* be a family. Maybe it would be this easy for it to fall into place.

Although Dan and I hadn't even discussed it beforehand, we didn't act like we were on a date. We acted like we were on a playdate. I wouldn't have wanted to walk around stealing kisses and snuggling at this point, and especially not in front of the kids. It just made more sense to let them get used to this semi-strange adult and the kid from daycare.

At around three, Maddie was starting to feel the effects of going napless, and even her good-natured personality was beginning to wane. We decided to pack it in, stopping at the food court for ice cream on the way out. Maddie was asleep in the car before we had even pulled out of the parking garage, and Dan had pulled up some YouTube video of Italian sports cars on his phone to entertain Lucas for the drive back.

Once the kids were taken care of, he reached over to hold my hand. I squeezed it back.

"So, when do I get to see you again?" he murmured.

"I don't know," I said. "Maybe the two of you can come over for dinner next weekend?"

"I'd like that," he said, lightly pulling on my fingers. "Although, I would really like to see, ahem, a little more of you."

"Might have to wait until next time Lucas is at his mom's," I said airily. "I'll see what I can do about getting a sitter."

"You better," he said, stroking my palm in a figure eight. "I've got big plans for you."

Oh, dear God. How the hell was I going to wait another two weeks?

Turns out we didn't wait that long. No, get your head out of the gutter—the kids were in the car. We went out for an early dinner for the next two Tuesdays in a row—I had suggested trading off sitting duties with Meg, who loved the idea of getting a date night out—and that way we were home by eight, in time to put our kids to bed.

Dinner was the least of the priorities, though. The first night, after Dan had pulled up to the curb, I jumped in the car before he could get out to open the door for me. I leaned over, gave him a long, deep kiss, and whispered, "I'm not hungry."

"Neither am I," he replied, moving his hand to my thigh.

"Let's find somewhere we can be alone," I said.

We drove around for a few minutes—not the easiest thing to do during rush hour in the city—and he said, "I know where to go." He weaved through the neighborhood, and drove to one of the few large, suburbanesque movie theaters in the city.

"Perfect," I said. We bought two tickets for a showing of a foreign film that had already started, and ducked into the theater. There were only two other couples there—it was a smaller theater as well—but they were both sitting toward the middle rows. He held my hand and led me to the very back row.

We took off our coats and lifted up the armrest between us. He put his arm around me and I snuggled into him for a moment before we started making out like teenagers. After a few minutes, we were both giggling, and the two other couples had both turned and given us disgusted looks.

"This isn't gonna work," I whispered. "Come on." I led him by the hand up to the exit behind us, and out into the hallway. We sauntered toward the lobby, which was completely empty. I opened the door to the ladies room and peeked in. Empty as well. We ducked in.

Let's just say the handicapped stall got a little more action than usual that night.

The next week, we went back to the movie theater. Except this time, we didn't bother leaving the parking garage. (Tip: at 6 PM on a Tuesday, no one parks on the top floor. You're welcome.)

After that second time, as I was pulling my leggings back on under my dress, he nuzzled my neck and started stroking my breasts. I unwittingly swatted him away.

"What?" he said, mock hurt. "I get to have every other part of you."

"I'm just...self-conscious about them," I said. Not to mention I still had a nasty milk blister on the right one, thanks to Oliver.

"You don't have to be," he said in between kisses. "I haven't even seen them yet and I can tell they're perfect."

"Then maybe we should just consider them forbidden fruit for now," I teased back. "I'll let you play with them. One day, when I'm ready." And when there's not a chance that he was going to get squirted in the eye.

When he took me home, he gave me a long kiss goodbye. He and Lucas would be heading up to Milwaukee the next evening to see his extended family for the week of Thanksgiving, coming home on Sunday night. I, on the other hand, would be spending Thanksgiving with my parents and Maddie in the suburbs. We had decided to forego cooking this year and planned to go to a restaurant instead, which I was kind of excited about.

"Text me if you get bored," I offered.

"I'll text you even if I'm not bored," he said. "Have a good one. Give Maddie a hug for me."

I kind of melted when he said that.

Mariela gave me the holiday and Friday as paid days off, and I repaid her with enough milk from my freezer stash to keep them set until Monday. I stuffed myself full of turkey and potatoes, ate leftovers for a few days and played nonstop with Maddie, and then it was back to work. As usual, Mariela went to the gym, Oliver cooed and napped, and Eddie was nowhere to be found. I nonchalantly mentioned something about Eddie's constant absence to Pierce, and he said, "Season's started. He leaves for the day by nine for conditioning, practice, and if he's not out of town for a game, he usually comes home around six."

"Makes sense," I said, and left it at that. "So, you know Mariela pretty well. Do you think she's happy with me and how it's all going?"

I was really curious. I was more than halfway into the original three-month contract I'd signed. Each time she paid me with a neat stack of Benjamins every two weeks, I nearly stood up and cheered. But, judging by the hours I kept and the lengths Mariela took to keep me under wraps, I had become fairly certain Eddie didn't know I worked there—and I was equally certain that I was getting paid under the table. I was a little nervous about how this was all going to shake out at tax time. I hadn't quite worked up the nerve to ask her about the tax forms she'd never had me fill out.

"Seems happy enough," said Pierce agreeably.

“Good,” I exhaled, relieved. I hoped that meant an extension on the contract. Maybe she wouldn’t keep me around until kindergarten, but she had to value what I brought to the table—other than my milk—didn’t she?

As it turned out, my nagging fears about Mariela letting me go once Oliver was weaned were unfounded. No, that wasn't what happened at all. About a week later, I had just put Oliver down for his afternoon nap. Mariela and Pierce were both out—she took him out for a birthday pedicure at Charles Ifergan—so I was alone, tossing Oliver’s toys that had been strewn about the living room back into the crate.

Suddenly I heard the door open.

“Back so soon?” I softly called out, still bent over.

“The hell are you?” demanded an accusatory voice.

I spun around. It was Eddie. And all seven feet of him were glaring at me.

“Oh!” I squeaked. “Mr. Tyson. Hi. I’m Amanda. Um. Mariela called me to babysit today so she could take Pierce out for a little while this afternoon.”

A look of recognition washed over his face. “Oh, God, it’s the Baby Whisperer!” he said, laughing. “I’m sorry. How you been?” He came over to shake my hand. It was surprisingly gentle.

“I’m all right,” I said, still red-faced. “You know, keeping busy. Getting ready for the holidays.”

"Right on, right on," he said. He shed his warm-up jacket and flopped on the couch. I finished putting the toys in the box, and out of the corner of my eye, I could see him sizing me up.

When I finished, I folded my arms across my chest as if chilled. "So. Um. Did you get out of practice early?"

"For sure. Three straight wins, so coach let us go with just a short practice and some conditioning today. I don't have to be back 'til game time tomorrow."

"Who are you playing?"

"The Heat." He looked at me slightly lasciviously. Oh, dear God. No.

"Well, good luck!" I said after a pause. "Anyhow, I should probably go check on Oliver and make sure he's still sleeping."

He plucked the monitor off the coffee table and clicked on the video button.

"Looks like it," he said, showing me a clear view of his comatose child.

"Oh," I said. "Do you still need me to stay now that you're home? I can certainly leave if you prefer."

"You should stay," he said, patting the seat next to him on the couch. "Why don't you relax?"

Fuck.

I sat down, as far away as I could from him on the couch.

He slightly scooted over.

"You look a little stressed," he said, concerned. (Maybe mock-concerned.)

I gave a tight smile. "I'm fine," I said.

He leaned in, "You know, Amanda, I'll let you in on a secret. If it hadn't worked out playing ball, I would have gone to school to be a masseuse."

I snorted. "Oh, I doubt that."

"For real!" he said, mock-hurt. "These hands are good for more than free throws. Let me show you, I give the best massages in this entire city."

"That's not necessary," I objected. But his hands were already on my shoulders. I stiffened.

"Just relax," he cooed.

My heart was pounding. I knew I was no match for his two-hundred-plus pounds of muscle, so I sat there, frozen, praying this was the extent of what he'd do to me. But he didn't get any farther. After three minutes, tops, the door swung open. Mariela's face went from shocked to furious and back to composed in no time flat.

Eddie immediately sprung up from the couch. "Hey, baby!" he said, dripping with charm.

Mariela dropped her large Louis Vuitton tote at the door, walked over to Eddie, and gave him a kiss on the cheek. "Hey, baby," she murmured back, and shot me the iciest look I'd ever seen.

Pierce then came in the door, trucking an armload of bags from the salon and blissfully unaware.

"Hey, Amanda," he said, then did a double take. "Oh! Hi, Eddie!"

"Hey, man," Eddie said, reaching out to shake his hand. Mariela still had her arm draped around his waist, and hadn't stopped glowering at me.

"I'll be going now," I said, and made my way over to the front closet, where I grabbed my coat, purse and pump.

"I'll walk you out," Mariela said drily.

Fuck.

She swiftly closed the door behind us, grabbed my arm,

and flung me toward the elevator.

"How could you?" she hissed, furiously jabbing at the buttons

I was aghast. "How could *I?*" I repeated. "I had no choice—he practically forced me! And that was all he did, Mariela. He made me sit there while he rubbed my shoulders."

She laughed bitterly. "Let me guess. Did he tell you that his alternate career plan was to be a masseuse?"

Clearly she'd been down this road before.

"I swear, Mariela, I did *not* come onto him. This was only the second time I'd even seen him."

"Yeah, there was a reason for that. Why do you think my permanent staff is made up of a twink and a grandmother? I have to have people around me that I can *trust*, Amanda. And obviously I can't trust you."

Now she had really crossed the line. "Mariela," I said through gritted teeth. "That's unfair, and you know it. And if anything, I could sue him for sexual harassment."

She gaped at me. "You wouldn't."

"Why shouldn't I?" I asked, folding my arms. "After all, that's what he did."

She looked up and tilted her head back, trying to keep her tears in.

"Because Oliver and I don't deserve that," she said quietly. "Again."

Sigh. She was right. She might be married to a total lech, but she—and Oliver, especially—didn't need to be in the press again. And I certainly didn't want that kind of attention for myself and Maddie, either.

I looked her in the eye. I might take the high road, but I was *not* stupid. Even if I liked her, and had grown to love

Oliver, I still had Maddie to think about.

"Three weeks severance," I said. "Cash."

She looked back at me. Not angry anymore, but sad. Tired. And a bit defeated. She reached into her purse, pulled out her billfold, and counted out three thousand dollars for me. The elevator dinged and the doors opened. I stuffed the money into my pump's pocket and walked out, not looking back.

That L ride was one of the longest in my life. I was slightly proud of myself for getting the cash from Mariela—okay, quite proud—but the feeling that gnawed on me was regret at my loss of Oliver. I hadn't even gotten to say goodbye to him. Much like I hadn't gotten to say goodbye to Esther and Eunice. It's like the record just scratched and it was over. How could their parents do that not only to me, but to *them*?

Or maybe the babies never even noticed, I thought numbly. Maybe I never meant anything to them, either.

After getting off at my L stop, the thought of going home was too depressing at the moment, so I wandered the few blocks over to Dan's.

When he opened the door, he seemed both genuinely surprised and happy to see me. "Hey, gorgeous," he said. "Aren't you normally at work now?"

I couldn't hold it in any longer. I burst into tears and buried my face in my hands.

Dan immediately put his arms around me. "Hey, hey, it's all right," he said. "Come on in."

He pulled me inside. I was trying to maintain my composure as best I could, wiping my eyes underneath my sunglasses, hoping I didn't look as splotchy as I guessed I did.

"You want anything to drink?" he asked once we took the two flights up to his condo.

"Just some water would be fine," I said dully, flopping onto his couch. He poured me a glass from his Brita and set it in front of me on the coffee table.

"Do you want to talk?" he asked.

"Not yet," I said.

"Okay," he said. "I'm going to get some work done in the office. Just take your time." He padded toward his office in the back.

I sipped at my water for a while, then took the throw blanket from the side of the couch. I had pretty much run out of tears at this point. Dan was being awfully nice about things. Probably just pity. Of course, he didn't actually know I'd lost my job yet, so I wasn't even sure what was going through his mind.

I went to his office, which was a small loft area in between the two bedrooms. He had both of his computer screens running, one with a series of logos for a new restaurant on the screen, and the other with his Outlook.

"I lost my job," I said, still feeling numb,

He whirled around and his face fell. "I'm so sorry," he said earnestly. "Come here." I sat on his lap, curling up like I was little. He stroked my hair and we were both quiet for a while.

"Did they give a reason?"

I snorted. "It's hard to explain. But they were paying me under the table, so I'm shit outta luck."

"That hardly seems fair."

"It's not. And every time I've lost my job, I've been blindsided. And it hurts more and more each time."

"I was laid off when Kyla was pregnant with Lucas," Dan admitted. "I'd been with the ad agency for almost ten years when it got bought out, and about a third of us got the shaft. If I didn't have a few good friends in the business, I'd never have been able to get my own thing going."

I half-smiled. "That's how I got started, too." I then told him the entire story—how Joy initially convinced me to do it; the months in confinement working for Alexandra and her elderly husband's secretly adopted children; how Mariela hid my presence from Eddie; how Eddie came on to me and I was dropped like a bad habit. I told him about everything...except the breastfeeding. I still just couldn't. *Guess I won't have to worry about his reaction to the wet nurse career,* I consoled myself as an afterthought.

Dan let out a low whistle when I was done. "And this has all gone down in the past year?"

"Past five months," I corrected.

"That's crazy," he said. "If anything, you've got plenty of material for your memoirs."

"Too bad they don't accept crazy stories as payment at Trader Joe's," I said.

"It'll work out," he said. "I'll help you with your resume. We'll find you something before you know it. Now, do you want to go back to nannying? Or do you want to go back to editing?"

"I'll do *anything*," I confirmed. "Seriously. Anything that will keep a roof over our heads and food in the fridge." But I doubted I'd find anything in the publishing world anytime soon.

"Do you want to start working on them today? We could do two different resumes—"

"No, let me just take a day to wallow in self-pity. I think I've earned it."

"Understandable. Do you want to get some lunch in the meantime?"

"Sure." We swung by the deli about halfway between our buildings for some sandwiches. I let him pay without protest. After eating, he walked me back to my apartment building.

"Want to come up?" I asked as we got to the glass door.

"I'm on a deadline, I should probably get back," he said, giving me a kiss. "I'll call you later."

"Sounds good," I said. "And thanks for everything."

"We'll get you back in the game," he promised.

13

As it turned out, there were a few pluses to being unemployed this time around. For one, since Dan was self-employed and worked at home, it made it a lot easier to get frisky without the kids around. Every day after dropping Maddie off at daycare, I'd wait for Dan to arrive with Lucas, or he'd wait for me, and then we'd head back to his place, where he'd work, I'd apply for jobs, and much of the day was punctuated by breaks for, well, you can imagine.

About two weeks after I'd been unceremoniously fired, I put Maddie down to bed, flipped on *Parenthood*, and poured myself a glass of Riesling, wondering which storyline was going to make me break into tears this week. There was a quick teaser clip to promote the NBC news after the show, and the voiceover said, "Eddie Tyson traded to Los Angeles! Details at ten."

I almost choked on my wine. I quickly grabbed the remote and rewound it to make sure I had heard right. I had. I ran to my laptop, did a quick keyword search, and found an article on ESPN's site:

In an unprecedented move, Los Angeles has traded veteran point guard Horacio Stearns, plus the ninth pick in the next year's draft, to Chicago for their star player, Eddie Tyson. This move comes only three years after Tyson left the West Coast following a contract dispute while the team was led by former coach John Jacobson. New coach Cade Peters *orchestrated the move, clearing an extra $2 million in his roster for Tyson with the exodus of Stearns...*

And then the article went on about a bunch of other sports strategy shit I didn't care about. The point was, the Tysons were moving back to LA. And I had an idea that was at least worth a shot.

I took a deep breath and texted Pierce: "Tell Mariela I'll sell her my milk. $2K for 100 oz."

He texted back: "You're crazy."

I texted back: "Enjoy spending your first week in LA hunting down his meals."

Five minutes later he responded: "$1K. Be here at 9 AM. We'll need you until 1."

When I got to the Tysons' the next morning with an armload of Trader Joe's bags filled with frozen milk, the door was already wide open, and a flurry of strange people were there. Movers were taking measurements in the living room and packing up the place. Mariela was nowhere to be found, but I did see Pierce, Edna, a few guys in suits yelling into their cell phones (agents, maybe?), and interestingly enough, Eddie. He was actually the first person to speak to me as I walked in, bewildered and bleary-eyed.

"Morning, Baby Whisperer!" he said, politely. "Thanks for coming to watch Oliver this morning while we get packed."

"Not a problem," I said, quickly looking around. "I'm glad I can help out in a pinch."

Pierce flew into the room and intercepted me. He whisked me and my bags away into the office, where he had styrofoam containers, UPS boxes and freezer packs at the ready.

"Where's Mariela?" I asked.

"Out. She had to close up her accounts at the stores, go to the gym one last time, stuff like that."

"Did she have an envelope for you to give me?"

He scratched his head. "No. Was she supposed to have?"

"I wasn't giving her the milk for free!"

He gave me an exasperated look. "I'm sure she'll have it for you when she gets back."

"When is that supposed to be?"

"How the fuck should I know?"

"Aren't you her personal assistant?"

"Whatever," he said, slapping packing tape on the box. "I have to take this to UPS. I'll be back in a while. Oliver's in his crib." He tossed me the monitor as he headed out the door.

Like hell was I going to let them get away with stealing my milk. I'd already been screwed over enough. I walked back to the living room, where Eddie was playing on his phone, occasionally answering questions from the movers with a, "just put it over there."

I mustered up all the confidence I had, cleared my throat, and said, "Pardon me, Mr. Tyson?"

He looked at me, then politely put his phone down. "What's up?" He was stiff, but cordial. I guessed Mariela had given him quite the talking-to.

"I hate to be a bother, but Mrs. Tyson informed me that you'd be providing the payment for my services today. She said I should contact you directly."

"Sure," he said, pulling a gold money clip from his pocket. "How much we owe you?"

"On such short notice, it will be $1,000," I said, keeping my voice as steady as possible.

He didn't bat an eye, and peeled off ten Benjamins. "Here

you go," he said, reaching for his phone again.

Shit. Maybe I should have asked for two grand. "Thank you, sir," I said, and scuttled away, as I heard Oliver starting to chirp over the monitor.

After I darted into Oliver's room, I locked the door behind me.

"Hey, buddy," I cooed as I leaned over his crib.

He immediately started grinning at me, and I felt myself choke up a little. I picked him up, cradled him into my arms, and fed him, stroking his slightly curled hair and humming "Yellow Submarine." Once he was full, I changed him, dressed him in one of his many adorable Baby Gap outfits for fall, and snuggled with him in his rocking chair. I felt more than a little sad that I wasn't going to get to see him grow up, to dip his toes in the water of Lake Michigan, or bring him to the Children's Museum at Navy Pier. No, I'd be very happy to get to do all those things with my own precious daughter...providing we weren't living in my parents' spare room or in section 8 housing by Christmas, both of which possibilities were seemingly infinitely more likely.

After about two hours of toys and Dr. Suess, Oliver started to squawk. I fed him slowly, letting him take a good half hour before he drifted off to sleep. I gave him a last kiss on the forehead goodbye. "I'll miss you," I said, as I closed the door and turned off the light.

Pierce was waiting for me outside the door.

"Mariela wanted me to give you this," he said coolly as he handed me an envelope and escorted me to the foyer. "She'd like you to leave. Now."

I hesitated for a second as the Meg and Leigh on my shoulder gave me a swift kick and screeched, "Take the money and run, dumbass!"

I wished I had it in me to do just that, but I handed it back to Pierce. “Tell her to keep it,” I muttered, and closed the door behind me.

PART FOUR

14

Through some serious budgeting and a really bare-bones Christmas, I managed to make my severance and the milk money last me through the rest of December and January as well. Dan was really sweet—he brought pizza or Chinese food for dinner over for all four of us at least a couple of times a week, and I happily pretended I didn't see it as charity. I kept posting my fliers around the city and sent off more resumes than I could count. I even enrolled with a temp agency, but was informed that I was on a waiting list three-months deep. And, I kept pumping.

Dutifully, every Monday, I'd take my week's worth of milk to the hospital milk bank. Lugging about two gallons of milk via public transportation never ceased to be a pain in the ass, even for a tax write-off and a chance for advertising purposes, but I didn't want to ask Dan to borrow his car—or ever let him see me with the milk. I tried my best to strike up conversations with the others in line, but after several weeks of odd looks and the brushoff, it became clear that meeting Pierce had been an extraordinary stroke of rare luck.

By the end of January, I was completely tapped out of cash. The 401K savings were gone. My credit card had reached its limit. I hadn't quite pulled the trigger on downgrading our health insurance, but I did have an AllKids brochure on the counter that kept taunting me. On February first, I realized I couldn't put it off any longer. I had to tearfully call my dad to see if he could spot me my rent for the month, which he thankfully did. And, in one of the most humbling moments of my life, in my next call I made an appointment to go on the following Thursday to register for WIC.

If you don't know, WIC stands for Women Infants Children. It's a "federally funded program implemented by the City of Chicago Department of Public Health that provides pregnant, breastfeeding, postpartum women, children and infants with nutrition assistance." It's exactly what it sounds like: I was going on public assistance to make sure I could continue to put food on the table for my kid. After I'd hung up the phone with the receptionist, I drank nearly an entire bottle of three-dollar wine, and ended up feeling twice as awful about myself. This was not the way my life was supposed to go.

On Thursday, I packed my diaper bag full of juice boxes, crackers, board books, a baby doll, diapers and wipes; called daycare to let them know Maddie was sick and wouldn't be in today; spouted the same lie via text to Dan; put on my big girl panties; and hopped a bus to Lakeview.

We got there about half an hour before my scheduled appointment. I checked in and Maddie and I took a seat in one of the last remaining plastic chairs in the overcrowded waiting room.

"Phone? Phone?" Maddie said, pawing at my purse. I pulled out my cell phone for her, opened her favorite YouTube video of a pirated Dora episode, and handed her a baggie of Goldfish. As she munched away in peace, I surveyed the room. Moms and kids. Lots of them. And most of them looked...like me. Normally dressed. Clean. Kids were sitting in their mothers' laps, or playing on the floor. *Well, what did you expect them to look like?* I snidely thought to myself. *For*

Christ's sake, we're all people. We're all trying to do our best for our families.

After about twenty minutes, I heard a voice call out, "Keane?"

I stood up, gathered my things, and walked Maddie over to a cubicle that held a waifish girl with a huge smile, black hair, and a sleeve tattoo on her arm. We sat down in the well-worn office chair.

"Hi, I'm Jane," she said kindly.

"I'm Amanda," I said, "and this is Madeline."

She smiled warmly at Maddie, who was regarding her curiously. "All right, looks like this is your first appointment, so we'll just make sure we have all your paperwork, and we'll get you set. Sound good?"

I nodded, and pulled out the large manila envelope I had prepared.

"Can I see your license, please?"

I pulled it out of my wallet and handed it to her. She began typing. I kissed Maddie on the head and bounced her in my lap.

"Do you have your birth certificate?"

I pulled it out of the envelope and placed it on the desk. She made a few more keystrokes on the computer.

"Shot records for your daughter, and a referral form from your doctor's office?"

I fished around and found both. More keystrokes. Getting the referral from the doctor's office had been another fine exercise in humiliation. The referral nurse was always such a cow, and I swear I had detected notes of glee in her voice when I put in the request last week.

Jane peered at her computer, scanning lines, and then her eyes widened with realization. "Oh! Sorry, I forgot to ask first. I need to see two paycheck stubs or your IDHS card," she said.

I chewed my bottom lip. "See, that's the thing...I don't have either."

"Did you leave them at home?" she asked, not unkindly.

"Er. No," I felt my face redden. "Well, I had a job and I was being paid as a contract employee by a family. So I was just being paid in cash. And then they let me go without any notice. So I have some money, but I'm just hoping to make ends meet temporarily while I look for a new job. I practically have one!"

She looked at me sympathetically. "Unfortunately, we can't register you for the WIC program until you register first with the Illinois Department of Human Services. Here's the number you can call for an appointment," she said, jotting down a number on a post-it note and passing it to me. She then reached into a desk drawer and pulled out an immense packet. "Also, here's a SNAP application. These you can fill out on your own and mail in, so you might be able to get set up in the meantime."

"What's SNAP?" I asked, furrowing my brow.

"Supplemental Nutrition Assistance Program," she said. "It's the revised name for the food stamp program."

"Oh," I said quietly. The thought of "food stamps" had a slightly different connotation than the thought of "a program designed to keep women and children healthy."

"It's all right," she said, noticing my discomfort. "It's actually in the form of a debit card now, so it's much easier to pay at checkout. Much more dignified, too."

I nodded and started shoving the forms back into my envelope. "I'll think about it," I said.

"I'll keep your file as pending in our system. Just make another appointment once you're set up with the state."

I scooped up Maddie, tucked her back into the Bjorn and adjusted my diaper bag. "Have a good one," I mumbled, not looking back.

"You, too," she said, calling after me.

We headed out the door, shivered in the flurries for a moment until the bus came, then boarded for home.

I absently stroked Maddie's hair while chewing my bottom lip. Shit. I really didn't know what I was going to do at this point. Getting an appointment at the state might take a few weeks, and then it might be a few weeks more before I could go back to WIC. It might not be until March or April that I'd start to receive assistance of any kind. And at what point did it become ridiculous for me to keep Maddie in daycare, in hopes that I'd be able to find a job soon, instead of spending that money toward rent? *It's already ridiculous,* I thought to myself. Never mind the fact that, if I took Maddie out of daycare to save money, her slot would get snapped up immediately. As a result, if I even found a job, I wouldn't be able to take it because it would be months before I found decent daycare for Maddie again. It was a vicious, shitty circle.

And for the first time ever, I finally felt a true wave of rage toward Eamonn. God. What a fucking asshole. *He* should be the one helping me keep a roof over our daughter's head. *He* should be splitting the cost of her daycare with me. *He* should be the one applying for food stamps if he has a problem making ends meet. *He* should be the one still in debt from the costs of her birth. Maddie's eighteen months old and he hasn't paid a single dime yet because I was too heartbroken to harass him for money. Well, not anymore. I felt the Joy on my shoulder stand up and do the wave with Meg and Leigh.

I glanced out the window and saw we were just passing Daly's, the bar Eamonn's uncle owned and where we'd infamously met.

Christ! Why hadn't I thought of this before?

I yanked on the cord above me and a few moments later, the bus slowed to a crawl and lurched to a stop at the corner.

I nearly ran the next block back, jostling a confused Maddie on the way. It was just about noon, so it should be open for lunch, and if it wasn't, I'd bang on the door until someone let me in. Luckily, that wasn't necessary. With my face red from the cold and wind, my hair a mess and no fear or shame to hold me back, I strode up to the bar, where Eamonn's uncle Colin was doing a crossword from the Trib.

"I need to get a hold of Eamonn," I seethed, getting right to the point.

He peered up over his bifocals and jolted up straight once he realized it was me.

"Amanda!" he sputtered. "What the...who's...I mean...Dear God! You have a baby!"

The rage left me for a moment as puzzlement washed over me. "Of course I do. This is Maddie, *Eamonn's daughter*," I said for emphasis. "Who else do you think she'd be?"

He cleared his throat. "Two years ago, his mother rang me to say you'd lost the baby and called off the wedding, so Eamonn wouldn't be coming back."

That son of a bitch. Both insults intended.

"Clearly that wasn't the case, Colin," I said with a snort. "He broke up with me over email the day he was supposed to fly back for the wedding."

He shook his head in disbelief. "That little prick," he said. "I'm stunned. What a ..." his voice trailed off and he sighed, rubbing his temple.

"Yeah, I know," I said, actually in agreement for the first time. "Look, I need to get in touch with him. He changed his cell phone number and either quit or blocked me from Facebook *when I was still pregnant*," I said, for further emphasis. "I never even knew his home address in Ireland, either. I'm going to file for child support, so I need to get his contact information." I didn't know if this was actually necessary, but it sounded right to me.

"Of course, love," he said. "My address book is upstairs. I'll be back in a moment with it. Please, have a seat. Can I get you anything? Some tea? Maybe some ice cream for the little one?"

Maddie's eyes lit up at the words. "I cream?" she asked. "I cream? I cream?" Colin grinned at her. She'd charmed him already.

"I don't know. She hasn't had lunch yet," I explained.

"Bridget!" he barked. A short, towheaded waitress bounced to the bar. "I'd like you to get these two whatever they like for lunch. On the house," he added, and excused himself to go upstairs.

"Course, Uncle," she said brightly, pulling a notepad from her apron's pocket. "What can I get you?"

I ordered a blarney burger and a side of champ—the Irish knew what they were doing when it came to potatoes, that was for sure—for myself and a kid's macaroni and cheese kid's meal for Maddie, who still was whining for "I cream." She returned less than five minutes later with the steaming plates, and Maddie and I tucked in. Colin joined us shortly with a scribbled piece of notebook paper.

"All right," he said, sliding into the booth across from me and adjusting his glasses. "I called my cousin Mary—Eamonn's mother—and she hung up on me when I told her you were here and had little Maddie with you."

"Wench," I muttered, stabbing my champ with my fork.

"You'd not be the first one to think so," he said. "So then I called cousin Aisling, her sister, and the one who knows all the family's business, and doesn't care to mind her own."

I leaned in, interested. "Do tell."

"She said she had heard a rumor that Mary had hatched the story to the whole family about you losing the baby, because she didn't want anyone to know what a sorry excuse for a son she had, leaving his poor fiancée like that. Aisling said she always thought it sounded like Mary was hiding something."

"Wow, Mary sounds wonderful," I said. "Grandmother of the year. I'm sure she'd have made a fantastic mother-in-law, too."

He gave me a wan smile. "I'd say you dodged a bullet.'"

"I'm sure I did," I said, and an image of Dan ran through my head. Thank God for second chances. "Does cousin Aisling happen to know where Eamonn is now?"

"Sadly, no," he said. "He's been traveling with his new band. She heard they have been making some rounds in Dublin at university pubs, but nothing steady. She doesn't know his address or mobile," he added apologetically.

"This is a good start, though," I said. "And thank you, this is really nice of you to help me."

"Of course," he said. "I do have to ask, though...why are you only looking to find him now? Why haven't you gone after his miserable arse in the past two years?"

I hesitated, then asked, "How much time do you have?"

"Bridget!" he barked out again. Once she trotted over, he said, "We'd like three dishes of vanilla bean ice cream, please. And two Baileys on the side."

Half an hour later, I'd told him the whole story. Maddie was in an ice cream and carb-induced sleepy state, back in the Bjorn, and I clung to her as I finished telling Colin everything (except for the wet nursing part. As far as he knew, I had just been a nanny.). Once I was done, he sat for a moment and regarded me, then cleared his throat.

"You've been dealt quite a hand, Amanda," he said, "and it isn't fair. Not at all."

"Luck of the draw," I said bitterly.

"Not when the draw is my family. I won't have my relations acting this way. I want to pay for your lawyer to file for child support," he said.

I choked for a second on my tea. "You what?"

"I want to help make this right. You're going to need a lawyer, yes? I want to make sure you're going to drain every last penny Eamonn's got if it means you'll be able to take care of little Maddie."

"This isn't why I came here," I said, shaking my head. "I wasn't trying to infer you owed me anything. *Eamonn* does, not you."

"I just found out I have a new little grandniece," he said firmly. "I'll not have her father abandoning her,"

"Well, when you put it that way, it makes sense," I admitted. "Thank you. That's really amazing of you."

"I take care of my family," he said. "I've never been lucky enough to have children of my own, so I've got to take care of the Daly children when I can, how I can. You can't take it with you, you know."

"Thank you," I repeated, overwhelmed.

I think the poor guy felt so embarrassed about Eamonn's behavior that he went so far out of his way for me. Colin held true to his word and helped me hire a lawyer—one of Jonathan's buddies from John Marshall that he highly recommended—and we filed the first of a boatload of paperwork to get Eamonn in check. As it turns out, Ireland is a country that respects "comity," or in non-legalese, they respect U.S. laws and judgments, meaning, if and when an Illinois judge orders him to pay child support, Eamonn's deadbeat, fiddling ass would have to pay it one way or another.

So in that sense, at least, things were looking up. Maddie was getting bigger by the minute (twenty-six pounds and out of the carrier for good) and adding to her vocabulary at a ridiculous speed. I'd bought some Sesame Street number flashcards, and she could recognize the numerals one through ten by Valentine's Day. And all the names of her 'Street friends. She also seemed to recognize all the Disney princesses wherever we went out. Not sure how that happened since we didn't have the Disney Channel. Maybe it's innate in little girls? I still wasn't sure how I lucked out with her. I liked to think that she got Eamonn's eyes, and the rest was a combination of me, and the influences of all the people who loved her. At least, that's what I hoped.

Embarrassing in college, and even more so once you're in your thirties, Dan and I had what Joy and I refer to as "The DTR"—the conversation where you Determine The Relationship—and he told me that he'd referred to me as "his girlfriend" the last time his mom had called, and "just wanted to run that by me."

I smiled and said, "You'd better be calling me that," in response. We still weren't ready for sleepovers—it would just elicit too many questions from the tots that we didn't want to answer— but on weekends when Lucas was with his mom, I'd occasionally finagle my mom or Joy into watching Maddie for a few hours while we went out...or stayed in.

But, I still kept pumping twice a day. I donated milk back to the bank every Monday, just in case. And every week, I kept on posting my fliers at as many wealthy-mommy hotspots as I could think of.

I'll admit, it was kind of a half-hearted attempt. I was no SEO expert, but my consultant website barely registered on Google searches. I had no idea how to improve it, but again, that was nothing I wanted to talk over with Dan. And as smitten as I was with him, I felt part of me holding back, because I was by now nearly certain that my days in the city were numbered. My credit card had been completely maxed out, and I'd had to take out a second loan from my dad to pay for rent and daycare this month. When he came by to deliver the money to me on March first, he voiced what I'd known deep down all along.

"Peanut, you can't keep going on like this," he said, patting me on the shoulder.

"I know," I said numbly. "But what else am I supposed to do?" I'd made an appointment for IDHS for next month, but again, I didn't know how long it would be before I'd get any kind of help. I'd done a Google search the day before to look up local food pantries, and then closed my laptop, too ashamed to even write down the addresses.

"I think it's time for you to move back home," he said.

And unfortunately, he was right. We talked it through, and he agreed to give me one more month to find a job. If I wasn't hired anywhere by the end of March, we'd break my lease, and Maddie and I would bunk in their second bedroom. Indefinitely.

I couldn't bring myself to tell Dan, about any of it. First of all, it was just too humiliating to admit; and second of all, I didn't know what that would mean for our relationship.

One morning in mid-March, I thought long and hard about it as I was cleaning out my collection bottles for the bajillionth time, and decided it was time to get rid of the pump. I didn't have any luck finding another job as a wet nurse, anywhere. I wasn't even producing that much milk anymore—ten ounces a day, tops, and even that was freakishly high for the average mother of a twenty-month-old—and my heart wasn't really in it anymore, either. I'd already donated so many thousands of ounces that I'd probably kept dozens of over-privileged babies up to their eyeballs in breastmilk for the first few months of their lives, and hadn't seen much of a return on it (although I was hoping it would help a little bit whenever I got around to filing my taxes).

So, the next morning—no sense in waiting until Monday to check out potential clients—I brought in my donations, and told Lindsey at the front desk it was probably the last time they'd be seeing me.

"Nooo!" she squealed. "Are you seriously quitting the pump?"

"Yeah," I said. "It's about time."

"I don't know how you made it this long," she said incredulously. "Hey, can I ask you a personal question?"

"Sure, I guess."

She leaned in. "Why'd you do it so long? I mean, after having your baby and all. Why on earth would you keep pumping for an extra *year*?"

I thought for a minute. I remembered the twins, the exhaustion I felt taking care of them for ten hours a day, never getting more than a thirty-minute respite, but the satisfaction I felt each time they'd burp and settle back into the crib for a snuggly snooze. I remembered nursing sweet Oliver, feeling his soft skin against mine, watching as he grew plumper and plumper over the weeks. And I thought about Dan, who looked at me like I was a Greek goddess every time I undressed, admiring the fullness of my breasts before cupping and caressing them.

"Weight loss," I answered.

"Right on," she said, nodding. "When I have a baby, I'm totally gonna nurse until all the baby weight falls off. I mean, even if it takes, like, six months." She fiddled with her engagement ring and admired it.

I smiled and nodded. "Take it easy, Lindsey," I said.

"You, too!" she trilled.

Before leaving, I texted Joy: Hey, I'm at milk bank. Time for a break?

She texted back: Sure! See you in 15 in caf.

True to her word, fifteen minutes later, she hobbled toward my table by the window in the cafeteria. Don't get me wrong, Joy made an adorable pregnant woman, but when they're short, there's not quite as much room for the baby to go.

"Hey, mamacita," I said, greeting her with a hug. "How's it going?"

"Ugh. Large. I'm thirty-seven weeks and feeling it acutely," she groaned.

"Seriously?" I said. "It's gone by really quickly...for me." Smirk.

Joy kicked me under the table. "Oh yeah, for me, too," she said. "I only wish I could have the heartburn and weight gain forever."

"'No matter how hard it is now, just remember, babies are a lot easier to take care of when they're on the inside.'"

"Thanks for quoting me," she grumbled. "And please tell me I don't sound like that to my patients."

"You probably do, but they love you anyway," I said. "Now they'll probably love you even more once you've gone through labor, too. Just try not to lose all the baby weight in one month and you'll be golden."

"At the rate I'm putting it on, that's doubtful," she said, taking a large bite of her panini for emphasis. "By the way, you're coming to the shower on Sunday, right?" Her sister-in-law was hosting her baby shower at her country club in Oak Brook.

"Of course," I assured her. "I'm catching a ride with Meg." Meg had graciously let me go in on Joy's gift with her—a massive swing—and even more graciously told me not to pay her back anytime soon.

"I know," she said. "She's actually coming in tomorrow for her glucose test." Meg had recently shared that she was pregnant with her second one, and due a couple of months after Joy.

"Excuse me, that's a violation of doctor-patient confidentiality," I teased.

"I'll file that under the category of, "Whoops, Don't Give a Shit," she said. "At least not in my last few weeks before I leave."

"How long are you taking off for maternity leave, anyway?" I asked, blowing on my tea.

She hesitated, then looked around the cafeteria. "I'm not coming back," she said, barely audible.

"What? You're kidding," I said.

"Shhh," she said, eyes darting around the room for colleagues in earshot. "Jonathan and I just decided last week. I'm going to take my twelve weeks as planned for my maternity leave, and then I'm going to quit. Barring any unforeseen circumstances, of course," she hastily added.

I let out a low whistle. "I can't believe it," I said, earnestly. "I never would have expected you to be so domestic, but that's fantastic. I think you're going to love it."

"I hope so," she said. "We just looked at our schedules, and our finances, and realized we didn't want to have someone else raising our baby ninety percent of the time. I mean, I know we could have gotten an amazing nanny—you, for example—but, I wanted to really commit to—"

"Wait, wait, wait," I interrupted her. "You wanted me to be your nanny?"

She looked sheepish for a moment. "Well, it did come up in conversation with Jonathan. But I don't know. I didn't know if that was even something you wanted to do."

I wasn't sure, either. Might have made the friendship a little weird. Hmm.

"Anyway, go on," I said. "You wanted to commit to...?"

"Right," she said, absently rubbing her ample belly. "I just wanted to commit to motherhood. The baby. Breastfeeding. All of it. We're lucky enough that we can live on Jonathan's salary, and maybe in a few years I'll be able to go back to work part-time. Or not. I'm not sure. But for now, we decided this is the route we want to take."

"Good for you," I said, and meant it.

"And hey," she added. "I'm sure I'm going to be hitting you up for advice, especially about nursing."

"I don't know that I can offer that advice anymore," I said airily. "This cow's going out to pasture."

"Seriously? You're hanging it up?"

"I'm hanging it up. As it turns out, there's no work out there in 'special nannying.' None that I could find, anyway. So it looks like I'm breaking my lease at the end of the month and moving back in with my mom and dad."

Her eyes widened. "You have got to be kidding."

"If only."

"What about your mothers' consultant thing?"

"No bites. Believe me, I tried. And the only ones who did follow up were turned off when I told them what I actually did. I really don't think that there's an actual market for this kind of work, or if there is, I'm clearly not running around in the right crowds to find it."

She took a sip of her latte. "How about getting back into editing?"

"I've been sending out resumes for a year now, and no luck," I said. "I'll tell you, it feels really useless to even try."

Joy gave me a sympathetic look. "It'll happen."

"How do you know that?" I said, wearily. "You have no idea what it's like to be out of a job, and worry about money, and you probably never will. I know I'm a victim of my own shitty choices, but it doesn't make it any easier."

"You can't mean having Maddie was a shitty choice."

"I don't mean that, at all. But God, it goes back to picking a useless major in college and going into a career field that's becoming more and more obsolete every day. I don't know why I didn't choose a career that could at least be profitable. Or recession-proof. Like a mortician or something."

"I don't know about that. At least a third of Jonathan's law school friends have been laid off too, or are still doing document review for years after they graduated. They all thought they'd graduate from law school and sail into this six-figure job, but no. And the ones who did—"

"Like Jonathan," I interjected.

She ignored me. "The ones who did are miserable, and doing the work of three lawyers for the price of one. No one's immune to this crappy recession. I think in a lot of cases, it just comes down to how hungry you are, how badly you want it."

We were both quiet for a minute.

Joy stirred her coffee for a moment, then sighed, laying the wet stirrer on a napkin. "What the hell," she said. "I'm leaving anyway. I was thinking of giving you a parting gift."

I cocked an eyebrow. "Say what?"

She pursed her lips. "Sonja Carey is coming in for her six-week checkup tomorrow at nine," she said.

"Sonja Carey, the lingerie model? Married to Chase Carey?"

"One and the same. She's been in a few times since having her daughter last month. She said she's planning to wean soon because she's under contract to get back to work, but she's pretty granola-crunchy in a Hollywood kind of way. You know—sustainable chic. Paleo dieter. She seems like the kind of person who'd be into a wet nurse."

"Interesting," I said. "When did you say her appointment was tomorrow?"

"At nine. Do with that information what you will," Joy said and winked. "I better get back upstairs," she said, hoisting herself out of the cafeteria chair.

"See you soon," I said, the wheels already turning in my mind.

15

The next morning, I arrived at Joy's office as prepared as possible. I was dressed in canvas flats, an oatmeal-colored wrap sweater, and yoga pants. I spent an inordinate amount of time doing my makeup that morning so I could look as makeup-free as possible. I'd tucked a copy of *Kiwi* magazine under my arm, and I'd even voyaged up north to Metropolis Coffee that morning to use a cup as a prop. And I had a few business cards in the Ella Vickers reclaimed sail tote (courtesy of Leigh's handbag collection) at the ready.

When I arrived at the office at a quarter to nine, my prey wasn't there yet. Good. I checked in at the front desk.

"The doctor said she'd try to squeeze me in this morning if she could. I just need her to look at ... something," I explained, not very convincingly to the receptionist.

She narrowed her eyes into slits. "Hold on," she said, and scrolled her mouse, eyeballing her monitor. "We can get you in at ten," she said.

"I'll wait!" I said, and whirled into a chair. There were five open ones left, all near me. I hoped Sonja would show up soon.

She did. All six feet of her glided into the waiting area, in skinny jeans, riding boots, and a cashmere poncho that I couldn't pull off if my life depended on it. And while I was happy enough with my own post-baby body, no one had the legal right to look as amazing and skinny as she did six short weeks after giving birth.

As I pretended to read my magazine, she wrote her name on the sign-in sheet and slid onto the chair directly across from me. She pulled out her phone and started to type away.

It was ten minutes to nine.

"I love your boots," I said earnestly.

She glanced up. "Thanks," she said with a half-smile, then looked back down at her phone.

Can't throw in the towel now. "They look vegan," I added.

She perked up. *Bingo*, I thought.

"They are," she said, "They're Stellas."

"They're gorgeous," I purred. "It can be so hard to find cruelty-free boots in the Midwest."

"Tell me about it," she said.

I took a sip of my tea so the label would show. "I've been looking for something similar for my one-year-old, but I haven't had a lot of luck. I've been to Piggy Toes and Psycho Baby, but I still haven't found just what I wanted."

"You should try LMNOP," she offered. "I always find something adorable for my daughter when I go."

"How old is she?" I asked, feigning ignorance.

"Six weeks today," she said.

"I can't believe that you had a baby six weeks ago!" I said, laying it on thick. "You look *fantastic.*"

Sonja shrugged, looking slightly embarrassed.

"I love that squishy newborn stage. My absolute favorite," I said. "I work with babies, and I love nothing more than getting to be with the really little ones."

"Oh, what do you do?" Sonja asked.

Here goes nothing. "I'm a wet nurse," I said, confidently and without blushing.

She looked taken aback for a second, and then....intrigued.

"Really?" she said, sounding fascinated. "You breastfeed babies. For your job."

"Absolutely," I said coolly. "There's no more rewarding profession than to help a child grow."

"Huh," she said, clearly mulling over the concept. "So who have you worked for?"

"I can't say—confidentiality clauses and all that," I said. "But," I lowered my voice, "I will say I have worked for the family of a certain professional athlete. And a certain designer who's been in *Architectural Digest* more times than I can count. I'm actually interviewing with another family tomorrow—a certain daytime talk show host."

(For what it's worth, Kate Alastair, Oprah's former protegé and host of one of the top-rated talk-slash-cooking shows in Chicago, had her baby the week Sonja had hers. Which I knew from reading in *Celebs* magazine. Kate and her son had been featured on the cover. Sonja had been relegated to page forty of the same issue, a small blip in the news shorts section.)

Her eyes gleamed. "You don't say," she said, drawing each word out.

"Sonja?" called the nurse, standing at the door with a clipboard.

She whipped her head back toward the nurse. "One second," she snapped. "Hey, do you have a business card, by any chance?" she asked me.

"Let me just check," I said, pretending to fumble in my tote. I pulled out a card and handed it to her. "I'm Amanda, by the way," I said.

"I'm Sonja," she said, standing up and gathering her purse. "But you already knew that." She headed toward the door.

She wasn't wrong about that. But I had piqued her interest, that was for damn sure. And around 8:30 that night, she called me.

"You'd mentioned that you were interviewing with another family," she said. "At what time?"

"One o'clock," I lied.

"Would you be interested in interviewing with us at 10 AM?"

"Let me see...." I said, pretending to flip through a nonexistent calendar. "I think I could be available at ten."

"Great," she said, and gave me the address. Based on what she said, I was pretty sure it was in Lincoln Park. Interesting. I'd pictured her husband as a River North kind of guy (or really, the "Viagra Triangle," full of wealthy, aging dudes and their bimbos), but maybe they'd moved when they had the baby.

"Is there anything you'd like me to bring? Resume, pump?"

"Sure, both would be good. You'll be meeting with me, possibly my husband, and the other nannies as well."

Plural? "Wonderful," I chirped. "See you tomorrow!"

After I hung up, I squealed and hugged myself. I had to get this. I had to! I called Dan to let him know the good news.

"Sonja Klitzki Carey!?" he said. "Oh, man! She's smok—I mean...I guess she's okay."

"Yeah, if you're into supermodels with legs up to their necks, she's all right," I teased. "I'm just hoping she pays well. She said that her 'other nannies' would be present at the interview."

"How many kids do they have?"

"I think just the one, right?" I said. "Wait. I remember some rumor from a few years ago that some other ex-model had a baby with Chase, but I don't think that was ever confirmed. It's probably still floating around as a blind item."

"I'm sure even if that's true, Chase just paid her off. He'd never be seen with that kid."

Probably true. Chase Carey was one of the biggest hometown celebrities in Chicago. He grew up in Wheaton, not too far away from me, but he's a good decade older than I am. He starred in a few indie movies in the mid-nineties, then made it big with a couple of comedies with fellow *Saturday Night Live* veterans, and has worked steadily ever since. He's cute—tall to the point of gangly, with a shaggy mop of blonde hair—and consistently cast as the idiot husband. A lovable, forgivable idiot, anyway.

He's kind of a dick in real life, though. When Joy and Jonathan got married about five years ago, the photographer took us to Millennium Park. This is where everyone in a downtown wedding goes for photos by The Bean, by the fountains, all the rest of it. We had just unloaded ourselves out of the trolley when Joy spotted Chase walking down Michigan Avenue, with Kurt Dean, the city's most famous running back. They were both in Sox shirts and hats, and appeared to be deep in conversation.

"That's Chase Carey!" Joy had yelled, a little champagned-up already.

Simultaneously, Jonathan had yelled, "That's Kurt Dean!"

Kurt looked up and tipped his hat. "Congratulations!" he called out, giving a friendly wave. The whole wedding party cheered back.

"Chase! Chase! Will you get in a picture with us? Please?" Joy shouted, waving her bouquet above her head.

He'd turned his head, sneered, and kept shuffling down the street, hands buried in his pockets and shoulders hunched. Kurt looked at him, shrugged and waved once more to Joy and Jonathan.

"Screw that guy," I'd said to a crestfallen Joy. "Anyway, don't you think he seems shorter in real life?"

"Why didn't you ask Kurt to get in a picture?" Jonathan had whined. "He would have done it."

"Who?" Joy had asked, genuinely confused.

That little episode had always tainted my opinion of Chase Carey. I get it if celebrities don't want to be bothered by the general public, but for pete's sake, then don't walk down Michigan Avenue on a Saturday in July in Sox gear. I read later that the two of them were on their way to the game and would be singing "Take Me Out to the Ball Game" during the seventh-inning stretch later that night. At any rate, I haven't shelled out eleven dollars to see Chase Carey in the theaters since.

"I just hope it ends up being a good fit," I said to Dan. "It would be nice to have some steady, full-time work again."

"Could be more than full-time, you know," he countered. "They might ask you to work some crazy hours."

"Maybe," I admitted. "Would you be averse to picking up Maddie from daycare now and then if I was going to be late?" Last month, I'd already changed the "Emergency Contact" to be Dan in Maddie's file at daycare. It made the relationship feel very official.

"That's no problem," he said. "I know how it goes. Sometimes when you're a single parent, it's tough to handle all the work-kid logistics."

"That's why I'm so lucky to have you," I said with sincerity. "Because you *do* get it."

He was quiet for a moment. "What if we didn't have to be single parents?" he finally said.

My heart caught in my throat. "What do you mean?" I said cautiously.

"You know what I mean. One day."

"Ah," I said. I didn't want to put the pressure on, but I didn't want him to think the idea wasn't on my radar, so I just said airily, "Sure, maybe. In the future."

"In the future," he agreed.

"Anyway, can I borrow your car to get to the interview?"

"Of course. Just wait for me at daycare and you can drop me off at home on your way there."

"Thanks, love."

"No problem. I better get Lucas to bed. Let me know how it goes tomorrow."

"Will do! Good night, you."

"Night."

Well. Shit had certainly just gotten real. It would have been helpful if I *had* known what he meant, too. Did he mean he wanted for us to live together at some point in the next five years? Did he want to go ring shopping for my birthday? Damned if I knew. But I couldn't worry about that right now. I had to get ready for tomorrow, and then get some sleep.

The next morning, I expertly reapplied my minimalist makeup, dressed in skinny jeans and my canvas flats again—didn't want to risk my Fryes in case she was *that* vegan—and an organic cotton blazer. Dan kissed me good luck, and about twenty minutes later, I was in front of a sprawling, buttercup yellow, Victorian house on a quiet street in Lincoln Park. With a *driveway*. And turrets. It was as if a giant claw machine had picked up a million-dollar home in Naperville, quadrupled the price tag midair, and delicately placed it on prime real estate in the city.

I was about ten minutes early. I rang the doorbell, smoothed down the front of my jeans, and waited. A moment later, a tired-looking redheaded woman about my age opened the door.

"Hello," she said, stifling a yawn. "Come on in."

"Thanks," I said, and came into the entryway. As I expected, the home was right out of a magazine, but not one that would have featured Alexandra's home. This one was more like an ode to the now-defunct *Cottage Living*, and incidentally, exactly how I'd decorate if I had unlimited cash and time. A rustic, reclaimed wooden bench with cotton throw pillows was to my left, against the stark white, beaded board wall. Further on led to the living room, where I saw overstuffed couches, built in bookcases with just enough tomes and a reading nook. It was so New England beach-house-beautiful. I couldn't wait to see the kitchen.

"Amanda, right? Can I get you anything to drink?" asked the redhead.

"I'm all right, thanks," I said with a smile.

"Sure," she said. "By the way, I'm Julie. I'm the night nurse."

"Nice to meet you," I said, shaking her hand. A night nurse. Of course.

"I'll go get Karen. She's upstairs with Delilah. Feel free to take a seat." She gestured toward the navy couch next to me. I did as I was told, as she headed up the creaking stairs.

A few minutes later, she returned with a willowy blonde who could have passed for Sonja's twin sister, carrying a little wisp of a baby, snoozing in her sling. I could barely see her head peeking out, but I saw a little tuft of downy golden hair.

"Hi, I'm Amanda," I stage-whispered.

"I'm Karen," she said, stage-whispering back. "And this is Delilah."

"I love that name," I said. "It fits her. She's gorgeous."

"Right? Just look at her mom, it's no wonder."

"Speaking of which—is she here?"

"She's just finishing up her bikram yoga session—the studio's upstairs. She'll be down in a couple of minutes."

"Oh," I said, unsure of what to say next.

About ten minutes passed while we waited. Karen and Julie made a little small talk with me. From what I gathered, Karen's true profession was a post-partum doula. Families hired her to help out for the first week or two at home after having a baby, and she'd do more or less whatever they needed—make dinner, play with the older child, take out the trash, rock the baby to sleep so the mother could nap, whatever. It seemed to involve very little care of the actual newborn, but she said she liked it well enough. She'd started out as the post-partum doula for the Careys, and after the two weeks were up, she was hired full-time indefinitely.

"Was there supposed to be another nanny?"

"No, Sonja was really committed to the idea of attachment parenting."

"How's that working out for her?"

She just smirked.

Julie had been a night nurse for a few years now. She explained that she started as an RN in a pediatric NICU, and had been working the overnight shift for as long as she could remember. One of her coworkers, Erin, had convinced her that there was a market out there for private night nurses, and the two of them started their own business. They usually alternated nights of twelve-hour-shifts, and had worked steadily for families not unlike the ones that had employed me last year. Sonja had hired both of them indefinitely, too. I was about to ask if they had to co-sleep with the baby, but just then the back door opened.

I craned my neck to see who it was. It was Chase. He cruised through the living room, wearing aviator shades and a hoodie that smelled of cigarettes, and carried a large iced coffee.

"Morning, ladies," he mumbled.

"Good morning, Chase," both of them chirped. He tromped up the stairs. They looked at each other and rolled their eyes. There had to be a story there, but I didn't get to hear it. Sonja came downstairs a moment later, cheeks flushed and a yoga towel around her neck. After her workout, she was radiant and glowing, which struck me as highly unfair to the rest of the human race.

"Hi, ladies," she said, fanning herself off and plopping on the couch next to me.

We all greeted her with hellos.

"Thank you for coming, Amanda," she said.

"Thank you for having me," I said. "Delilah is just adorable. What a sweet, little peanut."

She gave me a small, forced smile. "So, Amanda, tell me about your beliefs on raising a child."

"I believe in creating an atmosphere of 'yes' for the child," I said smoothly. "They're only small for so long. I feel that the world should be a positive place for them, and we should accommodate their needs, meanwhile challenging them to grow into unique individuals and explore their world."

She seemed to like that. I continued to answer her hippy-dippy bullshit questions with equally hippy-dippy bullshit answers as Karen and Julie busied themselves in the kitchen.

Sonja was sitting back in her chair, looking satisfied as I expounded to her about my daily breakfast of steelcut oatmeal and fenugreek supplements to keep my supply strong when Delilah woke up with a piercing, godawful cry. Sonja flinched, took a deep breath, and headed into the kitchen to get her from Karen.

"I'd like you to feed her," Sonja said, holding the baby toward me.

"Of course," I said, as I unclasped my nursing tank. She passed the squawking infant to me, and I deftly maneuvered Delilah into a football hold. She latched right away.

Sonja looked at me curiously for a second, then continued with her line of questioning.

"Have you ever worked with a baby with colic before?" she asked, sounding almost guilty.

"Several," I said. *Shit.* What was that stuff Meg had talked about when her son had it? "The poor things, they can't help it. It just makes your heart ache for them. I've found that nursing and...ah...gripe water! Yes. Gripe water. That helps."

"Somewhat," she said. "Anyway, she's supposed to be halfway through it by now." She looked blankly at Delilah, who continued to suckle away at me.

"Are you planning to wean soon?" I asked.

Sonja sighed. "Well, I *was* planning to nurse until she was at least two, but I don't know anymore. I don't think my body can keep up with the demand. You, on the other hand, might be able to."

"I hope so," I said with a wry smile. "Somehow lactating has become one of my greatest talents."

Delilah was slowing down, so I unlatched her and burped her over my shoulder.

"Would you like her back?" I said after Delilah delicately belched.

"No, you hold her," she said, vigorously shaking her head. "She should get to know your touch. Come on, let me show you around."

I carried Delilah close to my chest, facing her outwards, as Sonja gave me the grand tour. The downstairs consisted of the living room, an antique-filled dining room, an enviable cottage kitchen, a sitting room, and an atrium. In their backyard was a full outdoor kitchen on their patio, a greenhouse where they grew most of their own produce, a chicken coop, and a goat pen. I'd heard of urban chickens, but were goats even legal in the city?

Upstairs were four bedrooms: the master, the nursery, the guest bedroom—as of late, the room where the night nurses could stay when Delilah was sleeping—-and an extra room, which had been refashioned into Sonja's yoga studio, complete with its own climate control.

The basement had a laundry room and the media room, boasting a theater-sized screen—the only TV in the house, as far as I could tell—a large sectional sofa, a pool table, a wet bar, and movie posters of all of Chase's box office hits.

"So that's the place," she said, walking me back to the entryway.

"It's lovely," I said with sincerity. I spent about half the tour daydreaming about living here with Maddie, teaching her how to compost. Gathering eggs from the chicken coop each morning for breakfast. The only thing that could make the home more idyllic would be if it were moved to the scenic White Mountains of New Hampshire.

"Do you have any other questions for me?" I asked.

"No, I don't think so," she said. "Thanks for coming. We'll be in touch."

Hmph. I guess I couldn't expect an offer on the spot all the time.

"Thank you, Sonja. It's been a pleasure," I said with a grin, and handed Delilah back to her mother.

"Likewise," she said. She then barked over her shoulder, "Karen!" The nanny scurried over to take the baby off of Sonja's hands. I excused myself and headed out.

I kept my ringer at the highest volume and my phone in my pocket for the next week straight. I'd dutifully sent a handwritten note on a recycled paper card for which I'd shelled out six dollars, thanking her again for the opportunity to meet her and her family, and said what an honor it would be to help care for her child. Did I lay it on too thick? I hope she didn't think I was some kind of star struck stalker who'd sneak in her room and smell her bras.

Finally, the next Friday she called me, just after I'd picked Maddie up from daycare.

"Hello?" I answered, trying to collect myself.

"Hi, Amanda," she said. "Sorry it's taken so long for me to get back to you. We were out of town for a few days. I was working—photo shoot in Belize."

Must be rough, "Oh, that's no problem," I said. "Delilah must have loved the beach!"

"Sure. Anyway, I'm calling to tell you we think you'd be a great fit in our household, and we'd like to offer you the position of our wet nurse."

I shrieked on the inside. "Thank you," I said. "I appreciate you thinking of me." I didn't want to say the word "yes," just in case the offer sucked.

"My lawyer has an offer letter and some other paperwork for you. Can I have him email it to you, and then you can send it back?"

"Please do have him send it to me," I said. I gave her my email address.

"Great," she said. "He'll email it over now."

My phone pinged a few minutes later. I sat and read the attachments for the next twenty minutes. The highlights:

-Compensation would be decent—$1,100 per week before taxes, which was definitely enough to pay for rent, daycare, and anything else Maddie and I needed. I would be strictly the wet nurse, as they were keeping Karen on staff, so my baby-related duties were limited to feeding Delilah, feeding Delilah, and feeding Delilah.

-What I'd be doing the rest of the time that she wasn't eating involved "researching infant nutrition, optimizing my personal health and diet, and other duties as assigned." I'd have to ask about what this exactly meant.

-Hours were to be 8 AM to 5:30 PM, Monday through Friday, and evenings and weekends as assigned. Okay. Fingers crossed this would work out.

-The NDA was the bulk of the contract. In short, it swore up and down that I would regret it financially and personally for the rest of my very short life if I ever breathed a word to another soul in the entire universe that I was breastfeeding the baby of Sonja Klitzki Carey. Fine. I wasn't worried about Joy saying anything. Everyone else, I'd just tell them I got another nannying job, and that's all they needed to know.

That night, after feeding Maddie a celebratory dinner of her favorite foods—chicken nuggets dipped in honey, with sweet potato tots on the side—I put out some wooden puzzles for her to explore and busied myself with printing, signing and scanning the documents back to the Careys' attorney. I called my dad to let him know the great news, and he was just as thrilled and relieved as I was.

Then I called Joy.

"Hey," she said lazily, "What's going on?"

"I got a job with the Careys!" I sang.

"That's so cool," she said, slightly slurring her words. "I mean, really, really cool."

"Are you okay?" I asked cautiously.

"Oh, yeah, I'm fabulous," she said. "These drugs are great. I haven't felt this high since senior year in college."

"Joy...where are you?"

"Post-op," she said. "It's a girl."

"What!" I shrieked. "My God! Congratulations! When was she born? Name? Stats?"

"Almost an hour ago. Felicity Lynn. Eight pounds even. I went into labor this morning, and we decided to go for the c-section because she didn't progress the entire day."

"I can sympathize with that," I said. "I bet she is beautiful."

"Well, I only got a glimpse of her covered in birth cheese, but I think we'll keep her."

"Where is she? Have you gotten to hold her?"

"No, they're doing the screens now. Jonathan just came in a few minutes ago with my phone and ice chips. They should be wheeling her in any minute. You're actually the first to find out."

"I promise I won't leak the news," I said. "Can I come by tomorrow to visit?"

"You'd better. And maybe bring me some McDonald's?"

"You got it. Congrats, hon. I can't wait to meet her."

My parents had already planned to come into the city the next morning to take Maddie to the Shedd Aquarium—thereby giving me and Dan a brief date since Lucas was with his mom that weekend—so my next call was to Dan. After I told him about the new job, I asked him about the next day.

"Any way I can convince you to let part of our date take place at a hospital?"

"Sounds hot, but I'm not really into swinging with invalids. Why?"

"Joy had her baby today! It's a little girl. I'd love to pop by while my parents have Maddie today."

"That's great!" he said. "Of course we'll go."

Could this guy get any more perfect? Around lunchtime, he arrived to collect me from my apartment. We picked up enough fries and cheeseburgers for Joy and for ourselves, tucked them in my tote, and then made our way to the hospital.

"Hi, guys," Joy said, a little groggy. She was holding her swaddled little bundle in the standard supply flannel receiving blanket with pink and blue stripes on the edges. The baby had little black hair poking out from underneath her pink cap. Felicity had a tiny smattering of baby acne on her pudgy little nose, golden skin, full cheeks, and rosy little lips. She was perfection.

After we oohed and aahed over her, Dan asked, “Mind if I hold her?”

Joy obliged, and carefully handed her over. He sat in the rocking chair in the corner and cuddled her into his lap as if it were the most natural, everyday thing for him to do. My heart completely melted. I got a chance to hold her, too, and Joy recounted the last twenty-four hours for me. Her experience had been similar to mine, although she sounded like she already regretted the c-section.

“I keep wondering if I could have avoided it if I’d only waited it out or tried harder,” she said.

“Meh,” I said, shrugging. “I wouldn’t worry about it if I were you. I’d just concentrate on the baby and what happens moving forward.”

“I guess,” she said, with a yawn. “She’s eating every two hours already. I feel like I’m never going to keep up. How the hell did I tell all my patients that it was normal?”

“Because it is. And everything you told them was true. But, even the world’s best gyno isn’t going to know what it’s like until she experiences it for herself,” I said, giving her a small punch on her arm.

Just then, the photographer knocked on the door. “Are you ready for us?” he asked.

I looked at Joy. “We should get going anyway,” I said.

“All right,” she said. “Come on in.”

I gave both her and Felicity kisses on the cheek.

“We’ll see you soon,” I said.

“Hang in there,” said Dan. “It’ll get easier.”

Joy’s eyes watered a bit. “Bye, you two,” she whispered.

Dan and I were quiet, thoughtful, on the way back to his car.

"That was something," he finally said as we pulled out of the parking garage.

"It was," I said. "I'm so happy for them."

"That's probably the first baby I've held since Lucas," he said. "You forget how tiny they are."

"Ah, I get constantly reminded in my line of work," I said. "They're neat at this stage. Such little blank slates."

"Do you ever think about having more?"

My eyes widened and my head whipped around. "Excuse me?"

He half-laughed. "Do you?"

I didn't answer right away. Finally, I said, "Not really."

We were at a stoplight, so he looked at me. "You don't? Not even working with newborns all the time?"

"I don't, *especially* because I work with newborns all the time. I could never be a nanny and take care of my own newborn at a time. I highly doubt a family would grant me 'maternity leave.' I've had a pretty difficult time making ends meet for me and one child the past couple of years, so I certainly haven't considered adding another child to the mix. So, I repeat, the answer is 'not really.'"

"I heard you," he muttered. "Sorry I asked."

A moment later, I said, "I'm sorry. I didn't mean to get so defensive. It's just that having another child is not even on my radar right now."

"I said I heard you. Loud and clear," he said coldly.

A few more moments passed. "This is kind of unfair," I pointed out. "We've never even talked about the future before, and all of a sudden, in the last week you're dropping hints about marriage and babies, and then getting pissed when I don't automatically have a perfect response for you."

He was quiet, mulling it over.

"What's bringing this on, anyway?" I asked.

"Lucas asked me last week if he could start calling you 'Mom,'" he blurted out.

Whoa. "He did?" I didn't think he saw me in that way.

"And his daycare teacher told me the other day that he's telling them that Maddie is his little sister," he added.

"That's really sweet, I guess?"

"Yes, it's really sweet, but it's probably really confusing for him, too," Dan argued. "Maddie's too young to know the difference, but Lucas is starting to have questions that I don't know how to answer. How am I supposed to respond when he says, 'Why can't Maddie and Amanda live here, too?'"

"He asks that?"

"He did, a couple weeks ago," Dan confirmed.

I was quiet for a moment. "Is that supposed to be an invitation?" I asked cautiously.

"Well, not exactly. I mean, it's probably too soon. We've only been dating for a few months. We're not even engaged," he admitted.

"So I'm not sure how I'm at fault here," I said, crossing my arms.

"You're not at fault," he said. "It's just...I don't know what to tell Lucas. But, I think it's hard when he's thinking more about our future than we are."

"I'm not going anywhere," I said softly. "Dan. I love you."

"I love you, too," he murmured. I squeezed his hand, and held it for the rest of the drive back to my place.

As we pulled up to the curb, he said, "One more thing."

"What's that?"

"Do you love Lucas, too?"

"I adore Lucas. How could I not? He's a pint-sized version of you."

Dan smiled.

I added, "But while that's true, I'm not his mom. I'll be there for him in every way, but I can't encroach on his own mom's territory. He has to call me Amanda. Otherwise, it would break Kyla's heart."

"Kyla barely has a heart," he scoffed. "Someday, couldn't you see yourself as the kind of mom he deserves?"

I wasn't entirely sure how to answer that. True, I liked Lucas—how could I not? He was a sweet kid, and great with Maddie. I enjoyed the time all four of us spent together, but I thought I'd been pretty careful not to overstep my boundaries. He had a mom of his own, and I didn't want to disrespect that fact. Even if most of his weekends with her consisted of him being entertained by his grandparents so that Kyla could nurse a hangover or go out for pedicures.

For Dan, though, there were no lines to worry about crossing. Maddie cherished him as much as I did. Whenever we went to "Dan-Dan's" home, she bolted right to him and clung to his leg like a life preserver. Sometimes he'd put on a puppet show for the kids, or all four of us would snuggle on the couch, watching a movie and sharing a huge bowl of popcorn. Once, both the kids had fallen asleep on his lap, and he just let both of them stay there snoring, absently playing with Maddie's hair as he read a book. Like her dad. A part of me envied how easy his side of the relationship was in this sense. He never had to worry about stepping on Eamonn's toes. He was lucky in this way that he could just love her unconditionally, like she was his own daughter. Lucas deserved that kind of love, didn't he?

I leaned over for a kiss. "I hope so," I said, earnestly.

For the rest of the day, our conversation echoed in my head, and I felt pretty guilty. I remembered how I felt before I met Dan, so resigned to the idea of single motherhood, because A, who would want me, and B, no guy would come along that would love Maddie like I did. Here I was, wrong on both accounts, and how ironic that *I* was the one who wasn't fully opening my heart and loving Dan's son like I should. It shouldn't matter if his own mother was straight out of a 1950s handbook or if she was behind bars. I could love him like my own child, treat him like my own, care for him like my own. I just couldn't say he *was* my own.

For the moment, though, I couldn't keep worrying about this. I had a new baby to prepare for tomorrow, and I had to get my head in the game.

16

The following morning, I geared up for my first day at the Carey house. It was unseasonably warm for late March—over sixty degrees by 7 AM, and the air smelled damp, like spring should. I dressed in a nursing-friendly maxidress, ballet flats, and a light denim jacket.

"Good morning," said Julie, answering the door, shoes in hand.

"Hi," I said warmly. "Must be more like goodnight for you, huh?"

"You can say that again," she said, pulling on her coat. "Karen's with the baby in the living room. Sonja's outside getting some eggs. There should be some coffee in the french press if you want it."

"Oh, no thanks. I can't have caffeine," I added.

"Right, right. Forgive me, I'm a little brain-dead at this time of day," she apologized. "Anyway, I'll see you later this week."

"Bye, now." I put my tote down on the bench and came into the kitchen. Karen had Delilah in a sling, and was pointing out the different fruits in the bowl.

"Hi, Karen," I said.

"Hey, how are you?" she asked, swaying from side to side.

"I'm fine. May I?" I asked, gesturing to the pitcher of cucumber water on the table.

"Go ahead," she said. "Glasses are in the cabinet to the right of the sink."

I poured myself a glass and sipped it, watching a drooling Delilah suck on her hand. Karen seemed totally at ease, humming and letting Delilah wrap her other fist around her pinky.

Sonja came in the back door holding a basket of eggs, wearing a wide-brimmed hat, loose waves, capris, and a thin sweater. She stepped out of her flip flops and placed the eggs on the counter.

"Hi, Amanda," she said, giving me an awkward one-armed hug. "Nice to see you."

"It's nice to be here," I said, awkwardly half-hugging her back.

"Come on, Delilah won't need to eat for another hour or so. I have a project for you."

"Great!" I said enthusiastically.

She led me into the living room, where she had an iPad on the coffee table. She handed it to me.

"I need you to look up recipes for homemade laundry detergent."

"Oh! Sure," I said, thinking, *People make that?* "Any ingredients in particular you want or don't want?"

"It has to be chemical-free," she confirmed. "Let me know what you can find. Later, this afternoon, I'll need you to go out and get the ingredients."

"Will do," I said. Sonja went upstairs, and I pulled up a browser. An hour later, I'd saved three different recipes for her to review.

"Someone's hungry," Karen sang, bringing Delilah to me.

"Thanks," I said. Sonja was still upstairs. "Does Sonja have a preference of where I feed her?"

"I doubt it," she said. "She fed her anywhere. The couch is probably fine."

I adjusted myself and hooked Delilah on. About fifteen minutes later, just as I was switching sides, a freshly showered Sonja came down the stairs. She didn't even look at her daughter when she came over to greet me. I was starting to notice that she barely paid any attention to Delilah at all.

"So, did you find some recipes?"

"I did. I have them saved as documents on the home screen," I said.

She scanned through them, and pursed her lips. After a few minutes, she said, "Definitely the one with the lavender essential oil."

"I agree," I said.

"I'm going out for a bit. After she's done, just give her back to Karen so she can put her down for a nap. There's a Whole Foods a few blocks down. Just bring me the receipt and I'll reimburse you."

With that, she put on her sunglasses and headed out the front door.

Karen sauntered back into the room a minute later.

"Looks like she's about ready for a nap," she said, cooing at Delilah, whose lids were getting heavy.

"I'd say so," I agreed, passing the tot back to her nanny. "Hey, I have kind of a weird question."

"What's that?"

"Has Sonja...taken to the baby?"

Karen took a moment to choose her words carefully. "For some new moms, the adjustment period takes time."

"It does," I nodded. We regarded each other for a moment, and then Karen said, "I'm going to take her upstairs for our nap."

"Sonja lets us nap?" I asked, confused.

"She insists on co-sleeping," she explained.

"Gotcha," I said. Guess I wouldn't be napping, as it were. Which was fine. I had some shopping to do.

I returned about an hour later with some of the oddest purchases I'd ever made—twelve bars of a soap by the brand name Fels Naptha, a massive box of washing soda, an equally massive container of borax, and a tiny bottle of lavender essential oil. I felt like I was going to get some strange looks in the checkout line, but the dreadlocked cashier seemed to know exactly what I was doing.

"Homemade detergent, huh?" he asked excitedly.

"Yes. First time."

"That's awesome. Make sure you microwave the Fels Naptha first for about ten seconds. It'll crumble a lot more easily."

"Thanks for the tip!" I said gratefully.

"Good luck, yo," he said as I left.

When I returned, Karen and Delilah were sitting on the porch swing, enjoying the sunshine.

"How was the nap?" I asked.

"Delicious," said Karen, with a sleepy smile. "It's nice when Sonja has an errand or a pilates class. I much prefer the nap to scrubbing bottles or washing out the diapers."

"Ah, so they use cloth, too." Of course they did. I just couldn't get away from those things.

Karen lowered her voice, "Between you and me, they're a big improvement from what we did the first week Delilah was home. Have you ever heard of 'elimination communication?'"

"Do I want to?"

"It's the theory that babies give off natural cues when they're about to pee or poop. So the idea is to pay such close attention to the babies that you can rush them to the toilet in time."

"So the babies don't wear diapers?" I said, aghast. "How long did that last?"

"Just long enough to ruin about a dozen of Sonja's outfits, one couch and one mattress," she said. "I think it was two full days."

"Yikes."

She shrugged. "Sonja should be back soon. Just so you know, the guy in the kitchen is Rodrigo. He takes care of the greenhouse, the livestock and does all the cooking. He doesn't speak a lot of English, just a heads up."

"Got it." I headed inside and saw Rodrigo in the kitchen. He looked to be in his mid-sixties, with short-cropped silver hair, weathered skin, and a permanent smile. He was whistling and chopping vegetables for spinach and strawberry salads. I introduced myself and he grinned back.

Then, Sonja came into the kitchen through the back door, wearing her third outfit of the day.

"Oh, I see you two have met," she said. Rodrigo grinned at her as well. "Did you have any luck at the store?" she asked me.

"Yes, I was able to get everything," I said, pulling out each purchase from the reusable tote. I handed her the receipt, to which she immediately pulled out her purse and handed me three twenties.

"You can keep the change," she said.

"I couldn't," I said. "It wasn't even half that."

"It's fine," she said. "Okay, I'm going to need you to make the detergent this afternoon. Think you can handle it?"

"Sure, I can definitely do that."

"Great. Rodrigo will be out of the kitchen after lunch, so you'll have it all to yourself."

"Sounds good," I replied.

Rodrigo handed her a salad plate. "*Gracias*," she said. "I have some business to do, so I'm going to make some calls and take this upstairs," she explained. "Feel free to have some lunch, and please let Karen know it's ready, too."

"Thanks," I said. I could get used to this personal chef thing.

Just as Karen and I sat down to eat, Delilah started to wail. I grabbed the sling from the living room, tucked her in, and she started to eat, as well.

"So how long have you been a wet nurse?" Karen asked.

"Off and on, for close to a year now," I said. "My own daughter weaned around ten months, but my body never stopped producing."

"That's lucky," she said. "How do you like it?"

"Oh, you know. It pays the bills," I said with a laugh. "No, in all honesty, it is satisfying in a way that other jobs aren't. I like that I can fulfill a need."

And, as time had gone on, I found that I really meant that. I remembered when Joy first approached me about working for Alexandra, and the thought of nursing other people's babies was a little horrifying. But now, I don't know how anyone could be a wet nurse and *not* grow to love each of her tiny charges. Women did this for hundreds, if not thousands, of years all around the world, and no one passed judgment. At the same time, I knew it was an undeniably weird situation when looking at it with my twenty-first century eyes—which was partly why I wasn't telling anyone, regardless of the NDAs I signed.

"I know exactly what you mean," said Karen. "It's been different working for a family long-term like this, though. You get kind of attached." She looked lovingly at Delilah.

"Yeah, they're addictive when they're so tiny and sweet," I agreed. Once Delilah was finished eating and fully burped, I passed her back to Karen.

"Goodnight," she said, playfully tugging Delilah's hand into a small wave, and they tottered off.

I scraped the plates, wiped down the kitchen and pumped four ounces to give them for later. Then, I got to work on the detergent. Two hours, twelve potato-peeled bars of soap and a massive bucketful of white powder later, and I was done. I sure hoped it was right, anyway, but it looked more or less like normal laundry detergent to me. I went to the sink to wash my hands before showing Sonja my feat.

"What the hell is that smell?" said a voice behind me.

I whirled around and saw Chase. He was looking much sexier than he had the week before when he was bedraggled and hungover. No, today he was freshly showered and dressed in loose jeans and a gray polo. It actually looked like something Dan would wear.

"Homemade laundry detergent?" I said weakly. "Um, by the way, I'm Amanda. The, um, wet nurse."

"Yeah, the wife told me you'd be coming. About time she hired someone for that. Her tits have been off limits for almost two damn months now." He went into the fridge, pulled out the carton of organic milk and took a chug. He was immediately less sexy. Clearly he and Dan had a few key differences.

"Right," I said. "Hope that problem resolves itself."

He looked me in the chest approvingly. Before he could say anything else, Sonja wandered into the kitchen. "Hi, sweetie," she said, reaching up to give her husband a peck on the cheek.

"I just finished the detergent," I said. "I think it should be a success."

"Good," she said. "Let's test it out. Delilah's hamper is in the corner of her room. Toss whatever's in there into the laundry, and we'll give it a test run."

"You got it," I said, and went upstairs, glad to get away from Chase. I tossed the receiving blankets and onesies down the laundry chute, then headed down to the basement with the bucket to give it a whirl.

It seemed to do the trick—the clothes smelled fine, and were stain-free. Per Sonja's instructions, I took the washing out to dry in the sun on the clothesline.

Before I knew it, Delilah had one last feeding of the day, and I simultaneously pumped six more ounces to give them for the night.

"Is there anything else I can do?" I asked Sonja when 5:30 rolled around.

"Nope, don't think so," she said. "Thanks for everything. We'll see you tomorrow!"

"Okay then. Have a great night!" I said, letting myself out.

I power walked down the street, then caught the bus just in time. A minute before six, I got to the daycare, where Maddie was the last charge. She gave me a woeful look when I arrived, and whined.

"I know, sweetie," I said.

"Have a good night, ladies," Miss Kelsie said, shutting off the light in the toddler room as soon as I quickly slipped Maddie's shoes on and buckled her into her stroller.

I wasn't too thrilled about having to leave her here for close to eleven hours a day, but I wasn't sure what else I could do. It didn't seem quite right to ask Dan to pick her up every day. Was it? I didn't know. I couldn't worry about that just yet. As an apology to Maddie, I let her eat an ice cream sandwich for dinner.

The next three days at work passed in a similar fashion. Sonja would have a project ready for me each morning, and whenever I wasn't nursing Delilah, I was off purchasing the ingredients or attempting to make it. By the end of the day Thursday, I had made homemade deodorant (and tried it—not bad, if I do say so myself), diaper cream, and body lotion. The body lotion was the easiest—just a mix of shea butter and coconut oil, and it smelled like vacation. Before I left on Thursday, Sonja pulled me aside.

"I'm going to need you to come in a little early tomorrow," she said. "We have an at-home photo shoot scheduled for most of the day, so I'll need you to help out here and there."

"Of course," I said. "What time do you need me?"

"Would 6:30 be all right?"

Fuck. "Absolutely," I said. "I'll see you tomorrow."

I called Dan and explained the situation.

"You and Maddie should stay over here tonight," he said. "I'll take her to daycare in the morning."

"Are you sure?" I asked, uncertain. "Do you think that's going to lead to more questions for Lucas?"

"I'm positive it will," he said lightly. "I'll just let you answer them."

"Gee, thanks," I said.

But as it turned out, Lucas didn't have a single question about it. We set up Lucas' old playard in his room and put them both to bed around eight. I don't think they fell asleep until nine because they were yammering back and forth to each other, but all in all, it went fine on their end. Once Dan and I got into bed and switched off the light, he started to kiss my shoulder.

"Mmm, I don't know," I said. "What if Lucas wanders in?"

He hopped out of bed and quickly locked the door.

"He's slept through the night since he was three months old, you know."

"Ugh, don't rub it in," I groaned. Maddie still woke up overnight once or twice a week.

"Come on. We can be quiet," he insisted, and gently worked his way up to kissing my neck.

By the time he'd had his way with me, I certainly didn't want to be quiet. I kept giggling–it felt illicit, like making out with your boyfriend in his parents' basement during high school, hoping to God they didn't come down the stairs while his hand was up your shirt. Later, I fell into a deep, satisfied sleep, not waking until the alarm buzzed at 5:30. I quickly slammed it off, not wanting to wake Dan or the kids, and admired Dan for a few minutes as he slept peacefully. He slept on his back, one arm above his head, the other across his chest. Perfect for me to cradle my head into the crook of his arm. I just had to stay there like that for a minute, and then willed myself to get up and shower.

By the time I got out, Dan was already in the kitchen, making tea and toast for me, coffee for him.

"Good morning, beautiful," he said in a hushed tone.

"Morning," I said, kissing him on the cheek. "Kids are still sleeping, right?"

"Yeah. I peeked in there a few minutes ago. They're dead to the world."

"Good," I said, buttering my toast.

"I think our first sleepover was a success," Dan offered.

"Mmm," I said, taking a bite and giving a thumbs up sign. I swallowed and said, "I agree. And it is nice to wake up in the morning and see you there."

"Did you sleep well?" he asked.

"Like a baby. Or I guess like Lucas as a baby," I said.

"As it turns out, my bed is good for more than one thing."

"Ha ha," I said. "All right, I better scoot. See you tonight," I said, grabbing my keys and tote.

"Later," he said, waving to me from the kitchen island.

As I drove his car, borrowed for the day since time was of the essence, I thought about just how nice it was to wake up with him. I admit, I'd had a lot of daydreams about Dan in the past year, but most of them involved an isolated beach in Fiji, or a hotel suite in Paris, or a waterfall in Jamaica. The kind of daydreams I'd had about Eamonn—walking around the city, hand in hand, wearing a Baby Bjorn, or lazy Sunday mornings with pancakes and the newspaper while our toddler played with blocks on the floor—I think I'd willed myself *not* to imagine that kind of future for me anymore. Certainly not with Eamonn, but not with anyone else, either, because it hurt too much to have that dream taken away.

And I started to cry. I didn't think I could handle it if I gave my heart to Dan at this point, and it ended up not working out. So the question was, do I keep moving forward? Could I take that risk? Could I bring Maddie along for that ride?

I realized I wasn't one hundred percent sure, and I started to cry a little harder.

I pulled into a parking lot. Christ, I needed to pull myself together. I looked in the rearview, pulled a tissue from the crumpled packet I kept in my tote, and wiped my eyes. I reapplied some powder and lip gloss. It would have to do.

I pulled into the Careys' driveway at 6:30 on the dot and raced up to the front door. Julie was just leaving.

"Sonja's more than a little stressed out about this photo shoot," she warned.

"Got it," I said. "I'll do what I can to help. Is Karen here yet?"

"No, no, no," said Julie. "She's not coming today."

"Really?" I asked, confused. "On a day that Sonja *actually* has something to do, she wouldn't need her nanny there to help out?"

"As far as *Celebs* magazine is concerned, Sonja doesn't have a nanny. Or any staff, for that matter."

"What?" I said, narrowing my eyes.

"Just go inside," she said, waving me in.

Sonja was inside, running around like a mad woman, wiping down every surface in the kitchen. The house was already gleaming as usual, which was no surprise since her ninja of a housekeeper was there every afternoon, silently mopping or dusting in the background. Sonja was a little red-faced and unkempt.

"Morning, Sonja," I said. "Anything I can help with?"

"Yes!" she said, wide-eyed and a little too excitedly. "Yes. Delilah. Upstairs sleeping. I need you to put her in the sling and change the sheets in the co-sleeper. If she wakes up, you can feed her in the guest bedroom, but you *must* lock the door. Got it?"

"Delilah in sling, change sheets, lock guest room door if she's hungry."

"Perfect," she said. "The *Celebs* crew should be here at seven. See if you can get it done by then."

"Got it," I said, and turned for the stairs.

"Oh! And Amanda," she said. "You're Chase's cousin. Just helping out for *the day*. Understood?"

"Crystal clear," I said, turning around again.

"Crap! One more thing," she said, still flushed. "You have to wheel the co-sleeper into my room. Put it on the left side of the bed."

I nodded, then hightailed it upstairs. So that's how it all worked. It made me feel a little melancholy for Sonja. I liked her well enough—she honestly wasn't rude, or condescending, or unfair to any of her staff—and didn't seem like the kind of person who wouldn't be interested in her own child. I was no physician, but by now, I was fairly certain that she had post partum depression, at least to some degree. She clearly hadn't bonded with Delilah, and I couldn't think why that could be the case, with the exception of something hormonal going on with her. It was too bad that Joy was on her maternity leave, because I think she would have noticed it and urged her to get treatment. But, Sonja wasn't paying me to be her therapist. She was paying me to secretly feed her child, so that's what I'd do.

Delilah was just stirring when I got to her room, so I changed her, fed her and got her dressed. I deftly placed her into the sling, and she looked up at me and gurgled happily. I heard the doorbell ring—they must be here a little early. I quickly changed the sheets to fresh lilac-colored ones, then unlocked the wheels on her co-sleeper, and wheeled it into the master bedroom.

For fuck's sake. Chase was sitting on the bed, wearing gym shorts and smoking a joint.

"Hey, Amanda," he wheezed.

"Jesus! Sorry," I said, averting my eyes. "Sonja just wanted me to bring this into your room."

"Right on," he said, not offering to help. Dick.

"Okay," I said, after awkwardly maneuvering it around the room to Sonja's side of the bed. "We'll be downstairs."

He saluted me with the joint.

I returned downstairs, where a crew of about a dozen people had already set up shop. Over by the window, a pair of makeup artists were touching up Sonja's face as a hair stylist was putting Velcro rollers in her hair. Some lighting and camera guys were scoping out the house for where to film, and a couple of young girls with clipboards were darting around like lab rats. A statuesque woman with long, jet black hair and dressed in an olive blazer, jeans and holding a tape recorder, looked the most likely to be the journalist. She made her way over to me immediately.

"This must be Delilah," she said warmly, peeking into the sling.

I just smiled back. Why did she look so familiar?

"I'm Camille Pinto, *Celebs*. And you are?" she asked.

"Chase's cousin Amanda," called out Sonja from her chair. "She agreed to help out a little bit today."

I nodded, reddening slightly.

"I *only* trust family with Delilah," added Sonja.

"Family is the best," Camille affirmed.

Oh, my God. I realized who Camille was. She had seen me in the Langs' building on the day of the power outage last summer. When I was feeding Eunice. Fuck. I hoped she had a bad memory.

"It's pretty hectic here, so we'll just get out of the way," I said, looking for an excuse to exit the conversation. "We'll be on the patio."

"Sounds good!" Sonja chirped.

As I rocked in the outdoor rocking chair with Delilah, I sipped some cucumber water and people-watched the crew a little. I heard Chase thump his way down the stairs, and hoped for Sonja's sake that he'd had the good sense to drop in some Visine and shower first.

Then, the camera crew came outside. It was gorgeous out again—in the sixties and sunny—so they wanted to get as many outdoor shots as they could.

Soon, Sonja and Chase came outside, both looking like they resided on a supermodel hipster farm, which I suppose they did. The photographers spent about half an hour shooting them gathering eggs from the coop, tending to the plants in the greenhouse, feeding the goat. Sonja had her professional, glam-yet-accessible face on, while Chase had his trademark smirk, mixed with his occasional shit-eating grin.

They next got a few more shots of just Sonja, hanging some onesies on the clothesline, mixing a salad in a huge bamboo bowl in the kitchen, reading *Pride and Prejudice* on the window seat. Ha. I mean, I liked her and all, but *ha.*

"Okay, let's get some with the baby," said Camille.

I looked down. "She fell asleep," I said apologetically.

A glare flashed over Camille's face, then she gave me a saccharine smile. "Do you think you could wake her up so we can get some photos?"

My eyes darted to Sonja. "Sonja, what do you think? She's out cold."

Sonja thought for a second, and said, "Let her sleep. We can do the interview questions now if you can rearrange the schedule."

Camille checked her papers and gave a tight smile. "Sure," she said.

The team all shuffled into the living room, and Sonja went downstairs to fetch Chase from the media room, where he'd wandered off to, bored after the attention was off of him.

They situated themselves back in the living room, so I made myself scarce in the kitchen. I tried not to listen too much, but I couldn't help but overhear some of the more emphatic quotes:

"I think co-sleeping is *so* important to a child's development, and sense of security."

"Baby-wearing is the only way to go. We don't believe in having a bouncer seat or swing. Why would I *not* want for my baby to be held as much as possible?"

"We're locavores. We believe in knowing where the food on our table comes from."

"I plan on Delilah nursing until she's about two. Maybe longer."

Everything she said was true. It was just too bad that she didn't play an active role in any of it. I pondered how sad it would be to not feel like you could connect or bond with your own child, and then outsource every aspect of motherhood because of that. Then, for a real kick in the pants, have to put on a brave face to the public, and act like everything couldn't have been better.

Delilah woke up at the tail end of the interview, squealing and writhing.

"I think she's hungry," I said to Sonja, unsure of what to do next.

"I'll take her," she said. To Camille, she said, "I'm going to feed her upstairs for privacy."

"Of course," said Camille, nodding.

"Amanda, can you help me upstairs?" Sonja said pointedly. "I need you to help me pick out which outfit to put Delilah in for the photos."

"Right, of course," I said. She could think on her feet, I'd give her that.

We went into the nursery and locked the door behind us. Sonja passed Delilah to me, pulled down the shades, and I started feeding her.

"Are you all right?" I asked her.

"Fine," she said, surprised at the question. She threw open the door to Delilah's sizable closet, and pulled out a few options. After hemming and hawing, she decided on an amethyst-colored sundress.

"I think barefoot would be best for this kind of shoot, right?" she asked me.

"Oh, definitely," I said.

"Or maybe just in her cloth diaper in the sling?"

"That's pretty good, too. Maybe you should offer both choices to the photographer."

Sonja nodded. "I think I will. She about done?"

"Yep," I said, unlatching Delilah and placing her over my shoulder. She burped and spit up a little right away. I wiped her face on a spare receiving blanket, changed her diaper, and got her into her dress as Sonja paced the room. Once Delilah was photo-ready, we placed her back into the sling, then the three of us headed downstairs.

Even I was almost fooled by the family photo shoot. Sonja snuggled Delilah, kissed her on her head, played with her feet, tickled her tummy, as Chase looked on adoringly. Delilah looked like she was in seventh heaven. Sonja looked like such a natural mom. I wondered how hard it was for her to fake the affection, and how much it stung her inside. The whole thing made me want to cry, but I managed to keep myself together.

The following Saturday, while grocery shopping with Maddie, I saw the latest *Celebs* while in the checkout line. A photo of Sonja and Chase beaming at each other, with Delilah tucked between them, was plastered across the cover.

"At Home With the Careys" read the headline. The subhead was, "Urban Meets Country Inside Their Haven in Chicago." I snapped it up and could barely wait until I got home to read it.

It was a very flattering piece. Sonja was made out to be the second coming in attachment parenting, and seemed to be the perfect, adoring, sexy earth mother. Chase was the proud papa, finally shedding his lothario reputation to become a total family man. Delilah, of course, was beyond adorable. That much was accurate.

There was also a recipe for Sonja's "tried and true" homemade laundry detergent recipe.

From what I gathered, Chase would be starting press this summer for his first dramatic turn in a movie, *A Soldier's Honor*, so a magazine spread featuring his gorgeous wife and baby was par for the course. However, as it turned out, it was just as advantageous for Sonja.

17

About a month later, when I arrived at work one morning, Sonja greeted me at the door, pleased as punch. "There's something I want to talk to you about."

"Oh?" I asked. I hoped it didn't involve detergent. They'd had me make enough of that stuff to last Delilah through college.

"My agent called me last night. That *Celebs* article got some people talking, and she was contacted by a new Euro band. The Amateur Professionals? They're shooting a video in New York two weeks from now, and they want me to be the girl in it."

"That's great news!" I said. "Congratulations."

"Thing is...now that I've told the world about my attachment parenting...I need to bring Delilah with me. And I'm going to need you there to feed her behind closed doors."

"I see," I said. "When is this, again?"

"Two weeks from yesterday. I know it's Memorial Day, but it was the only time the studio was open. We would fly there Saturday night and come back Monday afternoon. Can you do it?" She looked at me expectantly.

"Well," I hesitated. "I think so. I'll just have to see about childcare for my daughter, and make sure my parents can take her."

"Oh," she said, a little unused to not hearing an immediate 'yes' from me. "Okay. Just let me know later today."

"Of course," I said.

Once Sonja was out gallivanting and Karen and Delilah were down for their morning nap, I called my mom and explained the predicament.

"Do you think you'd be able to take Maddie for Memorial Day weekend?" I asked.

"I guess we could," my mother said slowly. "It's just that she's never spent the night here without you, and I'm not sure how she'll do."

"I know, I've never been away from her overnight," I admitted. "I'm a little worried about it myself."

"Well, I don't want you to stress about it. We'll take her," Mom said.

My next call was to Dan, to let him know about the New York trip.

"That might be cool, getting to travel for work," he said. "And New York is always fun."

"I have a feeling I'll be spending the whole time in a trailer or a hotel room."

"Will she be paying you extra?"

"That's a good question," I said. "I didn't ask yet. I was caught pretty off-guard when she told me."

"When are you going?"

"Memorial Day Weekend."

"Seriously?" he said, annoyed. "Did you forget that we'd made plans?"

"What?" I said, momentarily confused. "Oh. Shit. Yes. I remember now."

About a week ago, he'd casually mentioned that his mom had asked if Maddie and I would come up to Milwaukee with the guys for the holiday so we could finally meet them. Dan's brother, sister-in-law, and kids were flying in from Texas, his aunts and uncles were going to come, his mom would be making an entire Polish feast, and all the guys in the family would be grilling the entire weekend. It was supposed to be a whole big thing.

He sighed. "My mom will never let me hear the end of it."

"I'm sorry," I said weakly. "But it's work. I have to." I still felt a little guilty about not fully explaining *why* I—and my breasts—absolutely needed to go on this trip.

The thing was, I'd been seeing Dan for over six months now, and I'd never worked up the nerve to tell him the truth. I'd always been a little scared of how he'd react. By now, I'd been keeping it quiet for so long that it seemed that if I ever did tell him...well, I just couldn't see how it wouldn't go over like a lead balloon.

"No, I get it," he said, still sounding peeved. "Well, whatever. I better get back to work myself."

"All right. Love you," I said.

"You, too."

When Sonja came back later that afternoon, the first thing she asked me was, "So did you get your childcare sorted out for next weekend?"

"I did," I said as cheerfully as possible. "New York's a go on my end."

She grinned. "Wonderful. The band's people will set up our tickets and hotels. I'll have my agent let you know once it's ready."

The next day, Karen and I were lounging on the back patio with Delilah, enjoying the sun and munching on some edamame Rodrigo had made for lunch. Sonja peered out over the dutch door.

"Hey, Karen, can you come in here for a minute?" she called.

"Sure," she said and headed in. I continued to feed Delilah in the sun, stroking her hair, which was growing thicker and surprisingly redder each day. I started daydreaming and promised myself that if I ever had a house, it would have a patio, and a yard, where I could sit in the sun every day. I wished I had a yard for Maddie. I'd hoped she'd have a good weekend at my parents' place where, they had a huge deck. And, I hoped the neighbors wouldn't send an angry letter to the association about them breaking rules with an overnight visitor under the age of fifty-five.

"Amanda? Hey, Amanda," Karen said, interrupting my zoned-out state.

"What's up?" I said. I looked at her, and she seemed to be holding back tears. "What happened?"

"Sonja just told me that they were going to end their contract with my agency, and that they wouldn't be needing me anymore," she said, slightly shaking. "Did you know about this?"

"No!" I said, utterly flabbergasted. "I had no idea! Did she say why?"

"She just said that now that Delilah was almost four months old, she thought she'd need less assistance now, and today would be my last day," she said glumly.

"Oh, man, I'm really sorry. I know how much you love Delilah."

She gazed at Delilah and wiped away a tear. "Like my own," she said. "I mean, with every other family, I only stayed for a week or two to get the family settled in. I never had a chance to get attached."

I gave her a sympathetic look. “Well, at least your agency will find you another job soon, right?”

“I guess,” she said, then let out a deep breath. ”Mind if I hold her a bit?”

“Go right ahead,” I said. She cradled her the rest of the afternoon.

Since my workload effectively doubled with the loss of Karen, I took over nap time, playtime and all the other times. It was easy enough, since Delilah was an easy kid, but still a little tiring. The next Tuesday before the holiday weekend, I came into work to find Sonja fiddling with an enormous, European-looking stroller. Delilah was inside it, looking confused about not being held.

“Wow!” I said. “That’s something else.”

“I know,” she groaned. “My parents sent it to me. It’s not really my style. But if you want to take Delilah for a spin around the block in it today, go ahead.”

I paused. “Really?” I’d never left the premises with her before.

She shrugged. “Why not? I’m just going to donate it next week. I’d feel better if they thought I at least gave it a try.”

“If you’re sure...” my voice trailed off.

She picked up her tote bag and put on her sunglasses.

“Feel free,” she said, stepping out the door. “I’ll be back around noon.”

All right, then! I waited about fifteen minutes, then I technically followed Sonja’s instructions by taking Delilah about a block away...to Starbucks. Soon, I was sipping a chai latte while Delilah looked at the amazing world around her, fascinated by the lights and the people. I had pulled out my Kindle and was enjoying the free Wifi, catching up on celebrity gossip and breathing easily for once. I could seriously get used to this. She seemed in no hurry at all to go, so I just pushed the stroller back and forth with my foot, and we had a fantastic morning. After about an hour, Delilah started to squawk for food. I thought about returning to the house, but then I realized that no one would suspect this kid didn't belong to me—and with a stroller that massive, certainly no one would think she belonged to the Careys. I pulled my long-unused nursing cover from my purse, situated Delilah, and continued to browse the celebrity gossip sites.

"Amanda?" said a confused voice.

I lifted my head. Oh God. What was he doing here?

"Hi, Dan," I said weakly.

"Hey," he said, holding a latte of his own and a laptop case under his other arm. "Are you....um..." his voice trailed off.

"Am I doing what you think I'm doing? Yes," I said.

"Oh," he said. He wrinkled his brow. "Nannies do that? Like, for other people's kids?"

"Not usually, but that's why they pay me the proverbial big bucks."

"Oh," he said again. I could watch him putting all the puzzle pieces together: me being a single mom, losing my old job, needing a new one—twice—and falling back on what was clearly my greatest talent.

"Does this weird you out?" I asked.

"No! No," he said a little too quickly. "No. I mean, it's cool. You gotta do what you gotta do, right?"

"More or less," I said. "What are you doing in this part of the city, anyhow?"

"Meeting a client. Potential one, anyway. I'm supposed to

be at their office in about ten minutes, so I should probably get going."

"Good luck, then!" I said brightly.

"Thanks," he said. "I'll, uh, call you tonight?" He awkwardly bent down to give me a kiss, as I couldn't move much without displacing the baby, or my cover.

"Bye," I said with an equally awkward smile.

When he left, I let out the huge sigh I realized I'd been holding in. Seriously, there had to be at least a few hundred Starbucks locations in Chicago. Why the hell did he have to go to the one I was at, the one time I left the Careys' house, and the one time I actually needed to *not* be recognized? I peeked down at Delilah and saw that she had completely fallen asleep. I unlatched her, moved her to the stroller without her batting an eye, and we left. On the short walk back, I convinced myself that Dan probably was a little taken aback to see me, ahem, at work, but he'd get over it. He probably thought it was slightly hot, in a way. A reminder that I was a MILF. Right?

But, he didn't call me that night. He didn't call me the next night, either, or respond to any of my texts. By Thursday, I was done feeling antsy and worrying about what he thought of me, shaking my imaginary magic 8 ball in my head and asking, "does he still like me?" No, by that point, I was just plain pissed off. He was avoiding me, clear as day. I was sure that as soon as I called him out on it, he'd make up some bullshit excuse about being so busy with a new client or Lucas, but no one's so busy or disconnected from technology that they can't take five seconds to check in with the person they've been fucking and bringing around their child for the past six months. Not to mention, the person they claim to love.

In my life before Maddie, I would have agonized over

whether I should even bring up how I was feeling when I was upset. I'd worry that I was coming on too strongly or seeming like a stalker, or making the relationship into something it wasn't.

Well, that person had been replaced by a new head bitch in charge. So Maddie and I were going to do a pop-in. At 6:30 PM on Thursday, I rang his buzzer.

"Hello?" his voice crackled over the receiver.

"It's Amanda and Maddie!" I said cheerfully. "We thought you guys might be hungry so we brought over some dinner."

"Oh!" he said, sounding surprised. "Um. Just give me a sec. I'll come get you."

He buzzed us into the building, and we waited downstairs for him to greet us. He had a few days' worth of scruff on his face and was wearing an ancient Illini tee and faded jeans. Damn. He couldn't look bad if he tried.

"How are my favorite girls?" he asked, giving me a small peck on the cheek.

"Great!" I said, over-enthusiastically. "You hungry?"

"We could eat," he said, leading us up the stairs.

"Hi, Lucas," I cooed when we entered. He looked up from his coloring book. "Look what I brought for you." I pulled from my purse the *Cars 2* Bluray that I had picked up for him.

"Coooooool!" he said, running toward it and my waving hand.

"He doesn't have this yet, does he?" I asked Dan. He shook his head.

"What do you say, Lucas?" he prompted.

"Thanks!" said Lucas, already getting the remote to set it up. I plopped Maddie on the couch next to him, and moments later, both of them were hypnotized.

"So," I said to Dan, as he fixed plates for us. "Haven't heard much from you this week. What have you been up to?"

"Work stuff," he shrugged. "You?"

"Just packing, getting ready to leave for New York, getting Maddie ready to stay at my parents," I said. "Quite frankly, I think you're avoiding me because I breastfeed other people's children for a living."

He stopped mid-bite. Then he swallowed. "Cut right to the chase, don't you?"

"I'm not wrong, am I?"

He didn't answer right away. "You have to admit, it's a little different," he finally said.

'What's so bad about it?" I asked, suddenly defensive. "I've only worked for families where the mother physically couldn't breastfeed. I am providing them with an invaluable service, and their kids are thriving because of it. They wouldn't be nearly as healthy or happy without me."

"Well, Lucas' mom didn't breastfeed him, and I think he turned out just fine."

"I'm not saying he wouldn't have—"

"No, you really just did," he said, crossing his arms.

"That wasn't my point. The point is, you clearly have issues with women breastfeeding. And I think maybe you're a little jealous," I added for good measure. I'd had a whole three days to rehearse this.

"I'm jealous now?" He raised an eyebrow.

"I think you are. That the babies I care for get to use my twins in a way that you don't."

"I see," he said.

"And the thing is, I *love* my job," I said. "And I'm not going to change what I do for a living. So you're just going to have to learn to deal with it, or move on. But I'm not going to bring Maddie into this anymore until you figure it out." I put my hands on my hips for emphasis.

"*Really*," he said, narrowing his eyes in a way I'd never seen before. "That's interesting. Because it crossed my mind that maybe I shouldn't bring Lucas around someone who's clearly a little dishonest."

"Excuse me?!"

"We've been together for six months and you never once alluded to what you really do," he said, equally hurt and angry. "Sorry, sweetheart, but a lie of omission's still a lie."

"I can't run around telling people I breastfeed for high-profile families," I retorted. "They make me sign an NDA, for pete's sake. The *only* person who knows what I do is Joy. Even my own parents don't know."

"Maybe you should think about getting into a line of work where you can actually tell your boyfriend what you do. You know, maybe a line of work where you're not selling your body."

That was it. I scooped Maddie up off the couch, and she started to wail a little at having to leave Lightning McQueen.

"Bye, Lucas," I said, opening the door.

"Bye," he said back, his eyes not leaving the screen,

I gave Dan what I thought was a very matter-of-fact look, and I shut the door behind us, taking Maddie back down the stairs, where her stroller awaited.

When I'd imagined this scene going down in my head, Dan had come barreling down the stairs while I was still buckling her into the stroller, apologizing, telling me he thought I was beautiful and confident and I should do whatever I wanted for a living, and then he kissed me passionately, and then everything would go back to normal. In other scenarios, Maddie and I had made it just to the sidewalk when it happened. (We never made it much further than that—he couldn't leave his kid at home alone, obviously.) So I went extra slowly in hopes that he would be only moments behind us. But, he wasn't.

And he didn't call that night, either. My pre-Maddie self would have cried myself to sleep, feeling like an idiot and wishing I'd had the good sense to shut the hell up and let him come around in his own good time. It turns out my post-Maddie self wasn't all that different, and she cried herself to sleep, too.

From Friday night until my mom came to pick her up Saturday morning, I barely let Maddie go. Without Dan—and by the radio silence, it certainly seemed that I *was* without Dan—she was all I had now. She pushed me away a couple of times, toddling off to find her babydoll or her blankie, but most of the time she was content to return right away to snuggle in my arms. I kissed her head and read to her from her growing collection of board books.

God, she'd grown so much in the past year that she was almost unrecognizable from the baby she'd been. She had a vocabulary of about a hundred words, could count up to ten and picked out her own clothes in the morning. I could put her hair in little pigtails now. She had climbed out of her crib once already, too, and I kept my fingers crossed that she'd stay in the playard for my parents overnight. But, she was growing up way too quickly for my liking. Sometimes it felt as if I'd missed out on everything by being away from her all day, every day. Other times I rationalized that it went by in the blink of an eye for every mother, working or not.

At ten, I took a taxi over to the Careys' house, where we'd all be taking a limo together to O'Hare. Even Chase. His agent had booked him an appearance on *The Chatter* to promote his movie on Monday, so he'd be accompanying us. I'd keep my distance as much as possible, but I didn't think that would prove difficult. I'd be more surprised if he didn't go out clubbing or gambling for the majority of the weekend.

There were some perks to this job, though. We flew first class—me included!—and even had a privacy curtain in our nook of the plane. I was able to feed Delilah with the rest of the plane unaware. Sonja took some herbal supplement, misted her skin with Smart Water, then dozed off most of the flight. Chase chewed gum loudly and watched a movie on his iPad. It looked to be soft-core porn. Delilah slept on me, with just a small break to scream upon takeoff and landing.

I had a lot of time to think on that flight. I knew that things were working out with the Careys, for the time being, but my days there were numbered from the start. Not that I'd done anything wrong, but a family with multiple nannies certainly wasn't going to keep me on past the nursing stage. I couldn't afford to be blindsided again. Maybe I should still consider my parents' offer to move back home—at least once the Careys let me go in the future.

And, I thought snidely to myself, *not like it would matter to Dan.* Half of me couldn't believe he'd reacted the way he did, but the other half could. Only because there was no way that a guy could be as perfect as Dan had seemed all these months, and it was only a matter of time before everything went downhill. I'd been let down by every other guy I'd dated—I'd sure as shit been let down by Eamonn—and it only made sense that the one guy I'd finally let into my heart, and Maddie's, would probably let me down most of all.

Sonja's agent, Cleo, met us at the limo. She had short, white-blond hair and large, eighties-inspired glasses, and wore a flouncy magenta dress, black stilettos, and a silk blazer. Somehow, she pulled it off, too.

"You must be 'Cousin Amanda,'" she said, shaking my hand.

"Er, that's me," I said.

"Don't worry, I know you're not the cousin," she said in a low voice. "But no one else is to know. Got it, Milk Jugs?"

I snickered. "Got it."

We buckled in Delilah's massive car seat—almost brand new, since evidently she had not been in a car since coming home from her water birth in the hospital—and piled into the limo.

"Okay, we're going straight to the set," Cleo said, whipping through the day's schedule on her phone. "The band got in last night, so their asses should be in shape by now. We can only hope. Hair and makeup will get started as soon as we get there. You'll have a dressing room, and we made sure it would have a bed for you and Delilah. No crib. We also had them get you a nursing pillow."

"Good," Sonja said.

"You," Cleo said, looking at me. "Your job is to stay in the dressing room with Delilah. Come out once in a while with her little earmuffs on and tell Sonja that the baby needs to eat. Parade her around here and there. Have some craft services. Go back into the room. Make yourself scarce."

"No problem," I assured her.

"I'm serious," she said. "*Celebs* is sending a photog and writer to cover the shoot. You see them, you take your ass right back into that dressing room *stat*."

"Got it," I said.

"And you," she said, eyeing Chase.

He looked at Cleo and raised an eyebrow.

"Don't get fucking arrested. And don't stay out too late. The paps are scheduled to catch the three of you at brunch tomorrow morning in Park Slope at eleven. Don't be hungover for it."

"Duly noted," he said, and started playing with his phone.

Soon, we were at the recording studio in a Brooklyn neighborhood that looked like it was straight out of *Girls*. I immediately felt my age and station in life. We went inside, and a bevy of Clipboard Girls greeted us and ushered us in, cooing over Delilah and subtly gazing at Chase with fuck-me eyes. I couldn't tell if Sonja noticed. If she did, or cared, it didn't show.

The beauty team got to work straight away, so I took the baby to explore our surroundings. I swayed Delilah from side to side, walking around the studio. Chase had already exited the building to find a bar. The lead singer of the band was also in hair and makeup—they were planning to rehearse mostly with him and Sonja today, and the other bandmates would show up later to film a few clips of the whole band together. The production people and cameramen were busying themselves with setup, and the Clipboard Girls were texting nonstop. I just tried to stay on the perimeter and out of the way.

Once Sonja was made up and dressed—she looked the picture of the hipster supermodel next door with her loose waves, floral belted dress and ankle boots—Delilah and I retreated to her room, where there was indeed a twin sized bed wedged in there. I locked the door, fed her, and we both conked out for about an hour. I felt her stirring in the crook of my arm and once she was fully alert, I changed her (thank God we were using dye-and-chemical-free disposable diapers for the trip; even Sonja couldn't justify the logistics of me handling diaper laundry for the weekend), tucked her back into a sling, and walked toward the set.

"Sonja?" I said. "I think Delilah's hungry."

She gave an apologetic smile to the director, who appeared to be futzing with the camera. "I'll be back in a few," she said, blowing him a kiss.

"Take your time," he said, not looking up.

I passed the baby to Sonja, who flashed me her *Celebs* smile, and they went back to the dressing room. I hadn't eaten since breakfast, so I wandered over to craft services, starving. As I filled up my plate with mini sandwiches, chips and crudités, I heard one of the Clipboard Girls say to another, "Band's here." They then swarmed toward the entrance of the studio. I finished fixing my plate, found an empty folding chair, and began to munch. I was about to pull out my phone to call my mom and check in on Maddie, when I looked up and saw the gaggle of Clipboard Girls surrounding the band and coming further into the studio. I'd never heard of them before, but supposedly they were the next big thing in Music That's Too Cool To Be Played On The Radio. As they advanced, I tried to only look out of the corner of my eye to check them out for myself.

And oh, dear God. There was Eamonn.

18

I almost choked on my sandwich. Literally. I started coughing, and then suddenly, all the Clipboard Girls turned their heads to stare, and the band followed suit. I managed to swallow and then sputtered out, "I'm okay." They all then turned their heads and went back to discussing the day's schedule. Except Eamonn. No, he continued to stare at me with a mixture of confusion, shock, and possibly fright. I stared right back. I was sure my face was fire-engine red. Finally, the Clipboard Girls led the band to their own dressing room, and I headed back to Sonja's just as she was coming out.

"I better get back to it," she said, passing Delilah to me like hockey players switch on the fly.

"Right," I said, trying to sound as calm as possible. "We'll be in here."

I locked the door behind us once again, and immediately called Joy.

"Hey, what's up?" she said. "Are you in New York?"

"You won't fucking believe this," I said. "Eamonn's here."

"Eamonn's there?!" she shrieked. A baby started to wail in the background. "Oh, fuck. Shh, shh, Mommy's sorry," she said to Felicity.

"He's in the band. They just got here to shoot the video."

"Did he see you?"

"Yep."

"Did you say anything to him?"

"No. But we made eye contact for about thirty seconds before he was whisked off to get ready for the shoot."

"Wow," she said. Felicity continued to cry. "What are you going to say to him?"

"I don't know!" I hissed. "That's why I'm calling you! What do I say to him?"

"How about, 'Show me the money, motherfucker?' That would be a good start."

"Very funny," I said.

By now the cries had escalated to a fever pitch. Even Delilah was giving the phone the side-eye.

"I better go," Joy said. "Keep me posted."

A few minutes later, my phone pinged with texts from Leigh and Meg. Clearly Joy had had the time to alert the troops.

Leigh's read: "Kick him in the balls for me!"

Meg's was a little more serious: "I hope you're okay. Let me know how it goes. Love you. PS Probably don't tell Dan."

Both of their texts seemed to have equal merit. I spent the next two hours rehearsing what I would say to him. What snarky comment I'd use as a greeting. I tried to figure out the most hurtful, insulting thing I could possibly say. I wondered if there were any isolated corners of the building where I could take him with the express purpose of kicking him in the groin and/or breaking his nose with the heel of my hand.

I fed Delilah once more, changed her, and poked out of the room again so Sonja could play the mom.

"All right, let's take ten, everyone," the director said, as Sonja happily swooped up Delilah. The guys all dispersed from the set, two heading to the water cooler, two others heading outside for a cigarette. Eamonn headed straight for me.

And he took me in his arms and hugged me, right in the middle of the set. And just like that, my anger melted away, feeling the warmth of his embrace. My throat tightened and I squeezed my eyes shut, but I couldn't hold it all in anymore. Three years' worth of hot tears started to spill out and I started shaking, overwhelmed at it all.

"Shhh, it's okay," he murmured. "Oh, Amanda. Amanda."

He led me by the hand to a quiet corner of the studio. We sat in some of the scattered folding chairs, and he briefly left to get us bottles of water. He returned a few seconds later, opened one and handed it to me. I took a large gulp.

We sat quietly, neither of us saying anything for a moment. He started to reach toward my hand but pulled back at the last moment, drumming his fingers on his thigh instead.

His hands were just as beautiful as I'd remembered.

"So," he eventually said.

"So," I replied. "It's been a while."

He looked appropriately ashamed. "I know. And I have absolutely no excuse for it, other than I was scared out of my mind. God, I'm such a shit."

I wiped my eyes with the back of my hand and half-snickered. "Well, admitting you have a problem is the first step."

He sighed. "Indeed."

"Looks like the musician thing ended up working out for you."

"Thanks," he said running his hands through his unkempt hair. "It took long enough."

"Is this your first video?"

"It is," he said, and took a swig of water. "We'd been playing the pub circuit in Dublin for the last couple of years, and a scout liked what we saw when he came to a show in February. We got a recording contract and it's been shenanigans ever since."

"That's great," I said. "I know that's always been your dream."

"Yeah, it feels grand," he said, with a wry smile. "At least I think it does. I haven't taken much time to think about it."

God, that smile. It still had the power to melt me. And seeing the way his eyes crinkled just like Maddie's did, made my heart pound even harder. God. I couldn't believe I was sitting here right next to him again after two and a half years. Part of me wanted to crawl back into his lap and have him cradle me for hours, rubbing my back and whispering that everything would be okay. A small part of me also wanted to wring his neck for all the heartache he'd caused, but mostly, I felt like a piece of me that had gone missing was finally back.

"How is it you're here, anyway?" he asked me, interrupting my reverie

I debated how much to tell him. "I work for Sonja," I said. "You could say I'm a mother's helper, and I entertain the baby when Sonja's busy on photo shoots or things like that."

"No shit?" he said. "How'd you meet her?"

"Through a....networking thing. Sort of a group for young *moms* in Chicago," I said pointedly.

Now he looked really ashamed. "How's Madeline?" he asked. When he said her name with his lilt, it almost sounded like a poem.

"She's perfect," I retorted. "She's almost two and she's this walking, talking, counting, giggling, amazing little miniature adult. She's the most charming kid on the planet."

"Do you have a picture of her?" he asked.

The Joy on my shoulder whispered, *Oh, now he wants to see her?* But I swatted her away, and instead said, “Here,” passing him my phone, where a picture of Maddie was my wallpaper.

He grinned. “She’s lovely,” he said. “She’s the spitting image of you.”

“She has your eyes,” I countered.

“She does?” he said, peering more closely. “Ah, I see it now.”

We were then interrupted by the unmistakable sound of a megaphone. “Everyone get your asses back on set,” barked the director. “We’re taking it outside for the golden hour.”

Eamonn handed my phone back to me, then didn’t let go of my hand. Oh, God. I still felt the electricity that I had nearly three years before.

“Look, I better get back, but...we still need to catch up,” he said, looking intently at me. “Are you going to have any free time this weekend?”

I thought for a moment. “Sonja and her family are going out to brunch tomorrow,” I said. “I could probably meet you for a quick breakfast.”

“Are you staying at the same hotel as us?” he asked.

“I have no idea,” I admitted. “I think it’s some little boutique place a few blocks away from here. We haven’t even checked in yet.”

“That’s the one,” he said. “Let’s meet in the café off the lobby. Around eleven?”

“Sounds good,” I said.

He gave my hand an extra squeeze. “I’ll see you soon,” he said, and gave me a peck on the cheek, as if we had rewound time. He then walked toward his bandmates and grabbed his violin.

Just then, the team from *Celebs* showed up. It was some photographer I'd never met and, lo and behold, Camille Pinto again. Wonderful. She made eye contact with me right away and headed over.

"If it isn't Cousin Amanda!" she said, giving me an air kiss.

"That's me," I said wryly. "Sonja needed someone to watch the baby while they're shooting."

"Of course she did," she said with a knowing look.

Cleo then carried Delilah toward me. "Good, you're here," she said to Camille and her sidekick. "We can get you set up outside. Amanda, this might be a while, so we're going to take you two back to the hotel for the night. The limo's out front."

"Perfect," I said. "Let me just grab my bag." I balanced Delilah on my hip and walked back to the dressing room and picked up my oversized tote.

Camille tugged at my arm when we were almost back to the set.

"Hey, Cousin Amanda," she said. "Might want to change—looks like you sprung a leak."

I gasped. She eyed me like the Cheshire cat. I then looked down and saw a wet spot on my left boob.

"Oh, gosh, it's spit up," I fibbed, repositioning Delilah so she covered my chest, and scurried to the door.

When I got to the limo, I heard the trademark sound of Eamonn's fiddle from halfway down the block.

I turned around, and saw him looking in my direction with an intense look on his face. I waved, then headed quickly for the door. I don't think I could have stayed a second longer without losing it. He was playing "All I Want Is You."

By the time Delilah and I were settled into the suite and had eaten (oh, room service, how I love thee), it was nearly nine. I called my parents' house to check in on Maddie.

"How's she doing?" I asked.

"Oh, fine," my mom said, laughing. "Does she normally ask for ice cream for dinner?"

"No, not really," I lied. "Can you put her on?" I heard the muffling as my mom transferred the phone to Maddie. I heard her heavy breathing.

"Hi, sweetheart!" I said.

"Mommy? Mommy?" she said, sounding worried.

"It's okay!" I said. "Mommy will be home soon!"

She started to whine. "Mommy coming? Mommy go home?"

"Shhhh," I said. "It's okay, Mommy will be home soon."

Maddie didn't sound convinced, and kept whining, I then sang the first verse of "Yellow Submarine," and it calmed her down a bit.

"Okay, let's say goodnight to Mommy," I heard my mom say in the background.

"GoodNIGHT!" Maddie squealed, and the line went dead.

I looked over at Delilah, fast asleep in the co-sleeper, which apparently Sonja (or maybe Cleo) had purchased and delivered to the hotel just for the weekend. Delilah was such a sweet baby, even more so now that she'd overcome her brief colicky phase. But she couldn't compare to my baby. She'd never come close.

My phone pinged a few minutes later with a text. It was Dan—the first time I'd heard from him since our fight.

"How's NY?" he'd written.

Was he calling a truce, maybe?

"Good. Tiring. How's the family?" I texted back.

Ping. "Good. Tiring. Lucas and I miss you."

"Miss you too."

And I did miss him. I couldn't help but feel, though, that maybe he'd been right about me when we had our blowout. I felt a little dishonest, and tossed and turned a lot that night. Plus, I couldn't stop thinking about Eamonn, and how he'd managed to turn my world upside again, and so fast. Part of me was anxious to see him again tomorrow, but part of me was petrified. What if I lost my cool again? What if I proclaimed my undying love for him, the love that I thought I'd finally buried for good, but maybe had only been dormant inside me? What if he wanted me back, wanted to be a family with me and Maddie? And if that was the case, where did that leave me and Dan, not to mention Maddie and Lucas?

It was too much to think about. I ended up taking a swig of Nyquil from the mini bar and as an afterthought, hoped it wouldn't mess with my milk supply.

I vaguely remember hearing Sonja shuffle into the suite around 1 AM. Then, around five, Chase came in like a herd of elephants. Delilah started to whine, and then I fed her, praying she'd fall back asleep. She did. It then occurred to me that Delilah had just slept for eight hours straight. Hmm. I wondered if she normally did that.

I told Sonja when we were all in the living room a few hours later how well Delilah had slept.

"She did?" she said, incredulously. "That's fantastic!"

"Believe me, for a three-month-old, that's amazing," I said.

"I think you've got the magic touch," she said with a smile.

"Doubtful," I said. "I'd say you just lucked out by having a wonderful baby."

Chase then cracked open a beer. Sonja shot him an annoyed look. "Hair of the dog," he said as an explanation.

Once the family was photo-ready again—the hair and make-up team had spent a good hour trying to make them look as just-out-of-bed-beautiful as possible—I fed Delilah once more, and then there was a knock at the door.

"Can you get, that, Amanda?" Sonja asked, riffling through her bag.

I opened the door and there stood Camille, looking smug as ever, and a tall, robust gentleman of about sixty with wire-rimmed glasses, large, ruddy cheeks, and a blue pinstriped suit. In one word: smarmy. In two words: functioning alcoholic.

Sonja's eyes looked startled for a second before she quickly regained composure.

"Kevan Riordan!" she exclaimed. "What a surprise! Please come in."

Whoa. Even I'd heard of Kevan Riordan. He was the group publisher of not only *Celebs*, but an entire suite of women-centric magazines: *Happy Housekeeper, In Shape, Your Best Self* and some others I'm sure I was forgetting.

"Sonja, darling" he said, kissing her on the cheek. "Let's talk business."

I quickly darted with Delilah back to the bedroom wing of the suite, where Chase was puffing one last joint and blowing the smoke out the window.

"Do you mind?" he asked me, irritated.

"Kevan Riordan's here."

His eyes widened. He tossed the joint out the window, coughed and headed into the living room.

"Kevan!" I heard his voice boom. "What's happening, brother?"

"What's happening is, the jig is up. Camille has caught on to you and your wet nurse, and your whole attachment parenting sham."

I froze. No.

"What are you talking about?" I heard Sonja ask innocently.

"I saw your nanny with a wet spot on her chest yesterday. And at that point, I realized where I'd seen her before—breastfeeding another baby last summer. Didn't take much to put two and two together," Camille said triumphantly.

Chase groaned. "Look, just tell us what the fuck you want."

"Exclusives—all unpaid—for the next twelve months. This is gonna mean family photos, more of your 'homemade' recipes that we're gonna put into a column in *Happy Housekeeping*, and a bikini shoot for *Hot Gears'* next swimsuit issue. And with that, no one will ever have to know about your 'Cousin Amanda.' For now, anyway."

After a moment, Sonja said stiffly, "Seems fair."

"One other thing," Kevan added. "We're starting a new charitable foundation. Chase, you're donating the first million out of your paycheck for *A Soldier's Honor*."

"The fuck I am!" Chase bellowed.

"The fuck you aren't," Kevan sneered back.

I heard some more mumbling, and then finally, Chase said, "All right, it's a deal." A moment later, the door closed.

Sonja and Chase both came into the bedroom, and my stomach dropped.

"How could you be so fucking stupid?" Chase shouted at me, red-faced. "Thanks a lot, Million Dollar Nanny!"

"Look, I swear she never saw me feed Delilah, and I just had some spit-up on my shirt—" I interjected.

"Oh, sure," he snarled. "Can't wait until this makes it into all the blogs by noon."

"Fuck," said Sonja. "I'm calling Cleo." She started furiously scrolling through her phone.

"And now I'm wasting twenty percent of my paycheck on a damn charity." He kicked the bedpost.

Sonja looked at the clock. It was 10:40. "I can't fucking deal with this right now—we have to be at brunch at eleven," she said, plucking Delilah from my arms. She then addressed me. "Get out. Now."

"Wait, we're not even going to discuss—"

"NOW," Chase sneered.

I hurried over to my suitcase, zipped it up, and threw my tote bag over my shoulder.

I shot one last look at Delilah, who had started to cry.

And the next thing I knew, Chase had opened the door, *shoved me out,* and slammed the door behind me.

I stood there for a minute, dumbfounded. Where the hell was I supposed to go now? And how was I even supposed to get home?

"Amanda?" said a startled voice. "I heard someone yelling. Is everything okay?"

It was Eamonn, peering out from his hotel room a few doors down.

"I'm—I'm fine," I said, unconvincingly. Then my shoulders started to shake.

He quickly stepped the few paces toward me and pulled me in for an embrace. He had just showered and his hair was still damp. He looked as sexy as he had the day I met him.

"It's all right," he whispered, ushering me back to his room.

When I got into his room, the first thing I noticed was the scent of the room, the very Eamonn-ness of it, and how comforting it was.

“What happened?” he asked gently.

I sighed. “I...well...I just lost my job. Sonja and Chase got angry about something out of my control, and they just let me go.”

“That’s terrible,” he clucked, holding my hand.

“You don’t know the half of it,” I said bitterly.

“If they’re anything like some of the Hollywood types I’ve met in the past few months, I’d guess that you’re better off now.”

I thought about that for a second. “Could be,” I admitted.

He stroked my fingers and gazed at me as if the last three years hadn’t passed. Those eyes, the ones I saw in Maddie every day, were so gorgeous, like the North Atlantic. God, it would have been so easy to throw myself at him right then and there.

“Well,” he said, breaking the tension and finally letting go of my hand, “I was about to head downstairs for breakfast—to meet you there, as it were. Still interested?”

“Sure,” I said. Looking down at my yoga pants and flip flops, I added, “I should probably get dressed first.”

“You want to use my shower?”

“That would be great, actually,” I said. “Thanks.”

“No worries,” he said. “Take your time, and just meet me in the café when you’re ready.”

What a gentleman. He gave my knee one last affectionate tap and was out the door.

I took a little longer than usual to get ready, dabbing on a little extra makeup and blow-drying my hair. Embarrassingly enough, I'd even dried myself off with his just-used towel...only because I could.

When I greeted him in the café about fifteen minutes later, suitcase in tow, I was as together as I could be.

"Morning, love," he said, then looked taken aback.

"Don't worry about it," I said. "Old habits die hard."

"I got you a cuppa," he said, gently pushing the teacup and saucer toward me.

"Thanks," I said, and perused the menu. I could feel him staring at me.

"What," I finally said, putting down the menu and staring straight at him, as if in a challenge.

"I'm so sorry," he burst out. "I really am. I was young, and a total arse, and completely unprepared to be a father."

"I know."

"You have every right to hate me."

"I know."

"And...I'm a sorry excuse for a man. I ran away, and I'm a complete moron, and I'm sorry." He looked really contrite. "You didn't deserve that."

I didn't say anything for another moment, soaking it all in. "I know," I said softly.

He took my hand and kissed it. And I let him. Then, I regained composure, pulled my hand back to grab the menu, and said, "So, tell me about your band."

We chatted for the next twenty minutes about what we'd been up to for the past few years. I left out the whole breastfeeding-other-people's children part, but I did tell him I nannied for wealthy families, and loved getting to be around babies. I showed him more pictures of Maddie, and his face lit up with each one.

It was easy, light, and made me feel like the stressful morning didn't even matter. It was like having lunch with an old friend. A really attractive old friend. Okay, a really attractive old friend that was bringing up long-buried feelings left and right.

Then, his phone buzzed. He looked at it, then said apologetically, "I better take it."

I nodded, and he excused himself to the lobby of the hotel. I watched him for a second, but couldn't get a read on who might have called. He scratched his head and frowned a few times.

Then, my phone pinged. It was an email from Joy. The subject line was "EFFING READ THIS NOW, AMANDA!"

So I did, a little concerned:

"Just saw this today on the *Celebs* website. Go to this link ASAP."

I clicked on the link, and the article was "Seven Things You Didn't Know About The Amateur Professionals!"

I scanned through each item, and then my heart stopped when I got to number six.

"Sexy violinist Eamonn Shaughnessy is a proud daddy-to-be! He's expecting his first child—a baby girl!—with longtime fiancée, aspiring actress Niamh Miller, in June."

Really.

Just then, Eamonn came back to the table.

"Sorry about that," he said. "Anyway—"

I cut him off, "You know what, my mom just texted me about Maddie. I better call her back and check in. I'm afraid it's my turn to be rude," I said. A plan had just hatched in my head. I couldn't believe I'd been so blind. I couldn't believe I'd compared Dan to him, had thought for a *second—*

"Not at all," he said. "Take all the time you need."

I flashed him a huge smile. "I'll be right back."

I went to the lobby, scrolled through my directory, and found the number I needed. When the male voice picked up, I said, "Can you make a miracle happen for me?"

A few minutes later, I came back into the café. Eamonn and I continued to chat, and each ordered another tea.

"So how long will you be in New York?" I asked, getting fidgety.

"I'm actually taking the redeye back to Dublin tonight," he lamented. "I wish I could stay here longer. With you," he added.

I looked down. "Me, too," I murmured.

"But now that we'll have a record coming out, I'm sure we're going to go on tour. Maybe not until the fall or winter, but we'll be back in the States by the end of the year. I'd love to see you again. And I'd love to meet Maddie, if you'll let me."

"Oh, you'll become part of her life. I'm sure of it," I said. I lightly traced his hand with my finger.

Just then, a tall, twenty-ish girl in a newsboy cap walked by our table.

"Omigod!" she said, wide-eyed. "Are you that violin player? From The Amateur Professionals."

"Yeah," he said, pretending to be embarrassed.

"Eamonn? Eamonn Shaughnessy, right?" she said excitedly.

"That's me," he said, eating it up.

Her face flipped to a cold glare like a light switch. She tossed a manila envelope toward him, and said, "You've been served."

"Wait, what?" he said, completely befuddled. I smiled and took a last sip of tea.

"See you in court, motherfucker," I whispered, then slipped out the door.

I darted into the elevator and hugged myself. My lawyer had faxed the papers to the process server he'd known in Brooklyn, and she'd cabbed it over right away. And just like that, I was on my way to getting Maddie taken care of. With any luck, Eamonn's shitty band would hit it big, and she'd be financially covered—who knows, maybe even for life. Finally. Finally. Finally. I was over Eamonn. When I'd read that article, I knew it. Every loving thought I'd had toward him just bit into a cyanide capsule at once. And I was finally free.

I got outside and hailed a taxi to the airport. While on the way, I texted my girlfriends the news about Eamonn, and they were ecstatic. I'd texted Dan to let him know I was on my way back early. No, I never mentioned the resurfaced feelings I'd briefly had for Eamonn. There was no point in hurting him like that, especially because now that those feelings were gone, I felt my love for Dan double. Triple. I was like the damn Grinch at the end of the movie.

When I got to JFK, I spent way too much money on a one-way ticket to Chicago that was leaving within the hour. Once I was on the plane, I also decided that no matter what Sonja, what Alexandra, what Mariela or any of my past employers thought my fate should be, *I* was going to be the one in control of it. I'd miss the babies, but I was done with my life as a wet nurse. For good. There was another little girl out there who needed me far more than another family ever could.

I landed at O'Hare on time, and headed to baggage claim. While watching the carousel for my suitcase, I suddenly heard a familiar voice squeal, "Mommy!"

I turned and saw Maddie in Dan's arms. Lucas was next to him, holding a bouquet of pink tulips. I ran toward them and embraced all three of them at once.

"I called your mom," Dan explained. "I wanted to surprise you. Hope that's okay," he said.

"Things couldn't be more okay," I said, kissing him full on the lips. I took my own daughter into my arms and hugged her tight, then tousled Lucas' hair.

"Let's go," I said. "Let's go home."

EPILOGUE

A few days after I returned from New York—after plenty of makeup sex and cuddles with Dan while the kids were in daycare—I headed over to Daly's to give Colin the update on Eamonn.

Once I'd finished, he let out a low whistle and chuckled.

"You're really something, Amanda," he said, "and I couldn't be prouder."

"Thanks, I'm kind of proud of myself, too."

"So now that your nannying job is over, what do you plan to do?"

"Not sure yet. I'll probably move back in with my parents in the suburbs. They live right by the outlet mall, so I may pick up a job there while I look for something better."

"You ever waitress before?"

"Never," I admitted. In college, I'd been the card-swiper girl at the front desk of the rec center for four years, and prior to that, I'd only babysat the neighbor's kids while I was in high school.

"Not much to it," assured Colin. "Long as you can carry a tray, smile and nod, I think you'll do fine."

"Wait—you want me to waitress for Daly's?"

"I'd certainly like to give you a shot."

We set up the schedule then and there—I'd work the lunch shift on Tuesday through Friday, and Sunday brunches as well to get started. I made a mental note to call Dan, my mom, and Meg to see if I could wheedle them into watching her for the weekend shifts. I hoped this would be temporary, but I was grateful for Colin's offer all the same.

And, long story short, the waitressing gig worked out just fine. Most Saturday nights, Maddie and I stayed at Dan's place so he could watch her the following morning when I tiptoed out to work; I didn't have to make a trip to IDHS or go back to the WIC office; I made enough in wages and tips to keep Maddie in daycare four afternoons a week, the rent paid, the lights on and the water running.

I was surprised to find how much I liked waitressing, too. After a year of working in other people's homes, with primarily just infants to converse with, I'd become a little lonely. I liked seeing the variety of people that came into Daly's for lunch—the tourists, the guys from the bank next door on their lunch breaks, the women's Bible study from the Presbyterian church a few blocks away. It was never terribly crowded for lunches, so I didn't feel overwhelmed, and I was pretty good at what I did. The Irish-born wait staff garnered better tips, but we split them at the end of the shift, regardless.

I'd gotten into a new rhythm and routine, and I'd just clocked out for the afternoon one Tuesday in July, when I turned my phone back on to see that I'd missed three calls from Joy and received five texts and an email from her that afternoon.

That's weird, I thought.

I quickly learned why.

In her email, she attached a link to an article from *The Huffington Post* titled, "The Careys Exposed: Behind Their Pretense in Parenting." And it was written by Camille Pinto.

Oh, God.

I read the article, word for word, paralyzed by fear. And everything she'd reported was true—the multiple nannies; the night nurses; Sonja's frequent absences from the home. Camille even mentioned their employ of a full-time farmer and cook.

I'd read nearly the whole article, holding my breath, when I finally saw it:

While not proven, it was also rumored that the Careys even hired an on-call wet nurse from time to time, from budding domestic services agency, Mother's Milk Consultants (www.mothersmilkconsultants.com).

I read the article three more times. Nowhere in there had she mentioned me by name—thank God. I had no idea where she got all the dirt—I'd found out via text from Karen that the Careys had ended up hiring her back immediately, so I couldn't imagine she would have spilled anything. Maybe it was Julie, the night nurse? I wasn't sure how Camille found out about my website, either. Had she gone through Sonja's things and found my business card? Or was she just *that* good of a journalist?

I read Camille's brief bio after the article. She listed herself as a freelance lifestyle writer, whose work has been published in *Celebs*. Ah, so that was it. I'm guessing that after things went south for her on the job front, she had a few celebrity axes to grind.

By the time I was done reading the article, and fairly certain the Careys wouldn't have any luck in suing me for violating their NDA (though I'd probably have to verify that with Jonathan), I'd received three more emails.

None of these were from Joy, though. All three had been written to me via the "Contact Us" feature on my website, inquiring about my services.

Huh.

The thing was, I couldn't have been a wet nurse any longer, even if I'd wanted to—without a baby to feed, I'd dried up a few days after getting unceremoniously fired by the Careys.

The wheels were turning in my head, though.

That night, after we put the kids to bed, Dan and I talked far into the night working out the details of my plan. I couldn't be a wet nurse, but I'd been around the block plenty of times, and there was a lot I could offer to new moms. Maybe thanks to this extra attention, I could turn this front into a real consultancy.

Colin graciously let me take the next few days off from the pub, and I spent every waking moment filling out forms, registering my business at the county clerk's office, drawing up a business plan and tweaking my website. Then, once I'd done as much as I could, and I was well on my way to becoming a legitimate, sole proprietor of the business, I started responding to the emails I'd received via "Contact Us." By now, I'd received nearly a hundred.

Most of them had directly referenced the article, so I had to address the issue as well:

"Mother's Milk Consultants does not provide wet nurse services to its clientele. Our consultants assist families during the transition period with a newborn, and can offer advice, techniques, and support to mothers regarding breastfeeding.

"All inquiries are held in the strictest of confidence. Information regarding past, present, and potential clients of Mother's Milk Consultants is permanently classified. For confidentiality reasons, Mother's Milk Consultants will not confirm nor deny reports regarding clientele."

And, with that text starting each email and now on the "Q&A" tab on the website, I got to work replying to each of my inquiries. The majority never wrote back to me, but I had more than a dozen who did. I scheduled initial free phone consultations with all of them over the next week, and many of them reminded me of myself in those early, overwhelming days of having a newborn—and some reminded me of my past employers, too. Some were like Mariela and were at the end of their rope, desperately trying to feed their child, and feeling like they failed at every turn. Some were like Sonja, too, and had high expectations of what motherhood would be like, and experienced an opposite reality. One of my consultations was even with a new dad, whose wife was clearly suffering from post-partum depression—much like I'd guessed Sonja had—and he had no idea how to help her.

Nearly all of the clients hired me for in-house consultations at three hundred dollars apiece—and many became repeat clients, as well. Each one was different. I'd help the mom by showing her different holds to try; show them how to use the pump more effectively; sometimes, I even just held the new moms' hands and rubbed their backs while they sat and wept. And, every one of them got a tutorial in my baby-quieting move, "the dip."

Fast forward a few months: It's now nearly Thanksgiving, and I've spent most of the week packing up my apartment. It's true. We're moving in with Dan and Lucas, because they're making an honest woman out of me. Dan proposed on the one-year anniversary of our first date. He gave me his grandmother's ring, an understated, square-cut stone that couldn't have been more perfect or meaningful. Maybe other people would think it was silly, but he proposed at the daycare drop-off. He'd arranged for the kids and teachers in Lucas' room to hold up signs asking, "Will you marry him?" After all, it was the place where we'd first met. I couldn't wait to start our life as a family of four. Who knows, maybe someday a family of five.

I'd stopped waitressing at the pub, and, thanks to referrals from my clients, my consultancy was booming. I was to the point where I'd have to cut back on my schedule, though, and only take a few morning clients per week, because I was going back to school in January. Between the money I made from consulting, and the crapload of back pay for child support that Eamonn was now paying me, it was entirely feasible. (For the record, Eamonn still hasn't met Maddie, and hasn't asked to, either.)

At any rate, yes, I was going to be a student. I have to take a few prerequisite classes in anatomy and chemistry at DePaul, and then I plan to apply for their Masters in Nursing program, so that in the next few years, I could become a board-certified lactation consultant. My breastfeeding days were over for the foreseeable future, but I took a lot of satisfaction in the services I provided for moms and babies. Soon after my consultancy was operational, I knew I wanted to become a legitimate professional. I wanted to share what I knew, to learn even more and to better support the moms who felt scared, overwhelmed or lost. Who knows, maybe some of the moms who had hired me—Mariela, Sonja—wouldn't have needed me if they'd had a better lactation consultant. I liked the babies well enough, but the moms out there—the moms who were wondering how in the world they were going to make it once they left the hospital—*they* were the ones I wanted to help in a more impactful way. I had my own babies at home. And that's where you'll find me, with my family, every night.

Acknowledgements

I would like to first and foremost thank the tireless and talented Claire Anderson-Wheeler, for taking a chance on an unknown writer. Claire could teach a doctorate-level seminar in the art of constructive criticism. Through her encouragement, I took this novel from the roughest of drafts to a publication-ready piece, for which she promptly found the perfect home. I'm mighty obliged to have her in my corner.

I would also like to thank Stacey Holderbach, for loving *Milked* as much as I do and treating it with such care. A kindred spirit and feisty writer in her own right, Stacey has welcomed me to the Simon & Fig family with open arms, and I'm grateful that my first novel is exactly where it belongs.

A big thank-you goes to The Office of Letters and Light. Without their annual National Novel Writing Month (NaNoWriMo) challenge each November, this book would not exist. Thank you for all you do to help writers around the world achieve their potential, and also for the panic-inducing deadline and thrill of victory in 2012.

Another huge thank-you goes to Jenny Chi and Sharon Reddy (my real-life Joys), for 20-plus years of friendship and endless material. Thanks also go out to my book club—Debbie Chun, Kate Darrow, Lauren Casella, Mandy Held, Sally Whitesides, Sarah Ramirez and Jenny Chi once again—for your invaluable guidance, support and girls' nights out. And, another round of thank-yous goes to the J10 Moms, for cheerleading me along the way. I'm eternally grateful to my other half, Tim, and to our sweet Colin, who never ceases to inspire me. Thank you for my daily dose of laughter and love.

And to my own mom, Georgiana Carollus: Thank you for

always believing in me.

About the Author

Lisa Doyle is a communications manager and freelance writer. She spent several years editing business-to-business publications for the personal care industry before moving to the nonprofit sector, and currently works in advocacy for homeless families. She resides with her family in the Chicago area. The only child she has ever breastfed has been her own.